"I need to see you alone."

"Then we must think of another dare," Eugenie said. She giggled mischievously. "At Miss Debenham's we visited the ruins of a nearby castle . . ."

"I thought finishing schools were all about manners and deportment."

"Miss Debenham was interested in turning out well-rounded girls," she retorted, with a twinkle in her eye. "The baron of this castle had a wicked reputation, prone to abducting any girl who took his fancy. He'd ride back to his castle and . . . well, the lesson didn't go that far. But I . . . well, my friends actually, found the idea of being abducted rather appealing."

Sinclair shook his head at her. "So that is your dare? For me to abduct you?"

For a moment he thought she was going to deny it. She was an innocent, he reminded himself, and more than likely a virgin. He was dabbling with fire. But Sinclair was too far gone to care.

"Not far, of course. Just a little way will do. Just to win the dare."

His eyes narrowed. "I am not in the habit of abducting young ladies in laneways," he drawled.

"I know. That is why it's a dare," she teased with a smile.

Romances by Sara Bennett

To Pleasure a Duke
A Most Sinful Proposal
Led Astray by a Rake
Her Secret Lover
A Seduction in Scarlet
Mistress of Scandal
Rules of Passion
Lessons in Seduction
Kissing the Bride
Beloved Highlander
Once He Loves
The Rose and the Shield
The Lily and the Sword

To Pleasure A Duke

SARA BENNETT

AVON

An Imprint of HarperCollinsPublishers

AVON BOOKS
An Imprint of HarperCollins*Publishers*
10 East 53rd Street
New York, New York 10022-5299

Copyright © 2011 by Sara Bennett
ISBN 978-0-06-133918-9
www.avonromance.com

First Avon Books mass market printing: November 2011

Avon Trademark Reg. U.S. Pat. Off. and in Other Countries, Marca Registrada, Hecho en U.S.A.
HarperCollins® is a registered trademark of HarperCollins Publishers.

Printed in the U.S.A.

10 9 8 7 6 5 4 3 2 1

To Pleasure
A Duke

Prologue

Miss Debenham's Finishing School, Graduating Ball 1837

Miss Eugenie Belmont waited in trepidation. Olivia and Marissa had spoken of their ideal husbands, and after the uproar they caused Eugenie felt her own qualms increase. Perhaps if she stayed quiet and made herself very small no one would notice her? The truth was she didn't have a choice of an eligible husband. Not a single, solitary one. Where on earth would she meet such a man in her circumstances? Eligible men were hardly likely to come calling at Belmont Hall, falling down as it was, and inhabited by her disreputable and rackety family.

Perhaps her friends would pass her over and ask Tina or Averil instead. Eugenie said a fervent prayer under her breath.

"Well, Eugenie? Are you going to tell us the

name of *your* future husband?" Marissa was smiling a teasing smile, and the rest of her friends leaned forward, their eyes bright with expectation.

Eugenie tried to smile, too, although her heart was clanging in her chest. The moment she'd been dreading for weeks had arrived.

"I haven't given it much thought, really. What about Tina? I'm sure she has someone really interesting to—"

"No, no," Tina retorted, "we want to hear *your* choice, Eugenie. Come now, don't be coy. Who is it? Do we know him?"

Eugenie took a drink of her champagne and violently choked on it. They patted her back, gathering around her. Desperately Eugenie tried to think of a way to escape their questions. She *could* tell the truth, but the thought of such an embarrassing admission made her squirm inside. Her friends seemed to know so many suitable men, all of them husband material. Eugenie longed to be like them, and she couldn't help but think that if they knew just how *un*like them she really was then they would no longer be her friends.

"There now," Olivia said, mopping Eugenie's cheeks and tucking her wild curls behind her ears. "All better?"

"I—I think so."

They waited expectantly. They exchanged glances.

"Come on, Eugenie. Is it really such a secret? Who is this man?"

"We all agreed to meet this evening and tell each other the names of the men we mean to marry. You can't change your mind now, Eugenie. It wouldn't be fair."

"Tell us, Eugenie, please!"

They weren't going to let it lie. Eugenie sought desperately for a name, someone handsome and wealthy and titled, someone who would impress her irrepressible friends. The one that popped into her head was completely unexpected and in her panic she gave herself no time to consider the consequences of uttering it aloud.

"Sinclair St. John, the Duke of Somerton," she blurted out.

Smiles wavered. Eyebrows were raised. "Good heavens!" cried Tina, always forthright. "Somerton is the most eligible man in the realm. Aren't you aiming a little high, Eugenie?"

"Why shouldn't she aim high?" Olivia spoke gallantly. "Eugenie deserves only the best. And she has royal blood!"

"Dear me, yes," teased Marissa, showing her dimple. "I had forgotten that. Was it your grand-mamma, Eugenie, who was a king's mistress?"

"No, it was my great-grandmamma. She was a maid in the palace, no great lady, and she wasn't at all pretty, so it is quite a mystery how she lured King George to her bed. Although he was rather ugly himself . . ."

They giggled.

"And then he made their son a baronet with property to go with it. The property and the money are long gone. All that is left to us of my great-grandmamma's liaison is the baronetcy, and my father's nose, which he insists is pure Hanoverian. We have no reason to boast about our royal connection, I assure you."

"But are you acquainted with the Duke of Somerton?" Averil, serious as always, dismissed Eugenie's self-effacing jests.

"Yes. I met him three months ago." Well, that at least was true.

"Met him only once?" Olivia gasped.

"No, of course not. That would be silly." Eugenie forced a laugh. "Met him for the first time three months ago, I meant. We have spoken many times since and—and written."

She was making it worse. Eugenie longed for her moment in the spotlight to be over. With any luck the Duke of Somerton would be forgotten by the end of the evening and then after a decent time she could bury him.

Averil was speaking. "I've heard he is rather particular in his choice of friends. A snob, in other words. I cannot see him sitting down to dinner with a mere baronet!"

"He is a pompous prig who believes himself too good for the rest of us!" Tina added hotly. "I have been cut by him. He looked right through me. Not that I cared, but I think you might do better, Eugenie. Why would you wish to spend your life with such a creature?"

"I, too, must express my doubts as to his suitability to be your husband," Averil went on, a little wrinkle of concern creasing her smooth brow. "He is not someone I know well, but what I do know . . . Eugenie, he is said to be arrogant and cold, quite unlike you!"

The final words burst out of her and there was a murmur of doubt from the others.

"We've all heard you speak about your family, Eugenie," Marissa went on in an understanding way. "Are you sure you haven't chosen Somerton because he is the exact opposite of them?"

Now Eugenie felt her skin flush, as it was prone to do when she was feeling emotional. She knew her wretched freckles would be standing out. It all came of having a great-grandmamma with red curly hair—the disreputable great-grandmamma! Although Eugenie's hair was more brown than red, she had inherited the tendency to freckle and to blush.

But it was true. Her rackety family was the bane of her life. Her friends knew the trials and tribulations she faced when it came to her family, and there was truth in what Marissa had said— she did dream of marrying someone who was the polar opposite of the baronet, her father.

"There is no point in denying it." Eugenie sighed theatrically. "You're right. I have a desperate desire to be conventional. And the Duke of Somerton is the most respectable man I know. Will he love me? Do I love him? I think I *could* love him and I *could* persuade him to love me. It might be fun to find out. Just think, I could be the first Belmont to be respectable."

They were silent and she knew they thought she was indulging in wishful thinking. Why would the most eligible man in England marry her? Eugenie knew she was no beauty. She was small and slender, with not much of a figure to speak of. Her hair was brown with red tints and curled wildly despite her efforts to subdue it, while her features were too sharp to be considered more than interesting. It was true that males did tend to gravitate toward her at balls and parties, but she thought that was because she laughed at their jokes and listened sympathetically to their woes. They felt at ease with her—thought of her as more like a sister than a possible romantic partner.

Why, oh why had she chosen such an unlikely man to be her husband? Why had that particular name popped into her head? But it was too late now. The hole she had dug for herself was too deep to get out of. She'd just have to continue on and hope that at some point she could wriggle out of the mess she'd created.

She lifted her pointed chin, fixing her friends with her clear green eyes. "Yes, Somerton is refreshingly different from my family and I agree he can appear rather stuck-up and—and proud. But that isn't the real Somerton. Beneath that chilly exterior is a man who is generous and kind; someone who isn't afraid to laugh at himself."

Olivia grasped her hand. "And, Eugenie, you are just the girl to bring out the best in him. But how do you know he isn't exactly as he seems to Averil and Tina? Are you *so* well acquainted with him?"

"I would not say I know him intimately, but I have seen him as few people can say they have."

It was true. She had seen beneath the pompous exterior of Sinclair St. John, the Duke of Somerton. Not in the way her doubting friends imagined, however. Now was the moment to convince them that plain and shy Eugenie Belmont was more than capable of ensnaring a duke.

She gave a secretive little smile.

"Eugenie! Tell us! Please!" they begged.

"It happened three months ago."

They all leaned closer.

Soon they were under her spell. Eugenie told a good story—her father, the baronet, said she was a chip off the old block, although she preferred to use her story telling for the pleasure of others rather than to swindle numbskulls out of their blunt, as her father often boasted. Now she did her best to amuse her friends, causing them to gasp and laugh by turns, and embellishing the scene to the point that even she began to believe that it really was possible for her to marry a man like Somerton.

" . . . and then he took my hand and said I was the most unusual girl he'd ever met . . ." It was mostly tosh, but her friends weren't to know that.

When her story finally ended, Olivia clapped her hands and Marissa giggled. Even serious Averil was smiling, while Tina gave an unladylike snort of amusement.

"So now you know why I want to marry the Duke of Somerton," Eugenie finished gamely, too flushed with her success to stem her flow of words. "Wait and see if I do not win him over."

"In fact by this time next year I believe you will be his duchess!" Olivia declared.

Eugenie believed nothing of the sort but they

were all watching her and she was forced to give a nod and a weak smile.

"How amazing," Marissa said, her eyes widening. "I think I will have to come and call upon you, Eugenie, and see this unfold for myself."

The others agreed, eagerly making plans, checking dates.

Eugenie's nimble brain sought a way out. She hadn't planned it, exactly, but she probably would have to wait a month or two and then pretend her romance with Somerton didn't work out. She would send each of her friends a sad little letter and hope they didn't arrive with the intention of reuniting her with her duke. She shuddered at the thought of them learning the truth. Bad enough that she didn't have a husband-to-be, but to have told them such lies! If they discovered the truth they would never speak to her again. For a moment she considered whether it would be simpler to persuade Somerton to marry her.

She pictured his handsome, aristocratic face, his black eyes resting on her in amazed disgust. *Marry you?*

The young ladies were raising their champagne glasses and she had no option but to raise her own and join in the toast.

"To Eugenie!"

"To the Duchess of Somerton!"

The champagne went down the wrong way. Eugenie began to choke. Again.

Chapter 1

Eugenie's first meeting with the Duke of Somerton
Three months earlier

Eugenie tugged at the rope. On the other end of it Erik, until recently the family billy goat, shook his head and gave her a pleading look from his pale blue eyes. At least, it appeared pleading to her, and that was because Erik knew he had gone too far this time when he'd broken through the wooden fence into the drying yard, and eaten an item of the family's clothing.

If he'd eaten the boys' underwear or even Eugenie's shift and petticoat, it wouldn't have mattered so much—they would have forgiven him. But instead Erik had chosen to munch on Mrs. Belmont's Parisian cap with cerise ribbons, a garment she treasured above all others. When she discovered the few remaining scraps Erik had discarded as unpalatable—a ribbon flower or what was left of it—she promptly threw hysterics.

"Take that animal back to Farmer Bartholomew," she'd ordered, her voice husky from shrieking. "I won't have it here any longer. The—the beast. I don't want to set eyes on it ever again."

Eugenie, whose task it was to put the weeping twins and ten-year-old Jack to bed, had hoped that the morning might bring a reprieve for Erik. But no amount of pleading would change her mother's mind and suggestions that Erik should be congratulated for his good taste in choosing that particular item were greeted with strangled sobs. In fact it seemed that a night without her beloved cap had only hardened her resolve.

The goat would have to go.

"Genie! Help!"

Eugenie looked around. Her twin brothers, Benjamin and Bertie, had been clambering in the hedgerow and were now caught fast in the prickly brambles.

"We can't get out, Genie!"

"Don't pull so, or you'll tear your clothing. What will Mama say then?"

The boys stopped struggling and Eugenie handed Erik's rope to Jack, who was trying not to cry. Erik was his special pet, and although the twins were fond of the goat, they'd soon move on to something new. It was Jack who was truly heartbroken and would need Eugenie's special care. The boy had always had an affinity with animals, something Eugenie tried to encourage. Jack's menagerie was famous—currently he was caring for a magpie with a broken wing and a mouse with one ear that the cat had brought home.

"Genie!" the twins wailed impatiently, as she

set about untangling them from their predicament. Eugenie pretended to scold, as she finally set them free from the brambles. Eight years old and full of mischief, they ran ahead down the lane.

What next? Eugenie sighed. It was as if she lurched from one disaster to another, soothing her mother, untangling her brothers, dreading her father's next scheme.

The sun was shining and the birds singing and it was a perfect summer's day. What were other girls her age doing? Visiting friends and going on picnics? Meeting handsome young men who made them ridiculous compliments and stole kisses when their chaperones weren't watching? As much as she loved her troublesome family she suddenly wished herself back at Miss Debenham's. She'd been looking forward to this break, to being home again, but now all she wanted was to be with her friends, who made her feel that her life was full of infinite and exciting possibilities.

"Eugenie!" Jack was wrenching at her hand, desperately trying to gain her attention.

Startled back to reality, Eugenie looked up. A horseman had just come around the corner of the lane and was bearing down upon them at speed.

He was a big man whose dark blue coat flapped behind him, while his face was a blur beneath his hat. He saw them a moment after Eugenie saw him and swerved to allow for such unexpected obstacles. However the twins had never stayed still in their lives and now they flung themselves across his path and into the hedgerow, shrieking with terrified excitement.

The horse tried to avoid the twins, and instead found itself directly in the path of Jack and Eugenie and Erik. Eugenie grabbed her brother tightly in her arms. Erik, his rope loosened, bolted down the lane, kicking up his heels and adding to the confusion. The horse reared with a shrill cry, like a dark angel of death above their heads, wickedly sharp hooves pawing, and then the rider regained control and turned him aside.

Despite her shock—her heart was beating like a drummer boy's drum—Eugenie could not help but admire the rider's skill. He'd averted disaster. Although, she reminded herself, if he'd been riding a little less recklessly in the first place none of this would have happened.

She watched him bending low over his horse's neck, speaking softly, calming the animal. Then he dismounted and Jack, as if responding to some unspoken command, ran to take the reins. Eugenie found herself staring. He had dark eyes in a long, handsome face, and they were narrowed as he strode toward her. With his boots so shiny and his clothing so well made, he could only be a gentleman, but he carried himself with a certain arrogance that went beyond that.

Eugenie's hands were trembling so she placed them behind her back; she sensed that this man would not respond to weakness. He was a great deal taller than she and now he looked down at her, making use of that height to intimidate.

"What in the blue blazes did you think you were doing, woman? I could have run you down!"

"If you had been more cautious—"

"Cautious?" he repeated, furiously, as if she were insane to suggest it. His eyes were dark and stormy, his hair the same color beneath his hat, and his lips curled. Plainly he'd like to throttle her. She glanced down at his hands, saw them clenched into fists, and took an involuntary step back.

Her movement seemed to bring him to his senses.

"You're unhurt?" he said, his voice dropping. "The children?"

The twins were standing nearby, watching, for once still and silent, while Jack murmured to the horse. "Shaken, that is all," she said.

His dark eyes swept over her and she thought for a moment she saw a spark of interest in them. But Eugenie knew she must be mistaken. She wasn't the sort of girl men found interesting at first sight.

He looked over his shoulder, as if suddenly remembering his mount, and Eugenie followed his gaze, and smiled. Jack had worked his usual magic on the creature. It was resting its chin on his shoulder, nuzzling against him.

"Good God," the gentleman muttered. "I've never seen him do that before."

"Jack has a way with animals," Eugenie replied, the pride evident in her voice.

Those dark eyes were back on her again. "And you are, madam?"

Eugenie gave a little smile and dipped a curtsey. "Miss Eugenie Belmont. And these are my brothers, Jack, Bertie, and Ben. We live at Belmont Hall."

He nodded as if he knew it but she could read the puzzlement in his face. "Somerton," he said brusquely.

"I beg your pardon?"

"Somerton," he repeated. "It's my name."

"How do you do, Mr. Somerton?" her wretched tongue joked.

He gave her a narrow look. "I beg your pardon?" he repeated her own words back to her.

"I'm sorry. Of course I know you are His Grace, the Duke of Somerton."

The most important man in the county and reportedly the most eligible man in England, she added in her mind but thankfully did not say it aloud.

He moved toward his horse without replying—he was probably used to people treating him with goggle-eyed reverence. But Erik the billy goat had no such respect for the duke's position in the realm and he chose that moment to come cantering down the lane and, head lowered, butted the duke square in the buttocks.

His Grace went sprawling most ungracefully, his long body thudding to the ground, arms and legs splayed out, his hat rolling toward Jack's feet.

"Oh my . . ." Eugenie gasped, shocked into a little giggle. "I am *so* sorry."

She hurried to his side, a sharp look at the twins stopping their loud hoots of laughter, or at least muffling them.

Bending down she clutched his arm and tried her best to help him to his feet. Irritably he shook her off, getting to his feet under his own power. After one glance up at his face she didn't look again; she did not dare. Instead she took hold of Erik's rope, gripping it securely in case he tried to escape, but the billy wasn't concerned. He looked completely unrepentant and didn't seem to realize that his future was looking very bleak indeed.

"Erik," Jack said in a wavering voice, "you— you very bad boy."

The goat rolled his eyes at his young master, as if inviting him to enjoy the joke.

"You know you're not to butt strangers. Apologize. Now."

Eugenie had seen Jack's magic before but it still amazed her when the billy goat went down on his front knees and bowed his head. The Duke of Somerton, who had never seen it, was clearly speechless. His mouth twisted as if he wasn't sure whether to roar with rage or shout with laughter.

"You have to forgive him, sir," Jack explained anxiously. "Otherwise he'll just stay there all day."

Eugenie didn't expect the duke to be impressed by this. In fact she had taken a step forward, to place herself between the duke and the now repentant goat. But Somerton surprised her.

"I forgive you," he said gruffly, eyeing the goat uneasily.

On cue Erik jumped to his feet, tossing his head, eyes rolling wickedly. Immediately Jack heaped him with praise. Somerton raised his eyebrows, catching Eugenie's gaze.

"Do you often take your goat out for a stroll?" he said, a mocking note in his voice. "I would suggest leaving it at home next time."

"There won't be a next time," Jack replied, before Eugenie could answer. His lip quivered. "Mama is sending Erik back to Mr. Bartholomew's farm, where he came from, and Mr. Bartholomew will sell him to someone else and we will never see him again."

"Or he'll cook him in a pot," one of the twins added, and a tear ran down his cheek. The other twin leaned against him for comfort.

Somerton took in their woebegone faces. "I see," he said, and Eugenie felt that he really did. "Sir Billy has been given his marching orders, has he? What did he do to fall out of favor with your mother?"

"Ate her Parisian cap with the cerise ribbons!" the twins shouted together.

"Her favorite," Jack said. "The one that reminded her of when she was young and pretty, before she was—was plagued with children."

Somerton considered this. Eugenie, expecting some remark along the lines of "serves him right" or "you'll find another goat" was again pleasantly surprised.

"Do you think he would like to come and live with me?"

Suddenly Jack was grinning all over his face and the twins were cheering. Eugenie, feeling a little dizzy herself, said, "You are very kind, Your Grace, but—"

"I have need of a good goat," he interrupted, before she could finish.

If he wanted to make fast friends of her brothers then he had done so. They were gazing at him as if he were the hero in a storybook.

"You—you are very kind," Eugenie managed, as Somerton took hold of his horse's reins. "I don't know what to say."

"Then say nothing," he retorted awkwardly, as if her emotion was unwelcome. The dark eyes swept over her again, and it seemed to Eugenie that he saw every flaw and fault, before he fixed on her own green eyes. He cleared his throat and added gruffly, "It is a small thing. Of no consequence."

"Can—can we visit him?" Jack asked anxiously. "I know he will be fed and everything, but he will miss us. And we will miss him."

"Naturally you must visit him." The duke mounted his horse, settling himself with a grimace. Eugenie wondered if Erik had caused any permanent damage but knew she could hardly ask. "I'll send someone to talk to your father." His gaze turned quizzical. "You do have a father?"

"Of course," Eugenie said rather sharply.

His gaze lingered but whatever it was he was thinking he kept it to himself, merely nodding, before he turned his mount back the way he'd come. A moment later he was cantering away and soon he'd vanished around the bend in the lane.

"You are going to a new home, Erik. A duke's home," Jack was telling his naughty pet, stroking the rough head. "And I will visit you as often as I can. Don't worry, I won't forget you."

Eugenie smiled. No, she thought, it would be

a long time before any of them forgot their meeting with His Grace, the Duke of Somerton. Who would have thought he could be so generous? And who would have thought the brush of those dark eyes could make her skin burn and her heart bump? Arrogant, yes. Aware of his own worth, that, too. He was a million miles out of her league.

But there was nothing wrong in dreaming.

The boys had a hard time convincing their mother that they really had met a duke. At first she declared it a make-believe story, designed to save the wretched Erik, but when Eugenie assured her it really was the truth, she cried that the whole world was conspiring against her, and retired to her room. Their father was more pragmatic and was already, Eugenie was sure, considering ways in which he could turn the situation to his financial advantage.

The next morning someone arrived at Belmont Hall as promised.

Eugenie was up early, as always, helping with the household chores and getting the younger boys ready for school. Of course, as soon as they knew the duke's man was there, they escaped her grasp and ran down the stairs and outside. With a sigh, tucking her unruly curls behind her ears, Eugenie followed. She had reached the back door and stepped out into the chaos that was their yard before she realized that the "someone" come to fetch Erik was the duke himself.

For a moment she was so surprised she could do nothing more than stare. He was speaking to her father, tapping his hat against his thigh, looking perfect in tight breeches and a coat from Bond Street—or somewhere just as posh. Only his hair was a little untidy, tangled from the ride, and his lean cheeks flushed from the exercise.

As if aware of her openmouthed stare, he looked up and met her gaze.

"Ah, Miss Belmont," he said brusquely, with a bow. "I have come for Sir Billy, as I promised."

The twins were dancing around him, and Jack was leading Erik from his enclosure, looking proud and miserable at the same time. "You must be on your best behavior," she heard him say, as Erik rolled his eyes.

"It is very good of you, Your Grace," she managed, with a curtsey, remembering she was wearing one of her oldest and shabbiest dresses and had yet to brush her curls or wash her face. Good heavens, what a fright she must look!

"Our Eugenie is to be a genuine lady," her father announced, tugging at his waistcoat where it bulged over his stomach. "She's currently attending Miss Debenham's Finishing School. We expect great things of her."

"I'm sure she will not disappoint you," the duke said, perfectly straight-faced.

"My grandmother was His Majesty King George the Second's mistress," he went on proudly, making Eugenie want to curl up in a ball and disappear into the earth. "Eugenie takes after her, you know."

The duke's eyebrows rose, as well they might.

"She was a house maid," Eugenie muttered.

"A palace maid," her father corrected her.

"How very interesting," Somerton said, tipping his head to one side and examining Eugenie carefully. "And you say your daughter resembles this woman?"

"The spitting image, Your Grace."

"Then I can understand why the king was smitten."

It was a gallant compliment. His coal dark eyes delved into hers and she felt the shock of his gaze right down to her toes. He looked startled himself, and the flush in his cheeks deepened. She thought she saw a spark of interest. A warm flicker of intention. Something equally warm blossomed inside her, spreading throughout her body.

"Erik is ready now," Jack was saying, handing over his pet's lead to Somerton. The duke quickly passed it on to his man, who Eugenie noticed standing behind him, and who petted Erik with the air of one used to animals. They prepared to leave.

"You may visit him whenever you wish," Somerton said to Jack and the twins. "He may be a little homesick at first, although I am sure he will soon settle in."

"And I will be sure to call on you about that little matter we discussed," the baronet said quickly, tapping the side of his nose.

Eugenie wondered what her father was up to and hoped he wasn't going to embarrass her yet again with one of his schemes.

Somerton made her a bow, a lock of hair tumbling down over his eyes, a serious cast to his lips.

"Miss Belmont, I do hope we meet again, after you have been finished at Miss Debenham's."

He was teasing her, as the king had no doubt teased her ancestress. She curtseyed again with wobbly knees. "Yes, Your Grace."

And he was gone, leaving the yard bleak and empty, and the day ahead looking endlessly long.

Sinclair left Erik to his groom, and rode ahead. There were estate matters requiring his attention but for some reason he found himself in no hurry to get home. His lips twisted as he thought about Eugenie Belmont and the revelation that she was the descendant of the second Hanoverian George and a servant.

He couldn't imagine his own family being proud of such a fact. His mother would probably put a sentence of death upon anyone who revealed such a scandal, and yet here were the Belmonts, shouting it out loud to the world.

Eugenie Belmont was no beauty and yet there was something very appealing about her, a mysterious quality that drew the eye. He laughed out loud as he recalled her frozen in the doorway in her faded pink dress, her abundant curls tumbling down her back, her green eyes as big as saucers. He could easily imagine how her ancestress might have captured the attention of the ageing king.

Briefly his thoughts strayed into lustful fantasy. He'd never been one for flirtatious behavior when it came to women, particularly those beneath his own station, and the idea that he may have flirted with Eugenie just now surprised him. He was not a rake, not by any stretch of the imagination. He was never easy in the company of women. Even during his youth, when suddenly he'd found himself with a surfeit of female bodies in his bed, he'd been uncomfortably shy once the lovemaking was over. Conversing with women did not come easily to him, and often made him seem stiff.

The last thing he needed was a liaison with Eugenie Belmont and her appalling family. His future, he thought with blind arrogance, lay in other areas.

Chapter 2

~~~∞∞~~~

Belmont Hall, Gloucestershire, England
Present time

As usual the eggs were overcooked, the sausages blackened, while the toast was soggy and barely browned. Eugenie viewed the table with resignation as she sipped her tea. Nothing had changed since she'd been away being finished at Miss Debenham's. Breakfast was always the liveliest meal at Belmont Hall, and she could see the strain on her mother's face as she sought to regain some control over the most boisterous of her brood while her father seemed to positively encourage them in more and more outrageous behavior.

To her cries of "Speak to them, dear Sir Peter, please!" he answered "Good morning, children."

They loved it, as Eugenie well knew, but she pitied her mother. Now that she was home it would be expected of her to take over some of the burden of caring for the family. The Belmonts were not wealthy, they could not afford more than two house servants, and as she was the only girl, Eugenie sometimes felt that the extra work fell upon her more than was fair.

"Genie, are we going to see Erik today?" Jack asked for the tenth time.

"Yes, we are," Eugenie answered patiently, while her insides were all aquiver as she considered the claims she'd made to her friends that last night at Miss Debenham's. Olivia and Marissa had already written. Although Eugenie managed to forget about her foolish words sometimes for an hour at a time they always returned. Like Marie Antoinette at the guillotine, Eugenie saw no way out of her situation.

Her father's chuckle brought her out of her gloomy thoughts. There was a suspiciously satisfied gleam in his eye. "I separated His Grace from ten guineas, thanks to that goat," he said.

"What do you mean? Why would he pay you ten guineas?"

"Father went to visit the duke," one of the twins piped up. "Tell her what you said, Father!"

"Tell her how you fleeced the duke!" the other twin added, bouncing up and down on his chair with excitement.

Sir Peter Belmont was nothing loath to share his triumph. "I explained to His Grace that I was giving up my finest billy goat, and that if he wanted to keep Erik then I'd need to be compensated."

Eugenie set down her teacup with shaking hands; a sick feeling was growing in her stomach. "Father, how could you? You know he was only taking Erik to be kind. And after the wretched goat butted him! I hope he refused to pay."

"Well, that's where you're wrong," her father retorted, barely ruffled by her criticism. "I admit he could have said no, in which case we would have had to come to some other arrangement, but he agreed that ten guineas was cheap at the price."

"Cheap at the price!" the twins echoed.

"Do sit still, boys!" their mother wailed.

Eugenie had the depressing feeling that she was the only member of this family who cared that a wrong had been done. How could she face the duke after her father's scheming? How could the most eligible man in England look favorably upon a woman whose own background was so obviously and completely *in*eligible?

"I will have to apologize," she said grimly.

"Oh, please don't purse your mouth up like that, Eugenie," her mother said in her long-suffering voice. "There was a time when you found your father's little tricks amusing. My sister Beatrix may have paid for you to go to finishing school, but how do you think we afforded the extras? Evening gloves, for heaven's sake. And the boys are always in need of new boots. They grow so quickly!"

"Speaking of which, Eugenie, my girl, I expect you to put to use some of those fine finishing school manners," her father interrupted. "Next time I go to the Torringham horse market you can come with me and bedazzle the customers."

"I'm sure I'll be far too busy to go to the horse market."

Eugenie's father had a not undeserved reputation as a shyster and a rapscallion—a man not to be trusted. She wasn't going to assist him in perpetrating one of his dishonest schemes.

Sir Peter found it easy to blur the lines between what was lawful and what was useful to him. After being thrown out of school he went on to gamble away most of his inheritance, apart from his title, and then marry a local heiress so that he could pay his debts—only now he was beholden to the heiress's hardnosed sister. He was charming, however, and it was charm that had carried him through life so far—much as it carried his grandmother into the king's bed. Terrence, the brother closest in age to Eugenie, was a great deal like their father when it came to that charm, and she worried that he would end up just the same.

She spent a lot of time worrying about her brothers.

When she wasn't worrying about the mess her wretched tongue had gotten her into and how she was going to get out of it. Apart from doing as she'd said she would and pursuing the most eligible man in the county in an effort to make him her husband.

Breakfast over, she led the younger boys outside to the stables. The twins were tumbling around like puppies as she loaded them into the old coach. It was like something out of the ark, and Eugenie tried not to notice how desperately the vehicle needed a new coat of paint or the alarming crick in one of the wheels.

"It's not as if we'll even see the duke," she comforted herself. "There'll be a groom to direct us to Erik."

That meant she probably wouldn't have a chance to apologize for her father's shameful behavior, but she could always write a letter, she told herself with relief. She should have written before, to thank him for agreeing to help with the billy goat, but she'd kept putting it off. What did one say to a duke who'd been butted by a billy goat?

The coach was just rolling past the front of the hall when Terrence came strolling up and forced them to halt. Eugenie narrowed her eyes at him through the open window, noting that his necktie was askew, his shirt and jacket were crumpled, and his eyes were shadowed from fatigue—at least she hoped it was fatigue. He was a handsome boy, a year younger than Eugenie, and took after their father in looks, but lately there was an air of dissatisfaction about him.

"Off somewhere interesting?" he asked, opening the door.

"Where have you been, Terry?"

"None of your business," he said, sneering in a way he probably considered rakish, and then spoiled it all by adding in an anxious voice, "Can you lend me a guinea, Genie? I'll pay you back."

"Have you been gambling down at the Five Bells?"

"There's little enough else to do around here."

"I thought you wanted to join the army?"

"What's the point? Father could never afford a decent regiment and I'd hardly want to go in as a foot soldier. I might as well resign myself to being trapped in this backwater until I die."

He sounded so forlorn that Eugenie felt sorry for him. Terry wasn't a bad boy, but with no way of achieving his dreams he'd begun to frequent places like the Five Bells and spend his time getting into scrapes with bad company. It wouldn't be long before he was in debt by more than a guinea.

"Do you think Aunt Beatrix will pay for my commission?" he said, a spark of hope in his eyes. "Like she paid for you to go to Miss Debenham's?"

"I don't know, Terry. I hope so. As long as father doesn't put her back up again."

Aunt Beatrix was an irascible lady who loathed Peter Belmont and didn't think too highly of his wife, her sister, who had been left a considerable amount of money by their father. But Beatrix had married well, a manufacturer of soaps and skin potions, and now she was a very wealthy widow. She was fond of Eugenie, probably because she reminded her of her sensible self, but Terry was another matter. Eugenie feared he looked too much like his father for Aunt Beatrix's liking.

"We're going to see Erik," one of the twins said now, bouncing up and down on the old, cracked leather seat. "We're going to Somerton."

"Are you indeed?" Terry gave them a thoughtful look. "Mind if I tag along?"

He didn't wait for an answer, climbing up into the coach and squeezing in beside Jack and Eugenie. She wondered why he should want to come on what he'd normally consider a childish outing, but she was so pleased to see him smiling for a change that she didn't make a fuss.

"We're going to see the duke, we're going to see the duke!" the twins yelled as they set off.

"I wonder if I will be allowed in the stables again," Jack said quietly, with a little shiver of excitement. "Last time I helped saddle one of the duke's best stallions. Would you believe it, Genie? The stable boys were frightened of him."

"You will all be good, won't you?" Eugenie said, looking around at her brothers' faces. "You will be on your best behavior. Do you promise?"

Of course they all did, even Terry, but although she wanted to trust them past experience warned Eugenie not to believe a word.

Sinclair St. John, the fifth Duke of Somerton, had business to attend to. Estate business. But business would have to wait until he'd dealt with the question of his sister. Annabelle was being difficult. At the end of last year she had become engaged to Lord Lucius Salturn but as the date for the wedding drew closer she'd become very restless and unhappy. Sinclair didn't know where she got her ideas from, but he knew their mother was depending on him to make her see sense before she arrived in London to attend prenuptial balls and soirees with her fiancé.

"I will *die* if I marry Lucius," she declared dramatically. "He does not believe women should read books. He told me so. How can I possibly marry a man who thinks such things, Sinclair?"

"It is up to you to change his mind," Sinclair retorted. "I'm sure you're more than capable of that, Annabelle. He thinks you are a goddess. He told me so."

That gave her pause, but not for long.

"I don't want to get married. I am too young. Just think of all the fun I am missing out on by being engaged to Lucius." Her voice wavered. "It isn't fair of you to make me do this. I *hate* you, Sinclair."

He sighed. Part of being an elder brother and the head of his family meant playing the disciplinarian. Sinclair knew the marriage was a coup where Annabelle was concerned, and Lucius was the perfect addition to their family. His mother had explained the importance of marrying within one's own sphere, of doing one's duty by one's family. Sinclair knew that his tough behavior was for Annabelle's own good, and any niggling doubts or sympathies he felt must be firmly quashed. But even so it was not easy to feel he was making her miserable.

"That's as may be," he said, steeling himself for her tears, "but you will be leaving for London on the first day of July and I expect you to be packed and ready. Do I make myself clear?"

His sister promptly fled the room, her steps ringing up the staircase and her sobs echoing up into the domed seventeenth-century gallery.

"Blast it," Sinclair muttered, and flung out of the French windows and onto the terrace, where he glowered at a gardener's boy who was staking lilies, frightening him badly. It was in Annabelle's best interests to marry Lucius. A year ago their

mother announced that Annabelle was growing far too wild and willful, and behaving in a
manner that was quite unladylike. She needed
curbing; she needed to be married.

"Marriage will sober her," said the dowager
duchess. "She must learn that people like us have
a position to maintain. We cannot do what we
wish. We must conform to our breeding."

It was only what Sinclair knew to be the truth,
for such pronouncements had been drummed into
him all his life. He no longer questioned them. He
no longer hungered for what he could not have.
Or so he told himself.

"We cannot have Annabelle turning into a
hoyden," he muttered to himself. "Like . . . like
. . ."

The name rang in his head.

Miss Eugenie Belmont of Belmont Hall.

His lip curled. It was his trademark expression
and others saw it as a sign of his disdain for those
less fortunate than himself. It was an affectation
he'd learned as a boy and now it came so automatically to him he didn't even know he was doing it.

But was Miss Belmont a hoyden? Surely it was
her family who were the hoydens! It still stung
him when he remembered the father trying to
ingratiate himself with Sinclair and then making
that outrageous offer. Sinclair didn't entirely understand why he'd paid for the privilege of keeping an animal on his estate that he hadn't wanted
in the first place. He supposed it was partly because of the boy, Jack, and the tears in his eyes.
And partly because he had seen in Jack a remark-

able talent for taming animals—in particular horses. According to Sinclair's groom the boy was a marvel. Within moments he'd had the wildest stallion eating from his hand.

Sinclair was very fond of his horses, and he told himself that by allowing himself to be fleeced by the father he was gaining the trust of the son.

As for Eugenie Belmont . . . her brother had artlessly told him that when his sister came home from finishing school her parents hoped she'd marry someone rich as a consequence. "Father is very proud of Eugenie. He says that when she comes home she'll be a lady and we need her to marry someone who can put money into Belmont Hall before it falls down," he went on, clearly too naïve to realize he was saying things he ought not.

"And has your sister a particular suitor in mind?" Sinclair inquired calmly, while a tingle of warning sharpened his senses.

"Oh, no, I don't think so. Not yet, anyway."

The tingle faded. Sinclair breathed a sigh of relief. Just for a moment he'd thought he might be the unlucky object of her desires! But surely Eugenie Belmont—royal blood or not—would be too canny to think she could ever be in the same class as the Duke of Somerton!

He wondered now whether it would be in his interest—in Jack's interest—if he found someone for Miss Belmont. A wealthy gentleman of lesser birth? Or even a businessman, a manufacturer, with money to burn on a rundown hovel like Belmont Hall? It was something to consider. Miss Belmont would be grateful to him, he was sure, and therefore Jack would look upon him favorably. The entire Belmont family would be in his debt and would not mind him borrowing their son for the sake of his horses.

And yet it was odd how often he had found himself remembering Eugenie Belmont during the past three months. The smile in her green eyes, for instance, and the way they sparkled. And how, despite her lack of stature, she had stood up to him in the lane, so straight, for all that she was barely up to his shoulder. As if she meant to protect her brothers at all costs. That pink flush in her cheeks and on her soft lips, her wild curls, and those endearing freckles scattered across her nose, as she stood in the doorway of her home. The sensation that he knew exactly what had attracted a king to make her commoner ancestress his mistress. Surely in normal circumstances her features should have faded from his memory? Instead they seemed to become clearer, more distinct. . .

"Your Grace?"

He almost jumped—as if he'd been caught doing something wrong. When he turned he found one of his servants hesitating behind him, loath to interrupt his cogitations.

"What is it?" Not Annabelle again, he hoped. He would be relieved when the girl was on her way to London and the welcoming arms of her fiancé.

"A Miss Eugenie Belmont has arrived, with her brothers, to visit Erik the, eh, goat."

The servant looked startled when Sinclair

smiled; he had expected the lip curl for which his master was so famous.

Well, this was providential, thought Sinclair. He didn't even consider avoiding them; the idea simply didn't even enter his head. He told himself he was keen to observe Jack with the stallion, and of course there was the question of whether finishing school had made any changes in Miss Eugenie Belmont. He hoped she hadn't become too conventional.

Is she still a hoyden?

He set off across the terrace with long strides which were undeniably eager.

Chapter 3

It was only the second time Eugenie had been to Somerton. The first time was when she and her parents had visited while the duke's family was away and the grounds were thrown open to the public. Although she had not been able to enter the house—that was locked up tight—and could only stand gazing at it from various corners of the garden, she had found it quite dazzling. And she took the time to discover a little of its history.

Somerton in its present incarnation was built by the first duke, in the seventeenth century, after he'd covered himself in glory during the wars on the Continent, but parts of an older house remained hidden behind the new, grand facade. The Italian Renaissance architecture was meant to impress—after all this was one of England's premier families—and one was not allowed to forget it.

"Are you sure you've got this right, Jack?" Terry ruffled his brother's hair. "You're not having us on? Are you really welcome here?"

Jack ducked away from his hand. "I've been

before, you know," he said irritably. "I'm allowed to visit anytime I like. The duke said so."

"I was there when Erik introduced himself to the duke," Eugenie reminded Terry. "And I think Jack has made quite an impression with the groom. You know how he is with horses."

Terry shrugged, playing at being unimpressed. His hair was falling into his eyes, his neck cloth was untied, and he lounged as if there were no bones in his body. It was all an act, she knew that, but she wished he wouldn't behave that way. She shuddered to think what the duke would think of him. Indeed she shuddered whenever she imagined the duke in the company of *any* of her family.

But then, she reminded herself, the duke wasn't likely to come out to meet them personally. Why should he? He must have far more important things to do. Just because her wretched tongue had set her on an impossible course—a husband who had everything she would never have, and who was everything she wished her family could be—did not mean he was going to fall into her hands. . .

And then her thoughts stopped.

A tall, elegant figure was moving toward them, a figure she recognized all too well, and she felt the drummer boy begin his rapid drumming on her heart.

He had come to meet them after all!

"*This is your chance, Eugenie,*" she heard her friends' voices in her head, as clear as if they had joined hands and were circling about her, urging her on in this madness. "*You must make him notice you. Fascinate him, ensnare him, wind his heart around your finger. Make him fall in love with you. You may not get another chance like this, Eugenie!"*

She felt quite giddy and took a deep breath. He certainly made an elegant and imposing figure. She couldn't help but admire him. If this was a novel he would find her equally fascinating in her ancient dress which was an inch too short at the hem, but unfortunately such things did not happen in real life.

Beside her Terry was still slouching. She dug her elbow into him, making him jerk upright just as Sinclair came striding up to join them.

He was impeccably dressed, his dark hair brushed into the latest style, his boots like mirrors. She felt no warmth from him, only that chilly reserve as he greeted them in measured tones. After Eugenie had dipped her curtsey, she introduced her brother.

"How d'you do," Terry drawled.

She wanted to elbow him again.

Sinclair lifted his brows and, ignoring Terry, settled his gaze on Eugenie. "Back from finishing school, Miss Belmont. Tell me, how did you find it?"

So he had remembered! She didn't know whether to be flattered or embarrassed that that awful moment had lodged in his memory.

"Most instructive, Your Grace," she replied breathlessly, ignoring Terry's snort. "I learned an awful lot."

His eyes were as coal black as she remembered. Strangely they no longer seemed cold. In fact a smile was lurking in them, a glimmer of something tentative, as though he wanted to reach out to her but didn't know how. Eugenie knew she must be imagining it. Why would Somerton want to be her friend? It was utterly preposterous. And yet she was aware of her own giddy feelings, that sense of having skipped over her last bridge.

Foolish and ill-conceived her plan may be but she was going to do it. She really was. She was going to go husband hunting for the duke.

The twins were led off by a young lad to find Erik, but Jack expressed a wish to see the stables first. Sinclair showed the way, with Eugenie hurrying to keep up.

"Thank you, Your Grace, for your generosity in allowing Jack to visit Erik. And your stables," she said raising her voice as he drew farther away. "He is very excited to see so many beautiful horses."

"Genie," Jack murmured, with a disgusted glance.

Now Sinclair did smile. "Just so, Jack," he agreed heartily. "These are not 'beautiful horses,' these are prime horseflesh. Come and I will introduce you to my latest hope for Newmarket."

Terry mooched along at Eugenie's side. "Must be easy to be generous when you have everything," he muttered, unable to hide his envy.

Eugenie frowned. "Do behave yourself, Terry. You promised me."

He gave a grunt but thankfully said no more. There was even a spark of interest in his gaze as he took in the sleek animals and for a short time he was almost the boy he used to be.

Jack was content to remain in the stables with the grooms, and Sinclair returned to the door, where Eugenie was standing, to ask if she would care for some refreshment. "Terrence, too, of course," he added, with a cool look at Terry.

"Thank you, that is very—" Eugenie began to answer for them both.

"Do you have any Moroccan punch?" Terry said eagerly.

Sinclair curled his lip. "Good God no," he said in what Eugenie could almost have called a sneer—a far more credible sneer than Terry's earlier attempt. "Surely that is only for bounders?"

They set off across one of the wide paths that crossed the immaculate lawn, shaded by old beeches and oaks. After his set-down Terry wasn't in a hurry to keep up with them, lagging behind like a sulky child.

"I've often remembered our meeting in the lane," Sinclair said, sneer gone.

"Oh?" Eugenie felt herself flushing at her own memories. "I hoped you might forgive and forget, Your Grace," she ventured.

"I never forget and rarely forgive," he answered swiftly.

She gave him a doubtful glance.

"Jack has shown himself an incredible horse handler," he went on.

Of course, he was talking about Jack! she realized, disappointed.

"I would be happy to offer him work here at

Somerton when he is of age. What plans does your father have for his schooling? I understand he has lessons with the local parson?"

He made it sound far direr than it was, and Eugenie sprang to the defense of her family. "Reverend Kearnen is an Oxford man. He taught Terry and will be taking on the twins soon."

Did Sinclair give a shudder?

How extremely rude of him! Even if his attitude was understandable, having met them on one of their worst possible days, she would have expected better manners from him. Sinclair may be the most eligible man in England but he was certainly not the most perfect.

"Do you think your father would be amenable to Jack coming to Somerton?"

Eugenie knew what Jack would wish to do, and she suspected her father would be more than happy to grant him that wish. If the price was tempting enough.

"You must ask him about that," she said uncomfortably.

His smile was enigmatic, as if he knew exactly what she was thinking.

The silence drew on.

"Your Grace, I want to apologize for my father's behavior regarding Erik. Asking for—for money from you, when you had been so generous. It was inexcusable. I hope you did not think I knew anything of the matter, for I assure you that I did not. I have told my father he should return your ten guineas immediately."

He looked down into her eyes, so green and

fierce it was difficult for him to look away. "Never mind that," he said gruffly, when only a moment before he'd been seething over the very same matter. "I was glad to take care of Erik, despite his propensity to send my gardeners flying." His lips curled, but this time it was into a smile. "Did you know he broke out of his yard and made a foray into the vegetable garden? We were worried he'd overeaten but he came through. He seems to have a taste for turnips and they don't like him. Or so I'm told."

Eugenie was trying not to laugh. "Oh dear," she said shakily, putting a hand to her mouth. "I *am* sorry. We should have p-paid you to keep him, not the other way around."

"Yes."

She gave him a sharp look and he wondered whether he'd overstepped the mark. He had a habit of putting peoples' backs up—not that it worried him particularly. Well, not normally. But in this case he found himself wishing to be thought well of by Miss Belmont. He much preferred her smiles to her frowns. And he felt an uncharacteristic urge to flirt with her and tightened the reins on it. The Duke of Somerton did not flirt, especially not with girls like Miss Eugenie Belmont.

"Would you like a tour of the house? The gardens are sometimes open to the public, but my mother refuses to have the masses tramping their muddy boots through the house." He spoke the words before he remembered she was one of "the masses."

She was looking at him with her deep green

eyes, as if she could read his very heart, and he held his breath. But all she said was, "We'd love a tour of your house, thank you, Your Grace."

We. He'd forgotten about the brother.

Despite what he'd said earlier Sinclair thought his butler might have the makings of Moroccan punch hidden away somewhere in his pantry, for the odd occasion when it was needed. Perhaps he should offer it to the boy and get him completely sloshed. Teach him a lesson.

But maybe not, he decided, glancing at Eugenie. If he wanted to keep in her good books then he'd best be nice to her brother. Brothers, he corrected himself. All of them.

It didn't occur to him to wonder why it was he felt he needed to stay in her good books.

Somerton was just as imposing inside as it was out. Eugenie gazed about, her awe mixed with terror. Could she ever be mistress of this place? Could she become used to ordering the servants and discussing menus and saying things like, "Yes, let's have a ball for the whole county and invite the queen!" as if the words came perfectly naturally to her.

Of course she was being wildly optimistic. But the thing was, whenever she looked into his eyes, she *felt* wildly optimistic.

And surely there was nothing wrong in placing a bet with long odds? Her father did it all the time, and sometimes, very occasionally, he won.

She glanced sideways at Sinclair, who had shortened his long strides to match hers, and tried to pay attention. He was lecturing her on the history of his family, and she could hear the pride in his voice, the arrogance. But surely arrogance was acceptable when one came from such an illustrious family? Although, come to think of it, she had heard exactly the same pride in her father's voice when he boasted about having fleeced someone too foolish to know he was being fleeced. But Sinclair's pride was different, surely? He would never do anything that was not respectable or proper, certainly nothing as underhand as selling a horse long past its galloping days as a prime racer.

He had stopped speaking and was looking down at her. He seemed to be waiting for her reply to some point he had made or perhaps he'd just noticed her attention drifting. Eugenie cast around for something intelligent to say.

"I suppose your lofty position comes with a great many responsibilities, Your Grace?"

"Naturally."

His lip curled. Earlier the sneer had been for Terry, but this time it was aimed at her. She felt like pointing out that the curl of his lip made him look less attractive, but perhaps this wasn't the time. He might take her criticism badly and she was trying to get him to think well of her.

"My father built several almshouses in the village," he was saying in a pompous tone, "and since I became duke I have built several more. I have tenants who need barns repaired and fences fixed, and villagers who depend upon our charity. The Somertons take their responsibilities to those less fortunate very seriously, Miss Belmont. It is part of being in a position of power."

"I suppose you think of Jack as a responsibility."

He appeared surprised. "Your brother is a remarkable lad."

"He is."

Sinclair gave her one of his quizzical looks, but at least he wasn't curling his lip at her. "I don't believe I think of him as a responsibility, although when he comes to Somerton in my employ then of course matters will change."

"If."

"I beg your pardon?"

"You said 'when he comes.' *If* he comes to Somerton, Your Grace. Such an outcome is far from being decided."

He said nothing for a moment but she thought that perhaps she had stung him a little. This was no way to go about capturing a husband. She should be flattering him and boosting his good opinion of himself, but she never thought it a good thing to puff someone up with flummery. Sinclair had quite enough consequence; he didn't need any more.

They were passing through a gallery where the ceiling rose high above them and was covered with a crisscross of ancient plasterwork and murals of heroes in armor hacking off the heads of vicious-looking creatures who had more to do with mythology than nature. Clearly the Somertons were a warlike bunch. Up ahead the statue of a horseman guarded the marble floor, and there were more statues and busts and portraits against or upon the walls. A fearsome array of weapons interspersed them, their sharp edges glinting in the light shining through the long windows.

So this was Sinclair's history, thought Eugenie, as she warily examined her surroundings. She doubted the Belmont heritage could have been set out like this to be admired. How would such things as gambling away several fortunes, running off with unsuitable women, drunken revels and being royal on the wrong side of the blanket be artistically displayed?

Sinclair was no longer behind her. Eugenie turned and found him standing stiff as a poker watching as Terry fought a mock battle with a sharp-looking sword, having taken it down from its place on the wall.

"Terry, please be careful!" she cried. "That doesn't belong to you!"

"It's only an old sword," he said scornfully, feinting a thrust at an imaginary foe. But the weight was too much for him, and the tip struck the marble floor with a loud ring.

"That 'old sword' belonged to the first duke," Sinclair spoke in frozen tones. "It is a family treasure and I would prefer it to remain in one piece."

Terry, his confidence dented by his almost accident, replaced it with an uneasy glance at the present duke. "I was only trying it out," he said sulkily.

"Learn to use it first," Sinclair snapped.

Behave yourself! Eugenie mouthed at her brother as she turned away.

She resumed her walk. A sideways glance showed the duke was not amused by her brother's antics, his mouth straight and thin, his chin jutting. "I apologize, Your Grace. Terry has hopes of joining the army. He imagines himself as a gallant officer fighting off the enemy."

"Hmm." He gave her a considering look.

Eugenie smiled. "He is young, Your Grace. Do you remember what you were like at that age? I'm sure he will improve with time."

He searched her face, a crease appearing between his brows.

"As yet there has been no suitable commission," Eugenie added, wondering what it was he could see that was so fascinating. The truth, probably. That they could not in fact afford a commission, suitable or unsuitable. She gave him another smile, and strolled on, nervous about the manner in which he continued to stare at her.

Eugenie was starting to feel as if this gallery would never end.

"Miss Belmont." His voice was abrupt. "I beg your pardon but . . . Have we met before? Not in the lane, of course I do not mean that. I mean some time ago. Just now I had the strangest feeling that we had met somewhere before. That would explain why I've been thinking about you all—" He stopped as abruptly as he'd started, his lean cheeks flushed.

Startled, Eugenie shook her head, meeting the intent look in his eyes. "I am certain we have not."

"Your smile . . . Yes, there *is* something familiar about it. I am not going mad," he went on, and now he was quite flushed. "Have we met? I demand you tell me at once."

"I assure you I would if I could. I can honestly swear to you that we hadn't met before the day in the lane."

"You have no sisters who resemble you?"

"I have not."

"Cousins?"

"Alas, no."

"Then I am flummoxed," he said. "Never mind, it will come to me."

Eugenie could not help but hope it would not. It was probably something uncomfortable, like being pointed out to Sinclair in the village as that Belmont hoyden or Belmont's ramshackle daughter. From experience she just knew it could not be anything good.

To her relief they were nearing the end of the gallery. A few portraits hung upon the walls, several enormous canvasses showing the Dukes of Somerton doing heroic deeds or seated on fat horses with small heads. There was even one of Boudicca—or at least she thought it was Boudicca—with her bosom barely covered with a flimsy robe and her hair streaming behind her as she drove her chariot toward her glorious end. The smile on her face seemed rather unlikely, unless she was laughing at fate.

"Aha!"

His cry made her jump. He was clutching her arm, his hand large and warm, his fingers tighter than was comfortable. With his other hand he pointed triumphantly at the vast painting.

"You see! I knew I had seen you somewhere before!"

Chapter 4

Eugenie stared up at the painting, trying to see what the duke saw. As far as she could tell Boudicca bore no resemblance to herself, none whatsoever. Perhaps the hair was somewhat similar, although far redder than her own, and the eyes had a hint of green in their mad glare . . . but the likeness was extremely nebulous.

"This came from an eighteenth century royal household, I believe," Sinclair was saying, dredging up his memory of the painting. "My ancestor bought it because there seemed to be very few women hanging among our ancestors and he considered Boudicca an acceptable addition. I wonder, Miss Belmont, if this might be your ancestress? George's mistress?"

Eugenie made a sound that could have meant anything. The woman in the painting was fierce and pagan, neither of which Eugenie considered part of her own character. Sinclair seemed rather excited by his conclusions but all she wanted to do was stroll on and leave her unsavory great-grandmamma—if indeed it was her—behind.

"Good Gad, Genie, is that you?" Terry was standing, mouth open, staring up at Boudicca.

"It's very like, isn't it?" Sinclair said, forgetting for a moment his dislike of the boy.

"Could be twins," Terry agreed obligingly.

"Well, I can't see it," Eugenie burst out uncomfortably.

Sinclair and Terry exchanged a look.

"No need to take it like that, Genie," her brother murmured. "You should be flattered."

"Well, I'm not," she said, and strode off down the final stretch of the gallery, not caring whether the duke followed her or not.

Sinclair found her in the yellow saloon, standing before the French windows and gazing out over the terrace and a fine sweep of the gardens. Her slim back was very straight, rigid almost, as if she was determined to show she didn't care about the painting.

Now that he considered the matter he realized the resemblance wasn't all that great. Just enough to strike a chord in him. Certainly not as apparent as her brother claimed, which was no doubt to repay his sister for her admonishment over the sword.

Sinclair rang for tea, and Terry threw himself in a chair covered in striped pink satin and yawned rudely. "I haven't been to bed yet," he announced with pride, as if he expected to be congratulated.

"Nothing ages a person more than lack of sleep," Eugenie said, turning from the window.

"I agree," Sinclair put in, meeting her eyes. She

looked a little pale but her gaze was as clear as ever. "I knew a man once, looked at least sixty. He was barely thirty. No sleep, you see. Wore him out before his time."

Her mouth twitched but she bit back her smile.

Suspiciously Terry glanced from one to the other of them. "You must think I'm an idiot. Lack of sleep isn't fatal."

"But can you be sure?" Sinclair retorted.

Now Eugenie did smile. He was back in her good books again, he thought with relief and then wondered why he cared so much. It was a mystery to him, just as most things to do with women were a mystery; it was just that normally he didn't care and with Eugenie he did.

Tea arrived and with it polite conversation. Eugenie took over the pouring of the beverage as if she'd done it all her life, handing out cups, sorting through the trays of cake and sandwiches so that both Terry and the duke were given their choice.

Here, she was in her element.

Eugenie knew polite conversation was one of her strong points—she was particularly good at putting others at ease—and she proceeded to do so. The awkwardness of the moment in the gallery was gone and, thankfully, the duke did not mention it again. They were getting on so well, chatting about this and that. Just for a moment she let herself imagine that Sinclair was thinking what a wonderful duchess she would make.

I knew at that moment I had to marry her.

She pictured the wedding, or tried to, but she

had never attended a society wedding and the detail eluded her. And things in her fantasy kept going wrong. When she got to the point where her brothers and Erik the goat were running wild down the aisle, she gave up on it and asked the duke if he wanted more tea.

Sinclair handed over his cup. He wasn't thinking about Eugenie's conversational skill or that she would make a wonderful duchess.

Sinclair was imagining what it would be like to kiss her.

The idea came upon him with shocking abruptness, like a dash of cold water on a hot day. He'd been staring into her green eyes, which really were like the clearest of ocean pools, and then his gaze wandered to the dear little freckles sprinkling her nose. After a moment he found himself watching her lips as she spoke—her words could have been babble for all he was listening—and trying to decide on their exact shade of pink. She smiled a great deal, her mouth curling at the edges rather delightfully. In fact her natural repose was smiling.

And that's when he knew he wanted to kiss her.

He, who never did anything which might undermine his importance or interfere with his lofty position, wanted to kiss a woman whose family were so far below his own they were almost invisible. He who never knew what to say to a woman once the social niceties were done wanted to get intimate with the by-blow of a randy old king and his chambermaid. He glanced across at her appalling brother and found he'd slipped out of the room. Probably gone to pocket the silver, he thought darkly.

"My mother is currently in London," he heard himself saying. "She enjoys seeing her friends and attending the opera and the theater. She is far more of a social butterfly than me, I'm afraid."

"You prefer the country, Your Grace?"

"Yes, I do. What of you, Miss Belmont? Are you heading to the metropolis now you've been 'finished'?"

To look for a rich husband, he almost said.

"My aunt has offered to put me up in London, but I haven't decided yet. I am required here for the moment—my mother needs help with the twins."

The twins would be too much for any woman, no matter how much help she had, Sinclair thought.

They were silent, sipping their tea. Eugenie was sitting up straight, her slim figure elegant, her profile turned to him as if she was deep in her own thoughts. Visitors to Somerton were often uncomfortable with its grandeur, overwhelmed by surroundings far above their own, but Eugenie did not seem overwhelmed.

"I wish I *could* go away from Belmont Hall," she said suddenly, passionately. "I wish I could leave my family behind and launch myself into a new life."

She gave him a flicker of a glance, as if uncertain whether her words would offend him in some way. He wasn't offended. While he did wonder why he'd been the recipient of her unexpected confidence he was rather pleased she'd chosen him.

"Why don't you?" he said cautiously.

She laughed. "I can see you do not understand the difficulties of common folk. How could you? You have everything you might ever want and if you don't have it then you can quite simply purchase it or find it or—or take it. You are a duke and everyone defers to you."

"I would have thought that brings its own bonds and ties. I have obligations and responsibilities, remember?"

"But don't you sometimes wish you could just throw aside all of it and head off on an adventure? Or do something completely out of character, something wild and dangerous? Have you ever done anything wild and dangerous and—and reckless, Your Grace?"

"Can't say I have, Miss Belmont."

She sighed. He found himself wondering what she was thinking. She seemed disappointed in him, as if he'd failed her in some way. Sinclair didn't want to be a disappointment.

"When I was a young boy, I considered being a tinker the most exciting life I could imagine. Wandering free through the countryside, sleeping under the trees and cooking rabbits over a campfire. No parents to insist I do my lessons or sit up straight at the table, no one to remind me of the heavy burden coming to me when I became duke. But when I began tying Cook's pots and pans about my person and affecting a tinker's accent my mother put a stop to my ambitions."

She smiled, and he felt pleased, as if she was rewarding him for effort. "I remember that tinker. He had long dark hair and a gold earring."

"I think it was the earring that I wanted most of all."

"I should think, now you are duke, you could wear an earring and no one would dare to comment upon it. They may think you eccentric, but the rich are allowed their eccentricities. Nice try, Your Grace, but I do not think I would consider that reckless behavior, not in your case."

Sinclair watched as she set down her teacup. What *did* she consider reckless behavior then? When she rose to her feet he felt his own stab of disappointment. "I'd better find my brothers before they wear out your staff."

He opened the French doors onto the terrace and she paused to admire the potted orange trees in flower, enveloped in their sweet, heady scent. The sunlight caught the red tints in her hair, where the curls were evading the confines of her straw bonnet.

She was no classic beauty.

Nevertheless there was something very fetching about her, something that drew him and made him want to . . . well, to kiss her.

A pulse began beating in his throat as she turned to smile at him, and he wondered what would happen if he did kiss her. Here. Now. Would that be wild and dangerous enough for her? Could he do it? Did he dare?

He leaned closer and she gazed back at him, her lips slightly apart, her pupils enormous and dark. Her scent came to him, an undertone to the orange blossom, sweet and fresh and womanly.

"Eugenie . . ."

But just before he took her into his arms, a familiar voice drifted toward them. Sinclair straightened up. Across the lawn and under a tree was his sister, seated on a swing, and pushing her rather too vigorously was Eugenie's appalling brother.

Sinclair leaped off the terrace and began to stride toward them with ominous speed.

Eugenie hurried behind, skirts held up above her shoes and stockings, more curls tumbling from beneath her straw bonnet.

"Whatever is the matter, Your—Your Grace?" she called, her voice fading as he outstripped her.

"Annabelle?" he said in his most glacial tone. "Where is Miss Gamboni?"

His sister stopped swinging and looked at him, her beautiful face mutinous. "I wanted some air, brother. Do I need a chaperone for that? Surely you would not begrudge me some air? There will be little enough to be had in London once I am residing there."

Sinclair eyed Terry with displeasure. "I see you have met Mr. Belmont."

"Mr. Belmont was kind enough to accompany me for a stroll around the garden," she replied primly, but with a sly sideways glance at her companion.

Eugenie arrived, breathlessly trying to straighten her bonnet. "Terry, I think we must go now," she said anxiously, reaching for his arm.

As if, Sinclair thought with surprise, she was

drawing him away from danger. Was *he* the danger? Did she think he was going to punch her brother in the nose? He might deserve it, certainly, for inveigling himself into Annabelle's company, but Sinclair knew he was far above such petty behavior. Still, he took a moment to calm himself.

"Let me introduce Miss Eugenie Belmont," he said in a milder tone. "This is my sister, Lady Annabelle."

Caught off guard, Eugenie gave a wobbly curtsey.

Just then a fair-haired girl came hurrying toward them, flushed, her gaze anxious. "Your Grace," she said breathlessly.

"Miss Gamboni," he retorted coolly. "We will discuss your failure as a chaperone for my sister later."

Eugenie felt sorry for the girl, but Annabelle was more interested in persuading her brother to let her have her own way. "Mr. Belmont says there is a ball in the village on Saturday night, Sinclair. Shall we go?"

"Annabelle, you know that is not possible."

"Why not?" Her voice had grown a little shrill. "He says they have a ball every year at this time and we have never gone. Don't you think that is a little odd, when we have lived here so long? I want to go, Sinclair. Just because I am marrying Lucius does not mean I cannot have a little treat. Indeed, I think I deserve a treat. Please. You know I love to dance. It is the one thing I miss about London. We have never attended the village balls and yet Mr. Belmont tells me they are a great deal of fun."

"Rather tedious, sometimes," Terry put in. "Very strict when it comes to manners, aren't they, Eugenie? No high jinks allowed."

Eugenie looked as if she might say something else, but her brother nudged her and instead she reluctantly nodded in agreement.

Despite all of his inner doubts, Sinclair felt himself waver. Annabelle was going to London soon. There would be no time to form a tender for the appalling brother, so what harm could it do? She would probably find the village ball boring and uncomfortable; she would not enjoy being jostled among so many smelly farmers and local worthies. And Sinclair and Miss Gamboni would be there to keep an eye on her.

"We shall see."

She pouted and tossed her head, but he thought it was more for Terry's benefit than his own. "You're so stuffy, Sinclair. You never have any fun and you want everyone to be as boring as you."

"We must go," Eugenie said again into the uncomfortable silence, with an urgent glance at her brother. "Thank you again for your invitation, Your Grace. We are most grateful for your kindness."

"Yes, thank you," Terry murmured, as he ambled in her wake.

Sinclair watched them go, their heads close, as if in serious conversation. It wasn't until Annabelle tucked her hand into his elbow that he realized she'd been speaking and he was miles away. Determinedly putting Eugenie Belmont out of his thoughts, he concentrated on his sister.

"You cannot have enjoyed being with Terrence Belmont," he said. "He's not up to your mark."

Annabelle smiled at him fondly. "Sinclair, you are such a snob. And the thing is you don't even know it."

Jack was back in the stables after a visit to Erik, but content to be loaded once more into the old coach. The twins were tired from a game of hide-and-seek with a stable lad and leaned against each other, sleepy-eyed. Terry waffled on about Lady Annabelle and how unaffected she was for a duke's sister.

"Do you think she'll come to the village ball?" he mused. "A guinea says she will."

"You owe me a guinea."

"Then we'll be even. If I could find a wife like Lady Annabelle I'd be made for life."

"Once she sees where the ball is held, in the rooms above The Acorn, she may not be quite so unaffected," Eugenie said dryly. "It is hardly what she is used to, Terry. I'd be very surprised if her brother lets her go. That poor girl . . . Miss Gamboni. Obviously Lady Annabelle gave her the slip."

"All the gossip about him is right, isn't it? He's an arrogant stuffed shirt. Did you hear how he spoke to me when I dared to touch his old sword?"

Eugenie wasn't listening. Her thoughts were drifting. Would Sinclair be at the village ball? And if he was, would he dance with her? The rooms above The Acorn were crowded and stuffy and couples were known to slip away for a cuddle and a kiss. Would Sinclair ever do anything so daring, something so far beneath his usual rigid code of behavior? If she could persuade him to do something so unlike himself then her chances of marrying him would surely rise a notch or two?

She wondered what it would be like to kiss Sinclair.

Her lips tingled, as she recalled the manner in which he'd looked at her when they were standing on the terrace, the way he'd moved closer, almost as if he was about to take her in his arms. The way he'd spoken her name.

Terry might think him stuffy and arrogant, but Eugenie saw something else in Sinclair's dark eyes. His Grace, the Duke of Somerton was lonely and quite possibly shy, hemmed about with his duties and responsibilities and his grand house. She smiled, remembering his boyhood wish to be a tinker with a golden earring. She was beginning to understand him. Whereas Eugenie wanted respectability her duke needed to do something completely undukelike and a little wild.

And Eugenie was the girl to help him do it.

Chapter 5

Jack was full of talk about the duke's stables and all that he'd seen there. Sir Peter didn't appear to be taking any more interest than normal, but Eugenie noticed he hung about after supper rather than retiring to his newspaper. She could almost see the cogs in his brain turning, formulating some plan whereby he would sell his services to the duke for a small fee. "I taught Jack everything he knows about horseflesh," he would boast, and then offer to share his expertise. Eugenie cringed at the thought, and hoped her father would think better of it. Unfortunately, knowing him as she did, she was more inclined to fear the worse.

As she'd grown up, her family had become more of an embarrassment to her. When she was young she was like Jack, naïve, believing there was nothing wrong in what her father did. But the years had changed that, and as Eugenie grew into a woman who found such behavior unacceptable, she felt the gap between herself and her family widen. She was like a changeling and sometimes she thought it would be a wonderful thing to walk away from these people who were so unlike her. Why, she asked herself, couldn't she have been born into a different family altogether—a respectable family with morals and ethics? A family she could be proud of instead of wanting to hide them behind closed doors?

But of course she couldn't walk away. Jack needed her, and the twins were not completely beyond redemption. She had a duty to them, to help them as best she could, although some days the burden was great indeed and she could not help but wonder if there would ever be a time for *her*. When would she be able to live her own life?

Eugenie tried not to give a sigh as she made her way upstairs to her small bedchamber. At least it was hers alone, she being the only girl in the family, and she treasured the small private space. With the door closed she could shut out the trials and tribulations awaiting her and lose herself in her books and her dreams.

She went to her wardrobe and stood staring at her few dresses. There wasn't much to choose from, but there was the ball on Saturday and she wanted to look her best. Her Sunday gown was too drab and serious, and she had grown out of many of the girlish dresses she'd worn before she went to Miss Debenham's. The truth was she needed something new, but that was unlikely to happen when the boys desperately required new shoes.

As she examined each garment, Eugenie imagined what Sinclair would think, and her dissatisfaction grew. How could she attract such a handsome, eligible man when he must be used to the most beautiful women in the most gorgeous outfits? Eventually she shut the door with a bang and flung herself back onto her bed, staring at the ceiling, and indulging in her favorite pastime of make-believe.

The make-believe world was always so much more satisfactory than real life. She could make the story end as she wished, and lately it always ended the same way. With herself happily married to the Duke of Somerton.

But today she couldn't seem to place the story threads to her satisfaction, and restlessly she turned over, her cheek on her hand, and gazed at the window. Downstairs she could hear the twins arguing and her mother's desperate and useless threats, and then her father's roar of displeasure, which worked better. It was no use. In a moment there would be a tap on her door, the long-suffering servant requesting she come and help.

Eugenie rose and left her daydreams behind.

Sinclair found his sister in a surprisingly good mood following the Belmonts' visit. He had his suspicions this was something to do with Terry Belmont, and the coming ball he'd let himself be persuaded into attending, but as Annabelle would be leaving for London soon he didn't concern himself too much. And he had had words with Miss Gamboni and instructed her sternly on the need to be vigilant when it came to his sister.

If there were tears when it came time for Annabelle to go, he would deal with them as he always dealt with her tantrums. By reminding her she had a position to maintain and a birthright to uphold.

He found himself thinking of Eugenie Belmont instead. *Don't you ever feel as if you'd like to do something dangerous?* He hadn't, not until that moment, or if sometimes he felt restless then he'd simply refused to allow such rebellious thoughts to form in his mind. He'd been born and bred to the title and everything had been sacrificed to it—that was just the way it was. He couldn't say he'd really felt dissatisfaction with his lot, not for years. Why should he? People were jealous of him, not the other way around.

But now he felt a stirring inside him, an urge—one he tried hard to quash—to do something reckless and wild. To show Eugenie he wasn't the stuffed shirt she imagined him.

He shifted restlessly, glancing down at the note on his desk. He'd written to his mother about the village dance and just received a reply, and now he forced himself to read it.

"Do be careful, Sinclair," she'd written in her neat scrawl. *"Annabelle is at an impressionable age and if you don't keep a close eye on her one of those yokels will make off with her fickle heart. A heart, which I should not have to remind you, belongs to Lucius!"*

Sinclair had no intention of allowing Annabelle to forget where her future lay, but he couldn't help but wonder what his mother would think if he told her how much his own thoughts had recently become preoccupied with Miss Eugenie Belmont.

She'd raise her narrow eyebrows and fix him with one of her cool aristocratic looks.

"Really, Sinclair," she would say, *"can't you do better than that?"*

He'd explain to her what it was about Eugenie that made her so fascinating, although because he didn't really understand the reason himself he'd probably make a hash of it.

"You have a duty not to make your family a laughingstock, Sinclair."

He thought about the painting in the gallery, the fierce Boudicca, bare-breasted, with her sword raised against the Roman invaders. Her red curls tumbling about her shoulders and her eyes glittering with purpose.

"You are lusting after Boudicca?" his mother would sneer. *"Dear me, Sinclair. Wasn't she a savage?"*

But he wasn't lusting after the woman in the painting; he was far more interested in Eugenie. She seemed to occupy a special place in his thoughts. And when Annabelle began speaking about the village ball and what she would wear and how excited she was to be going, he might tease her and roll his eyes and play the bored older brother, but in truth he was just as eager.

The cobbled square, on one side of which sat The Acorn, was alive with people and noise and flaring torches. The rain that had at one point threatened to spoil the evening was gone, leaving the ground washed clean and the air fresh and sharp. The Belmonts were on time, mainly because

Terry had harried them like a sheepdog a mob of sheep in his impatience to get here, although he was sensible enough not to tell his parents the real reason for his impatience. Eugenie felt frazzled, wondering if she was properly turned out. There hadn't been enough time to check her appearance as often as she'd wished to, and now it was too late.

Her tentative, "Do I look well?" was met with a chortle from her father and a teasing, "Are you hoping to catch a husband tonight, Genie? Make sure you ask him whether he is rich before you fall in love with him, because if he is poor then I will refuse to give my permission for the banns."

"This was where I first met and fell in love with your father," Mrs. Belmont said, sighing. "He was by far the most handsome man in the room."

"And did *you* ask him if he was rich, Mama?" Eugenie asked innocently.

Her mother pretended not to hear. The difficulties of her marriage to Sir Peter Belmont were well known, but Mrs. Belmont's manner of dealing with them was to always believe the best of her husband and to turn a blind eye to the worst.

Eugenie had always expected to meet her future husband at a ball like the one tonight at The Acorn. That was before she'd got herself into this scrape with her friends at Miss Debenham's and the Husband Hunters Club.

They went indoors and up the stairs to the rooms set aside for the ball. Eugenie swallowed her nervousness and smiled at her acquaintances, exchanging a word here and there, and gradually she began to relax and stop herself from worrying about what may or may not happen, and how she was going to play the part required of her if Sinclair did turn up.

Village balls were always great fun, even if sometimes matters got out of hand. Despite what Terry had told Lady Annabelle, there was certainly no stuffiness or grandstanding, apart from the landlord of The Acorn, who liked to remind everyone that it was down to his generosity that they were here at all. Whenever she had a moment, Eugenie glanced about her, but she could not see the duke or his sister. She told herself firmly that she wouldn't be disappointed if they didn't turn up, despite Terry's insistence that they would.

In fact I would be relieved.

But it wasn't true, not really. She wanted to see Sinclair again. She wanted to test her feminine skills on him. She wanted—she hardly dared to admit it even to herself—to kiss him.

"Annabelle promised," Terry said smugly, when she voiced her doubts to him, as if he knew her better than anyone.

"Lady Annabelle to you," Eugenie reminded him sharply.

He pulled a face at her. "She hates being Lady Annabelle. She says she'd rather have been born in a hedgerow."

"For heaven's sake don't encourage her," Eugenie hissed. "She sounds very young and impressionable. You're not planning anything silly tonight, are you, Terry?"

"Depends what you mean by silly," he retorted. "I'm going to show her some fun, that's all."

"Well, I hope that's all. The duke will lock you up in his dungeon if you do anything to compromise his sister."

Terry snorted and walked off to join a group of his friends, all of whom were slouching as if they had no bones.

Eugenie told herself that the duke was perfectly capable of watching over his sister and she was worrying over nothing, so she smiled and tapped her foot as the musicians struck up again and tried very hard to enjoy herself.

It wasn't until there was a stir at the door that she became aware that something out of the ordinary was happening. Eugenie looked up with the rest of the crowd. The tall, handsome figure of Somerton and his beautiful sister had drawn all eyes. The third member of their party was the fair-haired girl, Miss Gamboni, the chaperone for Annabelle, but it was the brother and sister who commanded the attention of the room.

"The Most Noble Duke of Somerton and Lady Annabelle St. John!" declared the doorman—the village constable—in his loudest and most official voice.

Sinclair bowed as he was introduced to the gathering and Annabelle curtseyed prettily. A crush of The Acorn's elite surged toward them, but already the duke's gaze was surveying the room over their heads, darting from face to face in the crowded room. Eugenie felt that familiar drummer boy begin his tattoo on her heart. She suspected that Sinclair was looking for her. Who else would he be searching for among this motley lot? With a smile she couldn't quite contain, she made her way toward him.

As soon as he caught sight of her, something sparked in his dark eyes, despite his face remaining cool and aloof. Annabelle, suddenly noticing her, clasped her arm to draw her into their intimate circle.

"Miss Belmont, how nice to see you again!" she declared, and then half turned aside to avoid her brother's watchful eyes and whispered, "Where is Terry?"

"I am certain he will find you," Eugenie whispered back. She wondered if she should offer a warning, but decided against it. This was her night, too, and she wanted to enjoy herself.

"So this is the famous village ball," Sinclair said, with that sneering curl to his lip she found so extremely irritating. When they were married, Eugenie told herself, she would insist he stop doing that.

When they were married. . .

A giggle escaped her at the sheer madness of the idea.

Sinclair gave her a baleful look. "Is it customary for one to dance or does one watch, Miss Belmont?"

"Well *I* prefer to dance," she said cheerfully. "There will be supper, too, later on. But do not expect a late night, Your Grace. The ball finishes promptly at midnight so that the farmers can rise to till their crops and milk their cows."

He gave her a sharp look but didn't seem to know how to answer her, or perhaps he was thinking up a suitable put-down.

"Will we stroll about?" Eugenie suggested, tucking her hand into the crook of his arm. "Then I can introduce you to some of the people present. Although I expect some of them are already known to you, Your Grace." She added, when he gave her a blank look, "Your tenants."

He looked down at her gloved fingers, resting so intimately upon his sleeve, and his mouth twitched. "Miss Belmont," he drawled, bending his head so that only she could hear. "I think you know very well I haven't come here to play polite with my tenants or eat what passes for supper at The Acorn. I'm here because of you."

Eugenie felt herself drawn into his dark gaze, like a small bird into a thunderstorm. She might have stepped away, to compose herself, but he'd placed his warm hand over hers to hold her exactly where she was. This was happening too quickly and she didn't know what to do, how to behave.

"Because of me, Your Grace?" she said, breathless, smiling to make a joke of it. "What could I possibly have to do with your attendance at our village ball?"

His eyes narrowed. Suddenly he looked very formidable and rather flustered. "I am no good at word games, Miss Belmont. Never have been."

"I'm not playing a game, Your Grace."

He frowned at her, looked away, but she saw the hint of doubt, of shyness in his eyes. Could the grand duke of Somerton be as uncertain of his next move as she? His vulnerability touched her as his arrogance never could.

"You asked me on the last occasion we met whether I'd ever done anything reckless . . . dangerous. I had the feeling you thought me a poor sort of chap when I denied it and I've been considering the matter ever since."

"I did not mean—"

"Of course you did!" he retorted.

Several heads lifted and he lowered his voice again.

"I have decided, Miss Belmont, that I would very much like to do something reckless and dangerous, but I need your help."

"M-my goodness, Your Grace."

He glanced about him and now she could see his frustration in every pore. "This is impossible. We should find somewhere private so that I can explain more fully."

She tucked an unruly curl behind her ear, giving herself time to think. "Your Grace, I am fully conscious of the honor you do me—"

"That is—"

Eugenie put up a finger, as if to lay it against his mouth to hush him, but stopped herself in time. She tucked the same curl behind her ear, blushing. His eyebrows rose. He was smiling at her.

"As—as much as I would like to speak with you in private, Your Grace, I don't think it would be appropriate so soon. You've only just arrived. Tongues would wag—they are probably already

wagging over the time you have spent with me—
and although you may think the manners of our
villagers quite antiquated I do have to live with
them."

Had she reproved him?

Sinclair believed she had.

It wasn't often a girl of no birth or family worth
considering reproved him for being too forward
and making tongues wag. In fact he could never
remember it happening before.

Well, it was certainly a step forward in his effort
to behave recklessly and dangerously. The tingle
of anticipation, the need to have his own way, was
growing inside him.

"How long do I have to wait before I can be
alone with you?" he said, and wondered if he
sounded as sulky as he felt. "I warn you, Miss Belmont, there is only so much of this I can endure."

She smiled up at him. She really was an en-
chanting minx. "Not long," she said.

"Do you promise?"

"Most sincerely," she answered, and he knew
she was teasing him. He couldn't remember a
woman being so free and easy with him, not for
a very long time. He didn't quite know how to respond to her.

While Sinclair was trying to think of a reply
Squire Richards came to join them. He knew the
man—a pompous fool—but he was claiming Sinclair like a long lost friend, at the same time giving
Eugenie a teasing reproof for monopolizing him.

A moment later he was being tugged away by the arm through the noise and the crush to a gathering of the squire's cronies.

He looked back over his shoulder, longing for Eugenie, feeling bereft. But she had already vanished into the sea of revelers behind him.

Chapter 6

Sinclair's frustration was growing by the moment. Here he was, forced to make conversation with any number of red-faced worthies, when all he really wanted to do was press Eugenie Belmont into a dark corner and kiss her. Thoroughly. Completely.

That is what I've come here to do, after all.

The force of his acknowledgement surprised him, even shocked him. Over more recent years he'd convinced himself he was a man of mild passions—women had tried to ensnare him but he hadn't felt the least bit in danger. Until now. This emotion he was experiencing didn't feel mild, far from it. Eugenie had brought him here—Eugenie and her dare—and now he wanted to collect his due.

Why not admit that she'd been in his thoughts ever since she laid down the challenge, and that the more he tried to shut her out, the more she returned to taunt him with her pink smiling lips and clear green eyes? He could tell himself that a man in his position had a responsibility to remain aloof from a woman so far beneath him.

But it was no use.

He even dreamed of her at night, and awoke hot and flustered and aroused. Sometimes he was surprised by the erotic fantasies he indulged in where she was concerned.

And now here he was in the same room as her and yet he might as well be in another country.

The music was giving him a headache. The fiddle player in particular was excruciating. Not that Annabelle seemed to care. He'd watched her dance every dance so far, although thankfully not all of them with Terry Belmont. Sinclair was keeping a close eye on *that* situation. If Eugenie was unsuitable for a Somerton then her brother was ten times worse. He had made some inquiries after their visit and learned that the boy was mixing with unsavory sorts at the Five Bells, drinking and gambling and probably carousing with the village girls. The consensus was that he was his father all over again.

The Belmonts were a thoroughly bad lot.

"Your Grace?"

His heart jolted. He would have spun around like a callow lad, except that at the last moment he remembered who he was and what was due to his position. So instead he turned slowly, in control of himself, and stared haughtily down into her flushed, smiling face.

And then he spoiled it all.

"Thank God," he growled. "Now can we talk in private?"

She pretended to give it due thought but he could see the laughter in her eyes. "First we'll need to dance."

"Dance?" he said, as if she'd asked him to stand on his head.

"Come, Your Grace, it is not difficult. I can show you the steps. Well, some of them. I am not so good at the more intricate country dances but I can waltz. Miss Debenham was very particular about the waltz."

"I am perfectly capable of dancing," he said. "*That* is not the issue."

But all the same he led her onto the floor and they took up their places. She was light on her feet and seemed to enjoy herself as they strove to find enough room in the sweaty crush to perform their steps. Grimly, Sinclair set himself to get through it, but after a while found it was not so bad. At least it gave him an excuse to hold her close, and he found the scent of her hair as intoxicating as the finest wine in his cellar. Lithe and graceful, her waist slim beneath his hand, he suspected she had underplayed her prowess when it came to dancing.

"Miss Debenham taught you well."

"Do you think so?" She flushed with pleasure at his small compliment. "I always enjoyed the lessons. Well, far more than embroidery or Italian."

"I promise not to start a conversation in Italian."

"Thank you."

"Or ask you to embroider me a handkerchief."

A crease drew her brows together. "You would be sorry if you did."

By the time the music finished he was smiling.

"Now, Your Grace," she spoke in an unnecessarily loud voice, "supper is this way." She preceded him through a door and into a narrow passageway. They paused to allow a group of giggling girls to pass through a farther door, which opened into a room even more crowded than the last. Inside, Sinclair could just hear the ring of silverware against china above the chatter and laughter. Behind them the music had started up again and his head began to throb. His headache, forgotten for a moment, was getting worse.

Eugenie had changed direction, darting down a small flight of steps, and he hurried after her. She glanced back at him and then opened a low door and slipped inside. He followed without hesitation, closing the door behind him, and suddenly found himself in a small, dimly lit anteroom. Above him the noise of dancing made the ceiling shake and his head pound.

Eugenie smiled at him. Behind her old bunting was stacked against the wall and what looked like a set of broken chairs was piled into a corner. An empty barrel sent out a reek of sour wine. The dust on the floor was a good inch thick.

Eugenie followed his gaze and grimaced. "I know. It's rather horrid, isn't it?"

"You little wretch," he said, surprising himself with his lack of good manners. "You've kept me waiting long enough. Come here."

It was her fault, he told himself, as he pulled her into his arms. She'd made him wait far too long and he'd be dashed if he'd wait any longer. It was her fault he had a headache, too. It was probably a combination of unrequited lust and the appalling music.

She was gazing up at him, startled, but not struggling. He took that as agreement and kissed her, his mouth pressing hard to hers.

She gave a little gasp and he almost let her go, but a moment later she relaxed into his arms, winding her own about his neck and clinging there as his mouth slid along the full warm sweetness of hers. Now he knew what her pink lips tasted like—ripe summer fruit—and he was relieved to discover she was not too shy to kiss him back. Perhaps she was not as innocent as he'd thought? But her next words disabused him of that.

She smiled and touched her lips. "I don't think I have ever been kissed like this before. In fact, my experience of kissing is rather limited."

"I can remedy that."

Eugenie searched his eyes with hers, as if trying to decide whether he was teasing or not. He'd sounded more serious than he'd meant.

"Well, have I won your dare?" he said. "Is this reckless enough for you, Miss Belmont?"

"I'm glad you decided to take up my challenge, Your Grace," she said with a husky laugh. "I like you better when you're reckless."

Her slender body was soft and pliant against his and he drew it closer, enjoying the feel of her, the fact that she was finally in his arms. He rested his overheated brow against her cool forehead and groaned.

She reached to touch his face, her fingers gentle. "You are very warm, Your Grace," she ventured.

"I have the devil of a headache," he murmured, squeezing his eyes closed. Even the dim light in here hurt.

She slid her arm about his waist, helping him take several steps, and the next moment he was sitting on the upended wine barrel. She stood before him, frowning at him, and he felt her hands cup his face, ecstatically cool against his overheated skin.

"I am rather good with headaches," she said in a quiet voice. "My aunt Beatrix suffers from them and she has a Chinese doctor who uses a special massage to reduce the pain. He showed me when I stayed with her some years ago."

Above them the music began again, but he concentrated on her fingers, stroking his head and face, finding little areas of pain and pressing gently against them. The pressure never became too much to bear before she released it, and gradually the pain began to slip away. Soon he felt able to open his eyes.

She didn't notice him watching her at first. She was too busy concentrating on what she was doing. She skimmed her fingers along his brow, massaging his temples with her thumbs in circular movements. He could see her slender neck and shoulders above the white lace of her dress, the pale sheen of her skin. The swell of her breasts were just visible above her bodice, and he wished he could see more. He wished he could undo a button or two and investigate what lay beneath all that clothing.

Instead he reached to encircle her waist with his hands and drew her into the wedge of his thighs and the heat of his body, his breath teasing wisps of her hair. "Thank you," he whispered against her ear, and felt her shiver. His lips caressed her earlobe and then her jawline, working their way toward her mouth. By the time he reached it her lips were parted, her own breath quick and sharp, and she gave a little moan when he took her mouth with his.

This time the kiss went on far longer and when she pulled away she was breathless, her eyes dark and dreamy.

"Is your headache better?" she said, and stepped back and away, out of reach.

"Oh yes," he growled, reaching for her again.

But she darted to the side, avoiding him. "Your Grace, we have been away long enough. It will be noticed."

"I don't care."

"I do," she said primly.

Frustrated, he strode to the door then back. "I need to see you alone again," he declared.

"Then we must think of another dare," she said. "Something more difficult. This was far too easy."

"Oh was it, minx!"

He was watching her, wishing his good manners weren't so ingrained in him. If he was one of his ancestors, the Norman baron perhaps, he would have no hesitation in snatching her up and riding off with her into the night.

"Why are you smiling?" she said with a hint of suspicion.

He told her and watched her eyes widen. "Ride off with me?" she squeaked. Then, her green eyes opened even wider and she cried, "I wonder if you dare. I wonder if *I* dare!"

He frowned with impatience. "What is it you are daring me to do?"

She giggled mischievously.

"Eugenie," he growled, taking a step toward her around the barrel. "I warn you, I am not climbing up the church steeple."

"Goodness, I would not ask that."

"Then what is making you laugh?"

"I'm sorry. It isn't really funny but you reminded me with your Norman baron. At Miss Debenham's we discussed history and visited the ruins of a nearby castle."

"I thought finishing schools were all about manners and deportment?"

"Miss Debenham was interested in turning out well-rounded girls," she retorted, with a twinkle in her eye. "Do you want to hear or not?"

He sighed. "Tell me then."

"The baron who once owned the castle had a wicked reputation. In those days there were very little manners and even less deportment. Not nearly as civilized as now. This baron was prone to riding about his lands on a big black horse and abducting any girl who took his fancy. He'd ride back to his castle and . . . well, the lesson didn't go that far. But I . . . well, my friends actually, found the idea of being abducted rather appealing, much to Miss Debenham's dismay."

He shook his head at her. "You really are the oddest creature. So that is your dare? For me to abduct you?"

For a moment he thought she was going to deny the whole thing. Doubt and a hint of fear clouded her eyes. She was an innocent young lady, he reminded himself once again, and more than likely a virgin. He was dabbling with fire where she was concerned. But Sinclair was too far gone to care. The vision of himself as a baron riding off with her to ravish her had taken hold of him and he was damned if he'd relinquish it now.

"I'm afraid I don't have a castle," he said quietly, "and I can hardly ride up the drive way at Somerton with you over my saddle. What would the servants say?"

She smiled, and he was relieved to see that her fear was gone. "You could meet me in the lane, where we first met."

"I could. Yes, that would be the perfect place to sweep you up onto my horse and ride off with you."

"Not far, of course," she added swiftly and a little breathlessly. "Just a little way will do. Just to win the dare."

His eyes narrowed, but excitement was already coursing through his veins. "I am not in the habit of abducting young ladies in laneways," he drawled.

"I know. That's why it's a dare," she teased with a smile.

"And when does this abduction take place?"

"Tomorrow? After the morning service?"

"You're not going to change your mind?" he said. "You're not one of those girls who promises something and then breaks her word?"

As he suspected, his words stung her pride. "Indeed I am not! I will be there."

"Then so will I," he said. Those feelings were stirring inside him. There was excitement. And lust. And longing. And a sense of coming alive after a long sleep.

"I demand another kiss, as surety," he said, and this time the barrel was shoved determinedly out of his way.

She had no time to struggle, as he wrapped her in his arms and pinned her against his chest and took her mouth, every inch of it, thoroughly. Despite her innocence there was a natural passion in her response—perhaps inherited from her wicked ancestress. Her efforts to kiss him in the same way he was kissing her increased his desire and numbed any conflict he may have felt for her position if he'd been thinking more clearly.

By the time he'd done she was having difficulty standing, and he was unashamed to feel an odd pride in that. Her eyes were sleepy, her lips reddened, her cheeks flushed. What he'd really like to do was lift her in his arms and find a bed, but Sinclair knew—as lost to reason as he was—that it was far too soon for that. Instead he bowed and backed away.

"Until we meet again," he said, his voice husky, and left her there.

Alone, Eugenie made a sound between a sob and a laugh.

Was she insane? She was playing a very dangerous game, a game to which she barely knew the rules. If she had any sense she would stop now, refuse to meet him tomorrow, tell him it was impossible for her to continue.

And yet her heart was beating fast and hard, his touch had brought her to life in a way she'd never known possible, and his lips on hers made her delightfully dizzy.

It seemed a shame to halt the game just now, when it was getting so interesting. Besides, what would she tell her friends? Wasn't the Husband Hunters Club all about using one's feminine wiles to capture one's prey? Of course there was a difference between capturing one's prey and *becoming* the prey.

Eugenie wasn't a naïve fool. Her family had been through enough scandals for her to understand what it was to step beyond society's boundaries and how that might affect her life. But it wasn't as if she had any great prospects, was it? And kissing the duke had been such a pleasurable experience.

"I will stop before anything really dreadful happens," she told herself firmly, ignoring the thought that perhaps her great-grandmamma had told herself the same thing, just before she climbed into King George's bed.

Annabelle was breathless from dancing. Her chaperone, Miss Lizzie Gamboni, steadied her and suggested she sit down for a moment, which was a suggestion Annabelle rejected. Of course.

Lizzie sighed. Her charge, a girl only two years younger than herself, was beautiful and headstrong, no doubt about that. Lizzie was beginning to think Annabelle was far too strong-willed for her. She supposed if she had had had so fortunate birth as Annabelle then she might believe anything in the world was possible, but Lizzie, the eldest daughter of a vicar in a family of twelve, knew differently. Her life had been sacrificed to the will of others, or so it sometimes seemed, although she tried hard to be grateful for what she had been given.

"May I have this dance, Your Ladyship?" a well-scrubbed farmer said, eyes bright with admiration. And Annabelle was off again before Lizzie could say a word. She had seen the duke watching them and hoped he wouldn't blame her for his sister's romp. She could not afford to lose her position at Somerton and she did not know where she might get another.

"Miss Gamboni."

Lizzie started. It was Terry Belmont, the very person the duke had warned her of, a handsome young man with a bad reputation, and—she admitted this secretly to herself—a heartbreaking smile.

"Mr. Belmont," she said, and hoped she sounded like a stern chaperone and not an insecure young woman.

But he wasn't looking at her, instead he was gazing across the bobbing heads to Annabelle. "Is Lady Annabelle's card full?"

Lizzie smiled. "I don't think she has a card with her tonight, Mr. Belmont."

"I did hope to have more dances with her," he said, longingly.

"I don't think that would be wise," Lizzie spoke sympathetically. All the young men fell for Annabelle and breaking hearts seemed to concern her not at all. "The duke is watching."

Terry smiled and she felt her heart do a little dance of its own. He really was very charming and she reminded herself once again that she must be the stern and grim-faced chaperone, or at least pretend.

And then he asked, "Do you ever dance, Miss Gamboni?"

Startled, she looked up at him wide-eyed. "D-dance?" she stammered, before she could stop herself.

He took that as a "yes" and, taking her in his arms, whirled her through the crowd and onto the dance floor. And Lizzie, who hadn't danced for ages, found herself enjoying herself very much.

The supper was as awful as Sinclair had feared, but he forced himself to make polite conversation and then he went to find Annabelle. She didn't want to go so soon but he insisted, so with a sulky pout she allowed him to escort her and her chaperone—looking suspiciously flushed—back to the carriage.

On the way home to Somerton Annabelle was quiet, but then so was he. He found he had a great deal to think about.

And an abduction to plan.

Chapter 7

Sinclair lifted the lamp and felt a wave of sadness as he saw the state of what had once been his secret room, his sanctuary, the hub of his dreams. He hadn't been up here in the attic for years and he should have expected neglect, but the dangling lace of cobwebs and the thick dust made the place appear even more forlorn than he'd feared.

Sinclair hadn't been able to sleep. He'd lain in his bed remembering kissing Eugenie Belmont, the flushed pink of her cheeks and the wild curls of her hair, and as her picture grew clearer in his mind he finally realized what that itching sensation was that was keeping him from slumber. So he'd risen from his bed, lit a lamp and climbed the stairs to the little room in the attic.

Had it really been ten years since he'd been here last?

The memories were still sharp of the day he'd locked that door on his hopes and dreams. Misery and defeat had followed him when he'd turned away and retraced his steps down the stairs; it had felt as if he was turning his back on more than a room. He was rejecting an ideal. He was walking away from the person he'd longed to be and the life he'd wanted to lead.

His mother had blamed his tutor at Eton.

At seventeen years of age, Sinclair had been lit by the fire of paint and canvas and the Royal Academy. He had talent—his tutor said so—and there was talk of him showing some of his sketches and paintings. He'd begun in high hopes, spending hours on his masterpieces, losing himself in the world of his imagination.

Until his mother put a stop to it.

Gentlemen didn't become artists, she said. Gentlemen rode to hounds and went into politics and gambled in gentlemen's clubs. An artist was a seedy Bohemian, a disgrace to his name and his family, and that was something she would never allow Sinclair to be. He was a Somerton and he should remember it and live accordingly.

There was no arguing with her, although he'd tried. His maternal uncle, Lord Ridley, had sided with him, but he was a bit of a Bohemian himself—a "loose cannon"—and according to his mother he didn't count. There was a bitterness in her recriminations, a gleam in her eyes, that frightened him more than he'd admit. She made him ashamed of his own dreams and afraid of the possibility that she was right. But he remained strong and determined, on the outside anyway, certain he could get his way. It was when she broke down in tears, sobbing about his selfishness and how could he do this to her, begging him to reconsider, that he knew she had won.

So he had locked the door on all that he'd longed to be, and turned into the Duke of Somerton, cold and proud and haughty.

Until now, when somehow Eugenie had brought back those boyhood dreams. The itch was there, the urge to pick up a pencil or a paintbrush, and it seemed as strong as ever. Stronger. He wasn't sure if this was a good development but he was eager to let it take its course. After all, what harm could it do?

Setting down his lamp, he uncovered the easel. The last canvas he'd worked on was waiting there, paint flaking from it, dust discoloring the surface. He wondered if he still had the talent to capture an image. Because he knew exactly who he wanted to paint.

Eugenie.

Eugenie as she was tonight in his arms, flushed and sensuous and beautiful.

And now that he was a grown man there was no one to tell him nay. Oh, if his mother found out she might act shocked, she might wipe a tear from her eye, but she couldn't stop him. Why should she want to? He'd proved himself a worthwhile duke and a responsible head of the family. No, she had no reason to. The only person who could stop him was himself.

He wondered idly what Eugenie would think if he asked her . . . if he dared her to sit for him. Would she laugh in his face or act appalled? He didn't think she'd do either. The Eugenie he was beginning to know would probably say yes.

Sinclair smiled. He would ask one of his more

trustworthy servants to tidy up in here tomorrow. The paints were all dried up so he would need new ones, but he could order them from London. He supposed his friends and acquaintances would think he'd lost his mind, but they needn't know about his little hobby. No one need know.

Sinclair closed the door softly behind him, feeling very different from the last time he'd been here. He was looking forward to renewing his acquaintance with the brush, and there was a sense of anticipation stirring in his soul. After all these years he was beginning to understand just how much he'd missed his Bohemian hobby.

Lizzie couldn't sleep. She wished she could put all of the nonsense out of her head and drift into nothingness, but she couldn't. She was worried about Annabelle; the girl was up to something. At The Acorn she had seen the glances that passed between her and Terry Belmont, and she was beginning to think there was something more serious to their friendship than a silly flirtation.

Lizzie knew it was her duty to report any fears she might have to the duke, but she also knew Annabelle would consider such tattling as treason and never speak to her again, or else insist she be dismissed. The thing to do was to keep a careful watch on matters without overreacting. Annabelle was marrying Lord Lucius soon. Surely she could not get up to any mischief before then?

Lizzie sighed restlessly and rolled over.

Unfortunately, knowing Annabelle, she could, and would!

* * *

It had been easier than Eugenie thought to escape the company of her younger brothers. All she'd had to do was make the excuse that she was taking a basket to "the sick" and after some face-pulling they'd gone off to play games, leaving Eugenie to set off with an appropriate-looking basket. Once out of sight she hid it in the hedgerow and, shaking out her grass green skirts and her white lacy cuffs, she hurried off to her abduction.

Trepidation made her knees tremble.

Would he come? He had last time. She couldn't help but remember the way his lips had fitted so perfectly to hers, the sensation of being held tightly in his arms. She'd never experienced such intimacy with a man before, never expected the sheer sensual pleasure of it. The way his body was hard where hers was soft, the manly confidence of his grip, the scent of his skin, and the faint roughness of his jaw against her tender skin.

Everything had been so new, and yet so perfect at the same time. She felt herself full of optimism and hope, although she wasn't convinced the duke would go down on his knees and propose marriage to her. Not yet, anyway. But for now she was happy to go in whatever direction fate was taking her and savor the unexpected experience of being pursued by a duke.

There was a drumming of hooves up ahead and then the silhouette of a rider approaching against the sun. Her heartbeat quickened. He'd come, as he'd promised. Perhaps, like her, he'd lain awake all night longing for morning to creep through his window and the church service to be finished.

Sinclair's horse slowed to a walk as he reached her, giving her time to take in his tight breeches and shiny boots, and the billowing white shirt open at the throat. He looked romantic rather than dangerous, with his dark hair windblown and the flush along his cheeks. When her gaze reached his, she found his eyes glowed with an emotion that echoed a chord in her.

"I thought about wearing a mask, but I didn't want to frighten the wildlife."

"I think you look very roguish," she replied, with a smile. "Just like a wicked baron riding about the countryside looking for wenches to abduct."

His eyes narrowed. His mouth curled into a wicked-baron smile.

"Then give me your hand, wench."

She did so. His fingers closed hard on hers, and then she put her foot on his in the stirrup and he swung her up behind him on the horse. She clung about his waist, relaxing against him, pressing her cheek against his shirt and feeling the muscles in his back tighten and shift. Once again she thought how nice it was to be in such close contact with a man, feeling him move and breathe, and drawing in his clean masculine scent.

Her irrepressible curls tugged against their pins and she shook her head so that her hair tumbled free. The wind caught the folds of lace on her bodice and at her wrists, and lifted her skirts to show her petticoats and stockings. It was shocking, she supposed, but she didn't care. She felt as if they were flying, the two of them, and the world was reduced to the simple equation of Sinclair and Eugenie.

But as they galloped further on, her determination to enjoy the moment began to give way to anxiety. The practical part of her brain took charge, reminding her that if they were seen, if they became the subject of gossip, then her reputation would be in shreds. She imagined explaining to her neighbors that she planned to marry him and the expressions on their faces. Disbelief, scorn, horror. They'd consider her a scheming hussy, or an innocent fool.

Why had she let herself be coerced by her friends' expectations into declaring her intention to marry the duke? Why couldn't she have chosen a lord or a baron, or even a plain mister? There had been a gentleman she met when she stayed with her Aunt Beatrix years ago who had paid her a great many compliments and she'd always thought . . . hoped . . . that one day he might seek her out.

It was probably the best Eugenie could hope for when it came to marriage prospects, or so her practical brain told her.

Slowly she withdrew her arms from about his waist, sitting back from his warm, muscular body. Time to put an end to this. Eugenie opened her mouth to tell him to stop and set her down, but just at that moment Sinclair turned his horse into the woods.

Taken by surprise, she clung to him again. He

slowed their gallop, as the branches and leaves reached out to enclose them, and the earthy smells of nature pressed upon her senses. It was shady in here, the light turned green and mysterious.

"Duck," he said matter-of-factly. Instinctively she bent her head and a low branch brushed over them. He glanced back at her with a smile. "Well done, Miss Belmont. A woman who can take orders without arguing."

Eugenie tucked her tangled hair behind her ears, ignoring his barb. "Where are we going, Your Grace?" she said, unable to hide her nervousness.

"Do call me Sinclair." His eyes sparkled with mischief.

"Where are we going, Sinclair?" she repeated breathlessly.

"A place I know. Ideal for our game of abduction."

It was a game, she reminded herself with relief. Of course it was. There was nothing to worry about.

Ahead of them the woods opened into a small clearing. The space was entirely enclosed by trees and undergrowth. The grass was sparse, the air a little chilled from the shade of the taller trees, and there was a hushed silence to the place that made her skin prickle. Sinclair dismounted and reached up to grasp her waist and lift her down. Her feet touched the ground and, suddenly shy, she stepped away, turning to examine her surroundings.

"How did you know of this place?"

"Jack mentioned it to me. Evidently fairies dance here when the moon is full."

"Do they?" She turned back to observe him. He looked very different from the polished and proper duke who'd appeared last night at The Acorn. Windblown and disheveled, he could indeed be a highwayman or a kidnapper. Someone to treat with caution. Someone to fear.

But Eugenie wasn't afraid. Instinctively she knew Sinclair would never hurt her, and she was the sort of woman who trusted her instincts.

No, he would never hurt her, but he may well try to seduce her.

That was what dukes did with women like her, wasn't it?

Her skin tingled at the memory of their kisses; the taste and feel of him in her arms. No wonder the village mothers warned their daughters about the dangers of the flesh! It was far too easy to become addicted.

He came toward her. Reaching out to take her hands in his, he raised one to his mouth and pressed his lips to her. She felt the warmth through her thin gloves and closed her eyes the better to enjoy the experience. When she opened them again he was watching her.

"You set me another dare and I have passed, have I not, Eugenie?"

"Yes, Sinclair, you have passed."

"Do I get my reward?"

Eugenie knew what sort of reward he wanted. There didn't seem much point in acting coy, especially when she wanted the contact as much as he did. Stretching up on her tiptoes she brushed her lips over his. With a growl he caught her up in his arms and held her tight against his body, plundering her mouth in a very ungentlemanlike manner.

This was the Sinclair she'd never imagined lay beneath his cold and aloof social exterior. The man few others knew. This was *her* Sinclair, passionate and fiery and very human. Eugenie wound her arms about his neck and kissed him back, giving herself up to the heat of passion.

When at last, breathless and dizzy, she drew away, the sparkle in his eyes had turned into a blaze.

Eugenie felt the same tingle of doubt begin to build again, the unease she'd been experiencing off and all morning. Was she really not afraid of him? Somerton had seemed the perfect gentleman but perhaps he wasn't as easy to manage as she'd imagined. Could she really control him? Could she really expect a man who'd had his own way all his life to listen to a woman like her?

Evidently he read her expression again because he gave a rough laugh and said, "Don't fear, Miss Belmont, I'm not going to ravish you. Not today. Although I cannot make promises about what I may do tomorrow."

"You're jesting," she said flatly. "Aren't you?"

"Am I?" His eyes narrowed. "Unless you want to be ravished?"

Warm pink flooded her face. "That is hardly something a lady would admit," she replied automatically. "Gentlewomen do not ask to be ravished."

"More's the pity," he mocked, a sulky droop to his mouth.

"Oh?" She found herself suddenly curious about his domestic arrangements. "I would have thought the Duke of Somerton would have plenty of women begging to be ravished by him. It is my understanding of the aristocracy—which I admit is limited—that they have a mistress in every house."

Laughter lit his eyes and the sullen little boy look was gone. "Is this your way of asking me whether I presently have a mistress, Eugenie?"

"I suppose it is," she said, with a mischievous smile.

He leaned against the tree trunk at her side, gazing down into her face. "You are making me wonder why you would want to ask so personal a question. Most young ladies of gentle upbringing would consider such a topic of conversation an abomination. They are taught not to notice such things and if they do to look the other way."

"Then I am not like most young ladies."

"No, Eugenie, you are unique."

His eyes delved into hers. He was very close now, and once again she felt that frisson. She was beginning to think it was a perverse sort of excitement. He was pursuing her in earnest now and Eugenie would have to make a decision soon. Did she want to be caught?

He reached out, his thumb against her skin, stroking her cheek. She sighed at his touch, closing her eyes the better to enjoy it, while his voice brushed over her like another caress.

"I am wondering, Eugenie, why you would ask such a question if there wasn't a reason for it. So I ask myself why would you want to know if I have a mistress? Can you be imagining yourself in that enviable position?"

His words penetrated her haze of pleasure. She stiffened and abruptly her heart turned leaden and heavy. The game had become serious. Of course she had known that eventually he would take this direction; it was the only direction he could take. Sinclair was a duke and Eugenie was . . . well, a nobody.

Sinclair was watching her, a frown between his brows. He seemed to know he'd said the wrong thing. His hand dropped to his side. "You appear shocked," he said, with a humorless laugh. "As the descendant of a royal mistress I would have thought you more broadminded, Eugenie."

She *wasn't* shocked. Not really. She was disappointed. She had been enjoying herself and now she would have to put an end to this game between them.

"Wait!"

Eugenie realized with surprise that she was already several paces across the clearing.

"Please, listen to what I have to say. Eugenie?"

He sounded ruffled, shaken. As if she'd pushed him into speaking of things he wasn't ready to speak of. As if he was in a position he had never been in before and didn't quite know how to handle it.

She waited, standing with her back to him, hearing his approach. He waited a beat, and then his hands rested lightly upon her shoulders. She felt his breath stirring her curls and longed to lean her head back against him.

"I accept you are a well brought up young lady of gentle birth, but even you must admit, Eugenie, that your family is far from top drawer. Your father is in debt, and when he does have money from one of his doubtful deals, he throws it away."

"You do not have to tell me what my father is capable of," she said angrily. "I do not want to speak of him."

"Forgive my careless words, Eugenie."

He took a breath, as if he would say more, but whatever it was he thought better of it. Instead he bent his head and kissed the nape of her neck, making her shiver. Again his tenderness tempted her to stay with him, but she reminded herself that he'd disappointed her. In another moment he'd be asking her straight out to be his mistress and suddenly she didn't want that. She didn't want their budding romance spoiled by such worldly considerations.

She moved toward the horse, and he allowed his hands to drop from her. She didn't look back. "Can you take me home now, Your Grace? Or do I have to find my own way?"

For a moment she thought he might be going to tell her just that, and then he was helping her up onto the horse. His face, the brief sight she had of it, looked closed and troubled, his lips white and thin. Perhaps she had insulted him as badly as he'd been about to insult her, but she didn't care. To be his mistress wasn't what she wanted. That wasn't what the Husband Hunters Club was about.

And yet Eugenie understood just how naïve she had been to believe even for a heartbeat that she could ever marry a man so far above her in station. Just because he liked her—and yes, he did like her—and just because he obviously desired her, did not mean he would dream of marrying her. It would not even occur to him.

As they rode back in silence, she still found herself hoping despite all evidence to the contrary that he might realize that to ask her to be his mistress would be a mistake. That, like a beam of sunshine falling on him, the truth would be revealed to him and he would throw aside all that held him back, and ask for her hand.

But it was another of her silly daydreams and Eugenie knew that this was one occasion when she could not twist the ending to suit herself. He was a duke and dukes took mistresses, usually dancers or actresses, women far below themselves on the social scale. That was how he saw her. As a woman far beneath him in every way.

When they reached the place in the lane where he'd abducted her, he stopped and set her down. Subdued, she thanked him and turned away. He did not speak and after a moment she heard him ride off.

Her heart still felt heavy and she knew it was partly due to disappointment and partly an acknowledgment of the cold, hard facts of life. But it was also because she'd become fond of him. She enjoyed his company and his conversation and the feel of his arms about her.

Eugenie clenched her jaw and told herself she would not cry. She would not! But a tear slid down her cheek, and then another one. Life was not fair. But at least she knew it now. She would make a new plan, and this time she would be practical about it.

Chapter 8

~~~~~~~

Terry Belmont glanced sideways at the girl beside him. Lady Annabelle's face was streaked with drying tears and her mouth was turned down at the corners. Although he would have loved to take her into his arms and comfort her, he didn't. He knew she wouldn't want him to. They were friends, companions in adversity, and it would be wrong to cross that boundary. If she thought he was just another rake trying to inveigle his way into her affections—or out of her fortune—then she would no longer turn to him for help. She would no longer trust him.

And Terry found he valued Annabelle's trust more than anything.

"I can't bear the thought of marrying Lucius and living in his house in London. I do not say he is a cruel man or—or cruel to me. He is a gentleman, but when I tell him all the things I want to do, he smiles at me as if I am a—a child. There is so much more to my life, so much to do. I never wanted to marry him, but my mother tells me I must and . . . She and Sinclair want me to be someone I do not want to be. Just because they only live for the Somerton name and care for nothing but our position in society, they think I should be the same. But I'm not, and I won't!"

Her passion spent, she mopped her eyes with her lacy sleeve like a child.

"What can you do?" Terry asked. "You say the wedding arrangements are all in place. Can you really back out now?"

Her dark eyes were almost wild. "I have a friend in Scotland, a girl I knew at school. We write often. She is married now, but she has promised to shelter me, if only I could get to her." She took a shaky breath, and reached to grasp his forearm, her fingers painfully intense. "Will you help me, Terry?"

Terry felt something major shift inside him. No one had ever asked him for help before. His younger brothers all turned to Eugenie if they were in need of help, while Eugenie never seemed to need help from anyone, especially not Terry. She still saw him as a little boy, someone who needed guidance and scolding, in equal measure. But now Annabelle was asking him for help as if he was the only one in the world she trusted.

"Of course I will help you," he said, and meant it with all his heart.

Her lips trembled into a smile. "Thank you," she sighed. "I wish I wasn't so ignorant of the world and how to make my way in it. I would run off to Scotland alone, but I fear I would lose my way or make some foolish error, and then I'd be captured and brought home to Somerton, and then they'd watch me so closely I would never have another chance." She gave him a confident look. "You know how to get to Scotland, don't you, Terry?"

Terry wasn't sure he did but he wasn't going to tell her that. He gave a worldly wise shrug. "Of course."

"Good. I'd better get back to Lizzie before she tattles to my brother."

Lizzie Gamboni had seemed small and insignificant to Terry, someone who needed looking after rather than someone inclined to cause trouble.

"I'm sure Miss Gamboni wouldn't tattle," he said without thinking, and then wished he hadn't when Annabelle gave him a narrow look. "I meant to say, she seems very loyal to you."

"Yes, well, I won't have to worry about her much longer." She sighed. "I'm so glad we met, Terry. I don't know what I would do without you to help me."

Terry felt like a hero—he was the soldier who took the hill fort single-handed, and saved the day. It was only later, on his way home to Belmont Hall, that doubts began to set in. He supposed, when she asked for help, he should have refused. That was the sensible course of action. Helping the duke's sister could only mean trouble for someone like Terry.

But how could he refuse? She needed his help and he needed to give it. Somehow he would have to get her to her friend in Scotland. Because Terry knew he couldn't tell anyone else. Eugenie would only scold him and insist he explain himself to the duke. And if he told his father . . . Mr. Belmont would rub his hands together and inveigle him in some devious scheme to make money from Annabelle's misfortune. No, there was no one he could tell. He must deal with this himself.

As he opened the door to Belmont Hall, Terry could hear the twins arguing interspersed with his mother's long-suffering wails. Avoiding them, he hurriedly climbed the ramshackle stairs to the room he shared with his brothers. Jack was there with his injured magpie sitting on his shoulder, his head buried in a book on horses.

"Benny and Bertie are at it again," he said, without looking up. "They decided to decorate the sitting room with some black dye they found in the washhouse. They thought Mama would be pleased."

They grinned at each other in horrified glee.

"Don't go down there unless you want to scrub walls," Jack advised, turning back to his book.

Terry had no intention of getting involved in the terrible twins' antics. He flung himself down on his bed, and stared up at the ceiling. With Annabelle he had a chance to show what he was made of, to be the sort of man he'd always wanted to be.

"Jack," he said. "If you were asked to help someone, someone you liked, someone who really needed your help, would you do it? Even if by helping them you might get yourself into lots of trouble?"

Jack thought about it while his brother waited. Although Jack was young, Terry had always thought him the cleverest of them all. "Yes," he said, nodding. "I would."

Terry smiled and lay down again. That settled it. He and Annabelle were going to Scotland . . . as soon as he sorted out how to get there.

Lizzie knew something was afoot. Annabelle made excuses and avoided her eyes, but she'd slipped away for an hour today and Lizzie was certain she'd had an assignation with Terry Belmont.

Surely she wasn't in love with him?

Annabelle, for all her spoiled and headstrong behavior, was at heart a girl who was very aware of what was in her own best interests. It pleased her to startle and upset her family by declaring all sorts of opinions that weren't really hers, but beneath all that she was really quite conventional. Or so Lizzie had thought until now.

Lucius was a perfect match for her, and she must know it, despite her declarations that she would die of boredom once married to him. Terry Belmont was not in her sphere when it came to the important decisions of love and marriage. Why, thought Lizzie, he was far more suitable for someone like . . . like herself.

But of course he would never notice her, no one ever did. She was like a little vicarage mouse, invisible, while all eyes were full of Annabelle. Not that she was resentful—she'd long ago accepted her fate. She just wished that for once in her life a man she liked would see her.

Really see *her*.

Chapter 9

❦

Wednesday was market day in the town of Torrisham, and Sir Peter had persuaded Eugenie to come with him and help with the sale of a horse he had been training up. "A fine lady's mount," he insisted, although Eugenie doubted any "lady" would be able to sit upon the beast for longer than a minute without being thrown into a hedgerow.

Usually it was Terry who went with their father to sell horses, but when it came time to leave he couldn't be found. "Probably with his friends at the Five Bells," Sir Peter muttered. "Never mind, Genie, you'll bring in more customers than Terry could. Just give them one of your smiles, and let me do the talking."

Eugenie wasn't so sure Terry was at his favorite hostelry. He had been different lately, absent in his thoughts as well as in body, and she had her suspicions he was up to something. Although, whatever it was, he wasn't telling her, and Eugenie had her own troubles to keep her occupied.

She hadn't heard a word from her duke since

his "abduction" of her. And although she'd told herself she wasn't going to think of him again, she found herself replaying the scene over and over in her head. In hindsight she knew she should not have allowed matters to go so far, so quickly. Her only excuse was that she was enjoying herself too much to stop.

At least she'd prevented him from saying the fatal words. He hadn't actually come out and said them to her face. Not yet, anyway. But Eugenie knew that it wouldn't be long before he did. The duke seemed determined to have her—to own her, like one of his horses. It wasn't as if he even knew her, not properly anyway, but he was evidently one of those men who made up his mind in an instant.

Eugenie could understand that. She'd done it herself when she'd seen a hat or a shawl she liked. But this was so much more intimate. Sinclair wanted to put her into some little cozy love nest he could visit, with Eugenie waiting patiently, perfectly dressed—or undressed—ready day or night in case he might pop around.

Eugenie knew she would never be able to bear such a hole-in-the-corner sort of existence. And what about when . . . *if* he grew tired of her and she was left with the truly awful choice of seeking another benefactor? She could not even imagine how one did that. Was there a special employment agency where discarded mistresses went? She tried to picture a line of women in doubtful dresses, their cheeks rouged, waving their handkerchiefs to attract the attentions of another line of gentlemen in need of new mistresses.

She shuddered.

No, far better to do as she'd decided in the lane as he rode away from her, and free herself of the whole mess and start again, this time with a proper plan.

But she would miss kissing him! Being with him was the most exciting thing that had ever happened to her.

Her father, sitting beside her in the trap as they bowled along, the horse trotting behind them, gave her a quizzical look. "You're glum today, Genie," he said. "What's up, girl? Was it the letter you received this morning? Not bad news?"

That was another thing. She'd had a letter from Averil asking how her husband hunting was going. *I have been perusing* The Times—*the engagements section—but haven't seen any news yet. Do tell me what is happening between you and the duke!* It was possible Averil was teasing, but maybe she was not. Whenever Eugenie thought she was about to escape the foolish vows she'd made about the duke fate conspired to dig an even deeper hole for her. Now she would have to write back and explain it was all over and the duke had broken her heart.

No, Eugenie thought. *She* had broken *his* heart.

"Just thinking, Father."

"Well, your thoughts don't seem to be making you very happy, do they? What were you thinking?"

"I was considering my future."

He chuckled. "Were you now? I'll tell you something to cheer you up. If we sell the mare for a good price today I'll buy you and your mother a new dress each. She's still in low spirits over the twins' shenanigans with the black dye and a new dress always cheers her up." He beamed at her. "What do you say, Genie?"

Eugenie knew only too well that there were unpaid bills galore but here was her father wanting to buy new dresses for his womenfolk, to cheer them up. She should remind him of his responsibilities, but what was the point when he'd never listened to her before? It was not as if he was ever going to change.

And suddenly Eugenie longed for a new dress.

"Thank you, Father," she said gratefully.

He nodded, pleased to have pleased her, and reached over to grasp her in a rough hug. "You're a good girl, Genie."

Eugenie wondered if that epitaph would go on her headstone when she was dead and buried. *Eugenie Belmont, a good girl.* Despite all her good intentions a wayward and wicked thought slipped slyly into her head: Did she really want to be a good girl? If being a bad girl meant kissing Sinclair?

Torrisham, with its golden stone buildings and narrow laneways, was a bustling place, especially on market days. Her father found the horse stalls and set about brushing down the mare and cleaning her hooves. The creature rolled its eyes but managed to control the urge to kick.

"Father, are you sure this is a lady's mount?" Eugenie said, eyeing it uneasily.

"You've ridden her."

"Yes, but I know what to expect."

"Nothing wrong with a bit of spirit," he said jovially.

Eugenie was about to say you could have too much of a good thing, when she happened to glance across the market square and spotted a tall and very familiar figure.

"Oh good Lord, it's him," she gasped.

"Who's 'him'?"

"The duke!"

Her father shot her a curious look, and then followed her gaze. "Ah, Somerton!" he called, as if they were the best of friends. "How do you do? Come to look at the horseflesh, have ye?"

If the duke had been planning to walk past then he could no longer do so without appearing rude. She watched him hesitate, considering his options, but he'd been seen and spoken to and he was not a man to turn and run—even if that was what he quite clearly longed to do.

He strode toward them, removing his hat as he bowed in greeting. Eugenie gave a quick curtsey, avoiding his eyes, keeping just behind her father as if he might save her.

"Sir Peter, how do you do? Miss Belmont, I trust you are well?"

He sounded awkward, and she could see that telltale flush on his tanned cheeks. No doubt he was replaying the scene in the woods, just as she was. Then his gaze slid over the mare, whose tether was in her father's hand. "You are selling today, I see. Is she any good?"

"A fine lass," Sir Peter said, enthusiastically. He stepped closer, assuring Sinclair in an undertone that he was only selling because he was a little "light" in the pocket, while Eugenie inwardly cringed. "Does your sister need a new mount? Something with a bit more go in it? I saw her riding a gray gelding last month—looked like it was one step away from dog food, if you don't mind me being frank with you, Your Grace."

Clearly Sinclair did mind.

"Lady Annabelle is perfectly happy with her gelding," he said shortly. "She is not an expert horsewoman."

"Not like my Genie here then. She can ride anything with four legs. If I had the funds I'd set her up with the hunt. She'd put the rest of them to shame, she would."

Sinclair's gaze flickered to Eugenie and away before she could read his thoughts. He probably knew that her father had attempted to join the hunt himself once, only to be refused, and it wasn't because of his lack of funds but rather his lack of good character.

At that moment her father's attention was claimed by another buyer, an elderly man who'd brought along his granddaughter, and Eugenie breathed a sigh of relief.

"Do you always participate in your father's schemes?" Sinclair said quietly, a note of deep disapproval in his voice.

"Terry was busy and Father needed someone to help with the mare," she said lightly, hoping he'd say goodbye and move on.

Because she knew exactly what he was thinking. She was a hoyden. She could not be expected to behave like a gentlewoman, like his mother or his sister. The curl of his lip said it all. Well, she told herself, let him think what he liked, she no longer needed to pander to his good graces.

Some children ran past, shrieking, and Eugenie spent a number of nervous moments quieting the mare. When she glanced up again Sinclair was still there, only now he was watching her, and his expression was a mixture of puzzlement and regret. Her own hurt and disappointment began to wane.

"I find myself missing your company," he spoke abruptly, and then seemed embarrassed he'd blurted out the words aloud. His explanation was equally clumsy. "I thought I'd apologized for anything I may have said to upset you."

"You did, but I find myself wondering how long it will be before you upset me again."

He frowned. "You are speaking in riddles, Eugenie."

"Last time we met I had the impression you were glad to be rid of me," she said.

"There, see! You say exactly what you think when I am surrounded by people who say what they think I want to hear. I miss your bluntness, Eugenie."

She laughed, she couldn't help it. "I never claimed to be diplomatic, Your Grace. I am not to everyone's taste."

"You are very much to my taste."

How could he do that to her? Make her stomach dip like that? Just when she was trying to convince herself she hated him he made her like him again.

He smiled, took a step closer, and she felt the power of his personality. "Do you think we could meet again? If I promise to mind my manners?"

Nervously, Eugenie glanced at her father, who appeared to be engaged in negotiations as to price. Sinclair took the opportunity to move even closer, and his voice grew more intimate.

"I want to set you a dare, Miss Belmont. It must be my turn, after all."

"I think I am reckless enough, Your Grace, without needing to prove it. I am through with dares."

"Nevertheless I dare you to meet me at the ruined manor on Goyen Hill. Friday at eleven."

"I am sorry but I must decline."

"Are you such a coward?" he growled. "You started this game, Eugenie. It is too late to back out now."

Eugenie opened her mouth to give him a piece of her mind, just as her father finished with the elderly gentleman and turned to them with a beaming smile and a handful of cash.

"Now, Your Grace, I'm sorry we couldn't come to some arrangement about the mare, but such a fine lass was certain to be snapped up. I do have other horseflesh almost ready for sale. Give me a day or two and I'm sure I can find something to suit Lady Annabelle."

"Father, the duke does not want to buy one of your horses," Eugenie murmured warningly.

"Thank you, Sir Peter, but your daughter is right. I have no need of a horse. Now, I will leave you to your business. Good day."

Sinclair tipped his hat again, giving Eugenie a meaningful look as he turned away.

She wanted to run after him and tell him there was no way in the world she was going to meet him tomorrow, but again she was prevented. The elderly gentleman was collecting his mare and Eugenie needed to quietly question him about his granddaughter's riding skills. Relieved, she discovered the girl was no novice. "She likes a firm hand," she said quietly and meaningfully, nodding at the mare. "Once she knows who's in charge she will settle. Oh, and she dislikes bright buckles, so tell your granddaughter to wear plain footwear when she's riding. And sometimes puddles . . . I think the reflections startle her."

Feeling more comfortable about the morality of the sale, she was able to spend the journey home worrying about Sinclair and his dare and Averil's letter and the mess she was in.

Was Sinclair still intending to ask her to be his mistress? All that talk of minding his manners and behaving himself was very well, but did she believe him? Well, he would have to learn that when it came to Eugenie Belmont he had met his match. Husband Hunters Club or not, she refused to be any man's mistress.

Sinclair finished his soup and nodded for the servants to bring in the next course. His dining table was full tonight with local worthies and friends of his late father come visiting from London. Not exactly riotous company, but a necessary evil for a man in his position and with his social status to uphold. He was the Duke of Somerton and people expected him to throw the occasional lavish dinner. An invitation gave them something to boast about to their friends.

Besides, the lack of stimulating conversation enabled Sinclair to dwell on a subject that was constantly in his thoughts: Eugenie Belmont.

She was beneath him in every way. If he hadn't known it before then he knew it now, after seeing her at the horse fair acting like a Gypsy, helping her father sell that wild mare to some poor unsuspecting fool. All of that should have given him a distaste for her, and yet it hadn't.

If anything his passion for her was hotter than ever.

"When will you be coming down to London next, Somerton?"

Sinclair gave the old gentleman some offhand answer. London wasn't on his agenda; he preferred the countryside. Would Eugenie take up his dare? And if she did, then she must know what he intended. Would that mean she was willing to listen to his proposal after all?

Sinclair knew after the abduction dare that he'd made his move far too soon. He hadn't been able to help it. He was a man who knew what he wanted. Where was the point in dilly-dallying? Eugenie was that rare jewel, a woman he enjoyed spending time with, a woman he could talk to and who made him laugh. And then there was the wild passion he'd developed for her. He couldn't remember meeting another like her and he didn't need to wait about to make up his mind.

He was a duke, he needed a mistress, and Eugenie was perfect.

In Sinclair's mind the offer he intended to make was absurdly generous. She would have everything she wanted, certainly a great deal more than she had now, and it wasn't as if she had a great deal to lose. Even so he would be careful with her reputation, such as it was, protecting her as much as he was able. Ensuring her life—and the lives of her family—were as comfortable as possible.

Which reminded him. Belmont Hall was afflicted by damp and rot and probably deathwatch beetle. The Belmonts would find themselves without a home if they didn't find some way of repairing that hovel. He could see to those repairs; he could even buy them something larger and less drafty. Something at a great distance from himself and Eugenie.

Arrogant he may be, but surely he was not being unreasonable in expecting a favorable answer? Considering all the benefits he was offering. She may be playing coy but he would win her around.

This uncertainty had put him in a foolish lather.

Oh, he had had his amours—what man in his position had not?—but none of them had meant more to him than a passing fancy. These days he was hard-pressed to recall their faces. There was a world of difference between how he felt about them and how he felt about Eugenie Belmont. The only way he could explain his feelings was that he felt himself when he was with her, as if he didn't have to pretend.

Surely that was reason enough to want to make her a permanent fixture in his life?

He'd begun waking in the night, awash with desire and longing. His body became hard as rock whenever he imagined her beneath him, naked upon his sheets. Sometimes he'd believe he caught a whiff of her scent, the fresh sweet smell of her hair, and his body would react with embarrassing promptness. He was beginning to think he was turning into one of his stallions, so eager to mate that he was liable to leap over fences to find his ladylove.

It might be a form of madness, but he wanted her. He wanted to clasp her in his arms and take her when and wherever the need took him. That was what a mistress was for, after all. He could sit with her in his arms and talk to her, or simply say nothing in companionable silence. And in return for being with him, she could have anything she'd ever wanted.

To Sinclair's fevered mind it was only a matter of time before Eugenie Belmont gave in to the inevitable.

Chapter 10

By Friday morning Sinclair was up and ready, his temper on a short leash. Annabelle eyed him uneasily over breakfast. He could tell she wanted to speak to him but wasn't certain how to broach the subject. If it was about her marriage to Lucius he would rather she remain silent, but Annabelle was not one to shirk a conversation just because it may cause difficulties to herself or others.

"I have had a letter from my friend Greta," she said at last, setting down her teacup on its saucer with a rattle of china.

"Indeed."

"She lives in Bedfordshire, Sinclair."

"And you are telling me this because . . . ?"

"Stop it, Sinclair. You are obviously in a bad mood but I will not let it affect me. I am telling you about Greta because I want to stay with her before I am hemmed about by convention as Lucius's bride-to-be. She has promised me a party and visits to other friends."

He raised an eyebrow. "I have no objections,

Annabelle, as long as your mother and your husband-to-be have none."

"What has Lucius to say to anything?" she snapped. "We are not married yet."

"If I remember correctly Greta was always a little unconventional. Perhaps this isn't the moment to visit her, Annabelle. We do not want a scandal."

She scowled. "You don't want me to have any friends. You want me to be miserable, Sinclair."

"Annabelle, now you are being ridiculous. You will have plenty of friends to see when you go to London. Who knows, you may even make some new ones."

She rose from the table and fled the room.

Miss Gamboni stumbled to her feet. "I am sorry, Your Grace," she began, but he waved a hand at her, dismissing her apology.

"Perhaps you could turn her mind in some other direction, Miss Gamboni."

"I will try, Your Grace."

He was getting used to such departures from his sister, and he didn't allow it to bother him for long. He had other matters to mull over.

His paints had arrived from London and he was itching to lock himself away in his attic room and begin painting. He'd already done some sketches of Eugenie from memory, and thought they were rather good. He still had to capture that sweet mischief in her expression, but he thought he could make a start.

Alas, after breakfast, he had to spend some time with his land agent, and then he needed to write several letters in regard to tenants who had asked him for help in the repair of their cottages or stone fences. As he worked he thought about how much responsibility his position placed upon him. For the past ten years he'd lived without complaint, doing as was expected of him, inhabiting his role as duke, not really thinking about what he was becoming.

Dull, boring.

And now, suddenly, Eugenie had changed that, challenging him to take risks and make changes, showing him that even the dullest life could be exciting. He couldn't imagine going back to the way he'd been without her.

He finished the last letter and tossed his pen aside, uncaring when it splattered ink. Done! At last, he was free to set out on his latest adventure.

Today was cool, with the threat of rain, but it could have been blazing sunlight for all he noticed or cared. He galloped all the way to his rendezvous, arrived half an hour early and had to wait, impatiently striding up and down beside the ruins of what had once been a grand manor house. During the Wars of the Roses there had been a battle fought here and unfortunately the building was in the thick of it. Now it was a picturesque ruin.

She was late.

He hated it when people were late for appointments. Then he began to worry she wasn't coming, the knot in his stomach twisting tighter. Should he leave, teach her a lesson in punctuality? Of course he knew he couldn't do that. He needed to see her, he wanted to see her . . . and then he heard a horse's hooves galloping toward him.

She came over the hill, her hair flying, her skirts barely decent about her stockinged legs. She was riding the mare from the horse fair! He laughed aloud as the creature came to an unwilling halt, rolling its eyes and stamping about nervously.

"I thought you'd sold that mare," he said, as he reached up to take her reins and hold the beast firm.

Eugenie was flushed and breathless, her green eyes bright. "They brought it back," she said, with a shrug. "No new dress for me."

His brows rose in inquiry.

"My father promised me a new dress if he sold the mare," she explained, as she landed on her feet on the ground and shook her skirts back into a more respectable form.

Impulsively he reached out and cupped her cheek. "I will buy you a new dress for every day we are together," he said hoarsely, "and every night."

And then he saw the expression in her eyes.

There was a tremble in her belly, deep inside. Eugenie conquered it, raising a hand to brush back her unruly curls. "I would need a very large wardrobe for all those dresses," she said coolly.

He didn't smile back. "Should I apologize again?"

To give herself time to think, Eugenie led her mare to the ruined wall.

She'd decided not to come but then she began

to think of writing to Averil, telling her she wasn't going to marry the duke after all, and what Averil would say to the others. They would think she'd made the whole thing up—which of course she had—but that wasn't the point.

Eugenie had her pride, too much sometimes. In the end she convinced herself she would give Sinclair one last chance to do the decent thing. Or maybe she was just too weak to refuse to see him again. Kiss him again.

She blushed as she began looping the reins through what appeared to be a hole made by a cannon ball. To fill the silence she began to tell him about the mare.

"The silly creature shied at a puddle and frightened her new owner, although thank goodness the girl wasn't hurt. I did warn them about puddles. Anyway, her grandfather wasn't best pleased with my father."

"I don't suppose he was."

"If I don't tie her up she runs away," she added. "But at least she runs home. It just means I'd have to walk."

"Rather inconvenient then."

"Yes. She doesn't mean any harm; she's just highly-strung."

"So I see."

The subject of the mare exhausted, she was forced to face him. He was gazing at her as if he'd like to eat her up.

"Eugenie, I think you can understand how much you would gain if you allowed me to look after you. Believe me when I tell you that you would want for nothing. I would treat you with the greatest care and consideration. I would protect your reputation. And if our—our association should falter—although I cannot imagine it, but these things must be thought of—then I would see to it that you retained all the benefits of your position until you decided whether you wished to marry or—or take up with another gentleman."

He was insulting her.

Take up with another gentleman.

She knew he didn't see it that way, but nevertheless in her heart this felt like a grave insult. "No," she said, striving not to let her voice to tremble for the sake of her pride.

"No?" He sounded surprised, as if he'd believed his offer was too good to refuse. "Just no? Nothing more? Surely you'd like to consider? Think it over?"

"I have never been asked to be a gentleman's mistress before. You must pardon my clumsiness . . . my lack of experience. I didn't expect a proposal such as this to ever come my way. I certainly would never have sought it."

"And I have never asked a woman to be my mistress before," he retorted, and then chuckled at the expression on her face. "Did you really think I had a dozen or so already? That's very flattering of you, Eugenie."

Eugenie was surprised and couldn't hide it. She'd imagined he'd some little dancer tucked away—innocent as she was, she knew that was the usual situation with rich and powerful men. And a duke could afford more than one, surely?

He read the questions in her eyes—he seemed able to see inside her head with startling ease. "I want you, Eugenie, and only you. I don't know why it is. Cannot fathom it. I find myself looking for you wherever I go. Looking forward to seeing you, speaking to you, holding you in my arms."

He didn't mean to flatter her; quite the opposite in fact. He spoke of his emotions reluctantly, as if he found them incomprehensible. And yet she was flattered. Not that she could take him up on his offer.

"We deal well together, don't you think?" he went on, clearly wanting an answer.

"We barely know each other," she said bluntly.

He rested his hand on the curve of her neck, stroking her skin softly, gently, as if she were one of his precious racehorses. "I know all I need to know."

The touch of his hand, the sensation of being caressed so, caused the trembling to increase inside her. Eugenie turned her head and met his eyes, seeking the heat in them, and knew a temptation such as she'd never known before—to place herself in his power and let him do whatever he wished with her.

For one wild, insane moment she actually considered accepting his offer. Jumping into the fire and letting herself be burned. But the next moment her powerful determination and her sense of self-worth bobbed to the surface. She could never take second best, and that's what being his mistress—any man's mistress—would mean. She'd rather remain a spinster all her life than accept less than being a wife.

Sinclair couldn't see it and probably never would, but in her heart Eugenie knew that despite her lower birth and her rackety family she would make him a perfect wife. They would be happy together—if they could get over the scandal that society was bound to make of them. A pity the gulf between the two of them was so insurmountable.

"Sinclair . . ."

His fingers were still brushing against her skin, lightly, back and forth. That surprising and tantalizing heat increased inside her, bringing with it a need that was building by the heartbeat. Building so strongly in fact that she knew she was going to have to exercise a great deal of willpower and fortitude to resist him.

She reached up to remove his hand, but he clasped hers, linking their fingers.

"Please, Sinclair, stop. You make me breathless," she said, and she sounded as if she'd been running.

"At least you haven't fainted. Does that mean you're willing to reconsider my proposal?"

"I'm not the kind of girl who faints."

He bent his head and despite her protests she found herself stretching up, lips apart, eager for his kiss. His breath brushed her skin, teasing. His kiss had barely begun before it ended, and she knew she wanted more. The hunger inside her demanded to be satisfied.

She made a sound, searching for his lips, and he laughed triumphantly and kissed her again, more forcefully this time.

"I want your answer," he said, his voice a low

growl in his throat. "Say you will be my mistress, Eugenie."

Her eyelids lifted slowly, sensuously. She reached to touch his jaw with her fingertips, enjoying the feel of his rougher skin. "No."

He stepped back, frowning, still holding her. He'd been so certain of her answer that now he seemed staggered. "No?" he demanded, his old arrogance surfacing. "Just 'no'?"

Eugenie glanced up at him in a manner at once shy and coquettish. It had the desired effect. He pulled her into his arms and kissed her again, and this time it was difficult for both of them to stop. It was as if he was placing his mark on her, claiming her as his in some primitive masculine way. When he finally drew away his chest was rising and falling heavily, and there was a flush on his cheeks.

"That doesn't feel like a 'no,'" he said huskily. "You want me, too, don't you? Be your blunt and honest self, Eugenie."

Eugenie didn't need a mirror to know her eyes were dark with desire. "I won't lie to you," she agreed, placing her palms against his chest. She could feel the heat of his body, and the heavy thud of his heart. "When you kiss me I feel as if I might do something dangerous. And to be your mistress would be dangerous, Sinclair. Whatever you might think of me, I am a gentlewoman. At Miss Debenham's Finishing School I learned how to make conversation and behave politely in all situations, how to dress, how to organize and run a household, how to stitch neatly and arrange flowers. I did *not* learn how to be a duke's mistress."

He moved to protest but she put her finger against his lips.

"Hush, I am not done."

When he seemed to be resigned to letting her continue, she went on.

"Sinclair, I am very sorry but the final answer must be no."

"I don't believe you," he snapped. "If you think a man like me cannot protect you from scandal, then you do not know me at all. I will keep your reputation safe, Eugenie. I can make it so that no one knows our true situation but you and I." His brows drew together and there was anger in his face as well as hunger. "I want you and I mean to have you."

"It always amazes me that men like you think they can have anything they desire. Well, you can't have me, Sinclair. My answer is still no."

She moved to walk away but he caught her, pulling her back into his arms. "Men like me?" he mocked. "You may fool yourself with your denials, Eugenie, but you can't fool me." His mouth swooped down, hot and hard against hers, as if he might turn her to his will by sheer force. Eugenie knew her lips would be bruised and swollen by his treatment of her—and she would have to hide that from her family—but the other part of her didn't give a fig for swollen lips. Indeed, she was reveling in his forceful passion.

And she was enjoying herself too much to stop. She gave her fingers permission to roam through his dark hair, mussing it up, exploring the texture of it. His skin smelled of sandalwood and man, and when she kissed him she could taste the passion for her on his mouth. He meant what he said all right. He really did lust after her.

His own fingers were cupping her face, his lips against her eyelids, her cheeks, then her throat and she found herself arching back, so that he could kiss the hollow there, before working his way down to the thin strip of lace that bordered her neckline. He dipped his finger beneath it, brushing the swell of her breast before encountering the well-laundered cotton of her chemise.

Eugenie's knees trembled. Her skin burned. She ached to have his hand delve farther, exploring the peak of her breast. She imagined his mouth closing over her, hot and moist, and experienced such a jolt of desire her head spun.

It happened so quickly. This loss of control, this need to give herself to him completely. The voice in her head was telling her that nothing mattered except this. Why worry? Everything would be all right. Don't stop, don't stop.

But she knew that she had to stop, that everything wouldn't be all right. She had to stop now. At once. Before it was too late.

Reluctantly, shakily, she dragged herself out of his arms, and then walked away, taking deep steadying breaths. When she felt able to turn he was standing where she'd left him, looking like a man who had just awoken from a dream and was still more than half asleep.

"Eugenie," he groaned, demanding and begging at the same time.

The temptation to run back into his arms was irresistible, but somehow she resisted. The distance between them was not wide enough, and she took several steps backward, increasing it until she felt calmer. Safer.

"I apologize," he said, running a shaking hand through his hair. "I was rather more brutal than I intended. It's your fault."

She laughed and shook her head. "My fault? You can't blame me for your behavior, Sinclair."

His stare was almost beseeching. One sign from her and Eugenie knew he would rush toward her and take her in his arms again, and then they would both be lost.

"I must go," she said quickly. "My mother will be looking for me. I have chores to do. We do not have quite as many servants as you do."

"We will meet again? How can I persuade you to change your mind if we do not meet again?"

"No. This is the end of the matter."

She went to where she'd tied her mare, not waiting for another argument. Suddenly his hands closed about her waist and, briefly, he drew her back against his chest, his lips pressed to her nape. She shivered as desire returned in full force, and then felt herself lifted and tossed into the saddle. Even that brief touch caused her to tremble and burn, but she fought for composure. It didn't help that his hand was resting on her stocking-covered ankle, possessively, as if she was already his.

"Good-bye, Your Grace," she said, with a cool nod.

He shrugged and stepped back, letting her go. She gave her mare its head, riding away without looking back, knowing he was watching her. A strange sort of feminine triumph blazed inside her but she damped it down. What was the use of having such a power over the duke when she could not gain the prize she wanted? He would not marry her. But someone else would; someone who saw her fine qualities and would love her for who and what she was.

Someone she was yet to meet.

Eugenie spent her time on the ride back thinking of her mystery man, of how she would wake up with him every morning and dine with him every night, of walking at his side as his wife. Bearing his children. Their days full of the small pleasurable moments between two people who loved and respected each other.

It was a pity that even in her daydreams her mystery man seemed to acquire the face and personality of Sinclair. Eugenie just hoped the duke hadn't spoiled her for anyone else.

Chapter 11

Sinclair was even more determined to get his way with Eugenie. Her lack of interest in his proposal stirred the coals of his desire into a roaring inferno.

Most men of his class and social standing had a mistress—it was expected, even if it wasn't spoken of in polite circles. A mistress was de rigueur and until now he'd denied himself that pleasure, but with Eugenie all of that had changed.

And by God, he deserved her!

As a man who was restrained and responsible, an almost-Puritan who'd always put his position and his family first, it was time he looked to his own desires. Yes, for once he was going to put himself and his own needs first.

And why not?

It wasn't as if he was going to marry her. He wasn't about to lose his head and create a scandal, like some peers were wont to do, making themselves laughingstocks in the process. He'd keep her private, a secret lover.

As Sinclair grew more and more determined to

make his wishes come true, the need to have Eugenie became a fait accompli, he was so certain he could persuade her—or if necessary bribe her—to say yes.

He'd come home from their meeting at the ruined manor and gone straight up to the attic room, beginning work on his painting. Hours passed, he became lost in the joy of his work, and it wasn't until one of his servants cleared his throat outside his door that he realized how late it was.

Hurriedly he dressed for dinner and joined his mother and sister at the table. But it was difficult behaving normally when he no longer felt like that man. Being with Eugenie had changed him, and he found himself thinking about their wild and passionate kisses, and squirming in his chair like a restless child. His body ached and throbbed with the need to have her in his arms again, only this time he would undress her, peeling her garments from her one by one until she was naked. Pale and beautiful upon his sheets, her wild curls spread about her, her green eyes warm and promising so much.

She represented a world that until now he had never known, and one that he was now desperate to enter.

"Whatever is the matter, Sinclair?"

His mother's chilly tones drifting down the long table brought him up short. She was watching him over her soup spoon, her arched brows even more arched, her thin nostrils pinched with disapproval.

"Nothing is the matter, Mother. Are you enjoying the soup?"

"Soup is much the same wherever one eats it," she retorted. "I was never overly fond of soup."

Sinclair stifled a sigh. His mother had decided to make a brief visit to Somerton on her way to friends farther west in the Cotswolds. They must be good friends to draw her out of London, which was her permanent home these days. She had always loathed the country, and their father's body was barely tucked away in the family mausoleum before she'd packed up and left, telling her son that he was the duke now and she was trusting him not to do anything to tarnish the Somerton name.

He didn't miss his father; it would be a lie to say he did. The old man had been stiff and distant and full of pride, and Sinclair had barely known him. Strange that it was often said that he was very like his father. He'd attuned his outward behavior to his father's on purpose, because he'd been brought up to believe that was the way dukes behaved. It was now second nature to him. He considered the chilly demeanor part of his heritage. Why not? The Duke of Somerton was a title to wear with pride.

But beneath the facade, Sinclair had become aware that he was lonely. With all his wealth and power, he was a man alone.

It had taken Eugenie to bring him to that realization.

"Sinclair, whatever is wrong with you?"

His mother was staring at him again. The servants were clearing the soup in preparation for the next course, their faces blank, pretending not to listen. He found himself wondering what they thought of him, of his mother—minutiae that had previously been beneath his notice.

"Sinclair is probably thinking of ways to increase his consequence," Annabelle quipped.

She'd been unnaturally quiet since their mother's arrival, and looking at her now he noticed her pallor and the shadows under her eyes. Was she fretting about her marriage to Lucius? Sinclair was aware it was unpalatable to her but the life of a duke's sister could never be as free and easy as a servant girl's. She must accept that lesson or expect heartbreak for the rest of her life.

Just as he had accepted.

"Of course the wedding will be at St. James's," the dowager duchess enthused. "And afterwards those guests we choose to invite can come to the London house for champagne and cake. I think we will have enough room. People are talking about it already, and once the invitations are sent . . . I do believe it will be the event of the year, Annabelle."

Annabelle smiled, her lashes sweeping down to hide her eyes. "Yes, Mama," she said like an obedient daughter.

Miss Gamboni gave her a sharp glance before looking down at her plate.

Sinclair frowned. Was there something in his sister's smile that should make him uneasy? What did Miss Gamboni see that he didn't? But before he had time to consider the matter his mother was talking again, describing how she intended to decorate the London house, the colors she would use, the theme she had in mind. Then she went on to describe some event she had recently attended, and who was there and what they were wearing. Appearance was all to her.

Suddenly Sinclair was bored with it.

Completely, utterly, and unbearably bored.

He stood up from the table. Three pairs of eyes lifted to his in amazement. "Sinclair?"

He was behaving completely out of character, but he didn't care.

"My apologies," he said, moving away. "I have remembered something I must do and I'm afraid it cannot wait."

"Sinclair, really! I'm sure you can get someone else to do it for you. You cannot rush off halfway through dinner—"

"I have apologized, Mother."

The door closed behind him and he took a deep breath. He'd actually walked out during dinner. Something he had never done before. Something he would never have thought of doing before. And he felt quite giddy with the thrill of it.

He wanted to see Eugenie.

Now! This moment.

"Have my horse saddled," he called to one of the servants as he strode across the marble hall. "I have an urgent appointment."

"Your Grace?" His startled gaze ran down over Sinclair's dinner clothes. "Aren't you going to change first, Y-your Grace?"

"Of course I am," he frowned, as if he'd never

forget such a minor detail. The fact was he had. Completely.

Upstairs he waved his valet away, dressing himself with unusual carelessness, and hurrying down the backstairs to the stables. By then his mount was ready and he set off at a gallop, out into the starry night, feeling remarkably free and reckless, and quite unlike himself.

Belmont Hall was not exactly ablaze with lights. Evidently the family kept early hours. It occurred to him that he hadn't had the foresight to discover which was Eugenie's bedchamber; however, by the use of his wits he saw one of the windows had a flowery curtain, more suited to a young girl. Probably it had not been replaced as she grew up, and he could not imagine Jack or the other boys with such a curtain on their window. Well, not for long, anyway.

It was a chance the old Sinclair would never have taken. What? Risk embroiling himself in a scandal? But this was the new Sinclair and he was a very different creature.

Standing in the darkness, below the faintly candlelit window, he knew he was behaving erratically. Some would say he had lost his wits. There was a moment when he almost turned away and rode home, but before the urge could take hold, before the old Sinclair could spoil his fun, he bent down and picked up some pebbles from the drive and threw them against the glass in the casement.

They made a satisfying rattle.

A shadow appeared against the candlelight, and

then the curtain was drawn aside and there she was. Eugenie. She stared down into the garden, trying to see who was there, and then threw open the casement and leaned out.

Her hair hung loose about her, a waterfall of tumbling curls within which her face was a pale oval.

An angel.

"Terry? Is that you?" she hissed. She sounded annoyed.

Not quite an angel, then.

"It's not Terry," he said.

She gasped, her hand creeping to her throat. Or maybe she was holding her nightgown up so that it didn't dip too far and disclose too much of her pale, curved flesh.

"Sinclair?" she whispered loudly. "What on earth—" She began to shut the casement. "Go away. I don't want to see you again."

"Come down. If you don't I'll ring the doorbell."

"You wouldn't dare," she hissed. Then she saw the stubborn expression on his face in the moonlight. "Wait there. I'll be down in a moment."

Sinclair decided he wouldn't wait under her window. The doorbell threat had been a bluff, and it suddenly seemed far too risky even for his new self to lurk about here. Good God, he wouldn't put it past Eugenie's father to demand he call the banns! He saw what looked like an arbor in the shadows behind him, set in the far corner of the garden.

It *was* an arbor. He ducked under the arch with its overgrown climbing rose, and sat down on a cold stone bench. Probably damp, too, he thought uneasily. He stood up, knocking his head against the arch and its thorny canes, cursed, and sat down again.

If Eugenie was anything like other women he'd known he could be waiting here until dawn while she primped and preened, trying on dress after dress, seeking to make herself beautiful for him.

But he already knew Eugenie wasn't anything like those other women and that was a big part of her appeal.

Just then she appeared from the shadows, in a simple dress hastily thrown on, a shawl cast about her shoulders, her hair still loose. For a moment she stood, looking all about her, and then he called her name, and she hurried through the garden to the arbor and, arriving breathless, stood before him.

"Sinclair," she said, sounding annoyed. "What are you doing here?"

The last thing he wanted was for her to find his romantic and impromptu visit annoying. For a moment he found his old awkward and tongue-tied feelings returning, as they always did when confronted by a woman he was attracted to. And then her scent reached out to him, warm woman and orange blossom, and he tried to draw her into his arms with a groan.

She pulled away. "I've rejected your proposal, Sinclair. You must believe me when I say I meant my no."

"I can't believe you," he growled, low and intimate.

He thought of telling her exactly what he had done, leaving in the middle of the meal to ride to her, before changing his mind. But one never knew with women—she might laugh at him. Better that she didn't know just how much he lusted after her. How much power she had over him.

"Sinclair . . . ?" She was peering at him, a frown creasing her brow. She reached out and touched his forehead and, drawing her hand away again, showed him the smear of blood on her fingers. "Whatever have you done to yourself?"

"The roses caught me," he said, gesturing at the loose canes on the arbor. "It's nothing."

She sat down beside him. "Is it safe for me to be outside with you?" she said.

"Of course," he retorted. "I am a duke."

She giggled. "That's more like the Sinclair I know." She reached to dab at his forehead with the end of her shawl, but he caught her hands and pulled her against him, kissing her. If she'd resisted he would have released her, but she didn't, so he lifted her onto his lap.

Her body was soft and unrestrained by a corset, and of course that meant he had to brush his hand against her breast and, when she didn't immediately protest, cup the firm flesh in his palm.

Her breathing had quickened.

He bent his head and breathed in the scent of her skin through the thin cloth. He could feel the jut of her nipple and covered her with his mouth, gently teasing with his tongue. Her fingers pressed him closer, tangling in his hair, and he could feel her breath, little gasps of sound.

Slowly, he warned himself. *Don't rush her. Don't frighten her. Don't break the spell.*

She arched in his arms, and then her mouth was searching for his, needy and hot. He kissed her deeply, drawing her closer still, her soft thigh against the hard thrust of his growing erection.

He felt his control slipping. Her bodice was loosened—had he done that? He slid his hand down and felt the warm swell of her skin. This was what it would be like, if she was naked in his bed. He'd come to her every night, and they would lie together and enjoy each other until dawn.

Eugenie moved upon his lap, her hands running down his chest, restless, eager. She pulled the shirt hem from his breeches and then her palms were on his stomach, making him catch his breath. He could see her eyes shining in the darkness, imagined the flush on her cheeks, the swollen pink of her lips.

His control was slipping but desperately, determinedly, he held on. He was a mature man after all, not some callow youth.

And then her fingers closed over his cock.

Chapter 12

He went stock-still, and Eugenia wondered if she had gone too far. Suddenly she was embarrassed by her own forwardness but when she tried to remove her hand, Sinclair fumbled for her fingers and clasped them tightly in his.

"Eugenie," he muttered raggedly into her hair.

She fitted perfectly into his arms, her head beneath his chin, her body curved to his, as if she was meant to be here.

"I'm sorry," she said. "You were touching me and it felt so nice that I thought I'd return the favor. Should I have waited to be asked? The etiquette of pleasure isn't something I was taught at Miss Debenham's."

"You did nothing wrong. It is just that I am trying to keep control and when you touch me I feel as if . . ."

"As if you might ride off with me like the wicked baron?"

His chuckle was husky. "Something like that."

She sighed. "I suppose you spend your time with blue-blooded ladies who would never dare to—to touch a duke. You forget I am a hoyden, Sinclair."

"I haven't forgotten. I'm beginning to think I prefer hoydens."

She smiled against his neck. "This must stop, Sinclair," she said, but he seemed to sense her weakness.

"Kiss me, hoyden," he growled, and she did so, spending a very pleasurable few moments lost in the hard promise of his mouth. Her body was growing more languorous, and she knew it was just a matter of time before she lost all strength to resist him.

This really was becoming extremely perilous.

His tongue tangled with hers, stroking her, and with each stroke the heat inside her body grew hotter. Just a little longer, she told herself. How could it hurt? Just a little bit more.

His hand was cupping her breast, and she felt the jut of her nipple against his palm, the sensation almost painful, but exquisitely so, as he used his thumb to rub against her. Her body jolted, her breath caught in her throat, and she made a sound she had never made before.

He bent his head and she felt the warm, wet cavern of his mouth close over her flesh. He played with her with his tongue. The pleasure was so new and exciting, she didn't at first realize his hand was on her thigh, beneath her skirt. Her heart began to bump more quickly as his fingers caressed her soft flesh, edging higher, closer to the moist heat she felt throbbing at her center.

And then his forefinger stroked down the

swollen flesh between her thighs, bringing to life even more dazzling sensations. "I don't think you should do—" she managed, but he didn't give her time to finish her protest, closing his mouth on hers, while his finger stroked again.

Her body seemed to have a will of its own, savoring every instant of pleasure, wishing it could go on forever.

But it couldn't and if she didn't stop him now then she would be lost.

With a soft gasp she slipped out of his arms and stood, a little unsteadily, in front of him. He seemed just as reluctant to let her go but he accepted her decision. And then he glanced down at her feet.

"You are barefoot!" he said, shocked.

"Of course I am. I didn't want to waste time finding my shoes," she said matter-of-factly.

"I'm not having you catch a cold," he retorted, and promptly swept her up into his arms.

"Put me down," she protested, struggling.

He held her fast. "Stop it. I'm being purely selfish. Kissing a woman with a cold is the very devil."

Irritably she said, "I have gone barefoot before, more times than I wish to remember."

"Well, when you are mine, Miss Belmont, you will always be shod, whatever the circumstances. You will have shoes for every occasion."

When you are mine.

The words were sweet, despite the fact that she knew they would never happen. She would never be his. Not in the way he imagined. Nevertheless she stopped struggling.

He was carrying her toward the house. "Speaking of something I want to do . . . I have a request to make of you, Eugenie."

"Oh?" She looked up at him suspiciously. "What is it?"

He seemed to be carefully considering his words. "I wasn't always a duke. Once I was young like Annabelle and I thought anything was possible. Lately I've been reliving those days, remembering how it was to be so caught up in my dreams that they were more real than this world we inhabit."

"Everyone should have dreams," she said quietly. "Just because we grow up doesn't mean we have to abandon them."

He gave a grunt of laughter. "You're an idealist, Eugenie."

"Am I? I'm not claiming that dreams always come true, you know. Just that there is nothing wrong in having them."

"I see."

She watched him, trying to read his mind as he seemed to be able to read hers, wondering what it was he was going to ask her. Something to do with his boyhood, his dreams?

"What did you want to ask me?" she prompted him at last.

He hesitated and then shook his head. "Never mind. I'll tell you next time. You're tired, Eugenie. You should be in bed."

His voice had turned suggestive on the last word and she forgot to remind him that there wouldn't be a next time. Her heart skipped a beat. Her skin was achy and sensitive, and the thought of him touching her again brought out goose bumps. Just for a moment she allowed herself to snuggle closer against him, breathing in his scent, and storing up memories.

When they reached the back door he set her down, steadying her a moment, before lifting her hand to his lips. "Goodnight, Miss Belmont," he murmured, ever so polite.

But his dark eyes were not polite. They were hungry and intimate, promising her so much. In a moment she'd be kissing him again, caught up in the magic that flared between them, lost to all her good sense.

She began to close the door.

"Will you come to Somerton tomorrow?" he said quickly. "Bring Jack with you."

She didn't answer him and then the door was closed. She stood and listened to his steps retreating, telling herself she would not come.

Eugenie was halfway up the staircase when a little voice on the landing made her stop.

"Was that the duke, Genie?"

With a start, Eugenie looked up. "Jack? Whatever are you doing up?"

"I heard voices."

She reached the landing and took his hand, steering him toward his bedroom. She lowered her voice, not wishing to wake the twins. Terry's bed, she noticed, was empty.

"It was the duke, but don't tell anyone. It was a—a secret visit, to invite us to go to see Erik tomorrow." Eugenie realized too late she had trapped herself again.

"Oh." His eyes were round. "The horses, too?"

"Of course the horses."

She finished tucking him in and bent to kiss his cheek. He rubbed off the kiss with his shoulder automatically, as all boys tended to do when they reached a certain age.

"Goodnight, Jack," she whispered.

His voice drifted after her. "Don't worry, Genie, I won't tell."

Back in her bed, Eugenie stared into the darkness. Jack had reminded her she was playing a dangerous game. If she was caught alone with Sinclair in such circumstances as tonight then her father would certainly create havoc. There would be a scandal and the person to be hurt the most by it would be Eugenie.

Annabelle giggled as they ran through the garden and into the copse of trees planted by her grandfather when the original wood had been chopped down to make ships for the navy.

"If Mother had caught you she would have exploded," she added, when they stopped to catch their breath. "Sometimes I am sure she will explode. She sort of puffs herself up." Her smile faded. "She can be very frightening."

Terry, watching her face, thought Annabelle truly was afraid of her mother, and yet she was brave, too, and willing to go against her wishes despite the consequences.

"We'll be safe soon," he said, trying to sound as if he weren't a little afraid, too. Although Terry found himself more afraid of Annabelle's brother than her mother. Something about the look in the Duke of Somerton's eyes when he settled them on Terry was quite terrifying. Not that he'd ever tell Annabelle so. She thought of him as her brave hero and he fully intended to live up to it.

He realized that until now he'd never imagined someone like Annabelle would have any reason to be miserable with their life. To have money and position and a grand house seemed perfection in itself and that Annabelle should wish for another life would have seemed bizarre to Terry only a short time ago. Now he understood that such a life came with its own form of bars and bolts—its own type of prison—just as his own life did.

He was beginning to feel quite grown up.

"Aren't you worried you'll be punished for running away?" he asked suddenly, and then wished he'd bitten his tongue when she gave him a strange look.

"Aren't you?" she countered.

He shrugged. "I'm nothing. You're the sister of a duke."

Annabelle smiled. "Then we must be certain not to let them catch us, mustn't we?" She clasped his hand in hers and held it tight. "I'm so glad you're my friend, Terry. I don't know what I would have done without you to help me."

A wave of pride swept over him, and with it a kernel of shame. Because the truth was Terry did not think of Annabelle as his friend. Well, not really.

In the beginning he'd thought of her as an opportunity for himself, a pattern of thinking he now realized he'd learned from his father. Then, when he got to know her and understand her, he began to like her for herself and not for who she was. And now, well, he loved her.

Not the sort of lustful love that he'd felt for girls before, a feeling that was more like a physical urge than anything emotional. This was something far more pure. He wanted to help her, save her, make her happy. He wanted to sacrifice himself for her well-being.

He knew he was a bloody idiot. His friends would soon tell him so if he tried to explain to them. But he couldn't seem to help it.

He wanted to be her hero.

"Lady Annabelle!"

The hero jumped, but Annabelle faced their discoverer with a raised eyebrow and a cool smile.

"Lizzie. I hope you haven't told Mother I am out here."

"Of course not," Lizzie Gamboni retorted.

Terry thought she looked flushed and cross, her fair hair fluffy about her face, the buttons on her pelisse crooked as though she had dressed in the dark in a hurry. And yet there was something oddly endearing about her.

"Well, now you have found me what are you going to do?" Annabelle dared her. "You know how miserable I am. Will you give me up? They will keep me prisoner until the wedding if you do. Lock me into some horrid little room with only bread and water."

"Annabelle, I won't give you up," Lizzie said, and Annabelle's shrill voice quavered to a stop. "I would never do that. But I do wish you would be careful and—and think before you act."

Annabelle sighed and took her hand. "You are a true friend, Lizzie." She turned and smiled back over her shoulder at Terry, reached to claim his hand, too. "You are my only friends in this cruel world."

Terry found himself looking into Lizzie's pale eyes. Was there a plea in them? A plea to take care with her charge? Well, there was no need to ask him that. He would never harm Annabelle; he would only ever do what she wished him to.

"We had best go indoors now," Lizzie said, lowering her gaze and turning away, leaving Terry feeling strangely bereft. "Come, Annabelle."

Annabelle went without argument, and Terry watched them disappear into the starlit darkness, Annabelle's hair dark as a raven's wing, Lizzie's fair as a dove.

Chapter 13

"I'm sure you've been overfeeding that goat,"
Eugenie greeted Sinclair at Erik's compound the next afternoon. "He's grown quite fat."

Sinclair raised his brows. "I will tell Barker," he said.

"Genie," Jack murmured, uncomfortable. "Somerton has been very kind to Erik. Perhaps Barker just doesn't know what sort of food is good for goats."

"Should you be calling His Grace by his name, Jack?" she said sharply.

"He asked me to," Jack retorted, puzzled. "Why? What should I call him?"

Sinclair's brows were still raised as he waited for her answer.

She changed the subject. Just because she was cross with him didn't mean she should be rude. "Here I am berating you for making our goat too comfortable when I should be thanking you for taking him in." She looked up at him from beneath the brim of her straw bonnet, a wry smile in her eyes. One of her wayward curls danced against her cheek in the summer breeze.

Sinclair smiled back, as if she'd reacted exactly as he expected. "Barker mentioned to me that he thought your goat might like several lady goats to keep him company. What do you think of that, Jack? Should I ask your father's permission to go ahead?"

Eugenie bit her lip while Jack deliberated.

"No, you needn't ask Father," he said at last. "He'd only make you pay him again. Genie says that wasn't fair, and I think she's right."

Eugenie sighed with relief. Jack *was* right. She could just imagine her father demanding a fee for Erik's stud services. "If Barker believes that is best for Erik then that is good enough for us," she said firmly.

"Father says we were lucky you didn't take us to the magistrate for having a dangerous animal," Jack went on blithely.

Sinclair was suddenly looking very dukelike.

"My meeting with your goat is probably a constant topic of conversation in your household," he said coolly. "I imagine it causes you all a great deal of hilarity."

"No," Jack said thoughtfully, before Eugenie could stop him. "That isn't Father's favorite story. Do you want to know what his favorite story is?"

"I'm sure the duke would much rather not," Eugenie said, putting a restraining hand on Jack's shoulder.

"But indeed I would," Sinclair retorted, his lips

growing frighteningly thin. In a moment he would
be curling one of them in that hateful sneer. "Tell
me, Jack, what is your father's favorite story?"

"You tell him, Genie," her brother begged. "You
tell it better than I do."

Eugenie sighed.

"Yes, please tell me, Genie," Sinclair mocked, a
light in his eyes she found discomforting.

"Very well. But don't say I didn't warn you."
Eugenie settled herself, gazing out over the green
pastures. "Long ago there was a bereavement
in a wealthy family. As was proper, the coffin
with its sad occupant was returned to the house
and placed in the parlor on the night before the
burial was to take place. The family retired for
the night, but they'd hardly begun to sleep when
they were woken by a terrible wailing from the
parlor. When one of them crept downstairs to investigate they saw a white shapeless form. Terrified, they remained upstairs, huddled together,
awaiting the morning and convinced that their
departed loved one was taking some sort of revenge from beyond the veil. When the dawn
finally came they ventured downstairs, armed
with all manner of weapons to protect themselves against the physical and the spiritual, only
to discover they had been burgled. The so-called
ghost had in fact been a thief, keeping them
upstairs, while his accomplices went about the
business of robbing them."

When the story finished there was a silence,
and Jack—who normally laughed along with
his father—glanced uncertainly from one to the

other. "Don't you think that was a good trick, Somerton?"

"I think the family must have felt very sad, Jack. First they lost their loved one, and then they lost their precious possessions. I wonder how you would feel if it happened to you."

Jack shifted uncomfortably. "I don't have many precious possessions," he said at last. "Only my mouse and the magpie with the broken wing, but he's nearly well now." He glanced over toward the stables and his face brightened. "Can I go and look at the horses?"

Sinclair touched his shoulder. "Of course you can."

Jack set off, soon breaking into a run, and Eugenie wondered whether he was eager to get to the stables or eager to escape the dawning realization that his father wasn't Sir Perfect.

She turned to Sinclair, perhaps to excuse her brother's naivety, or her father's disreputable sense of humor, but before she could speak he put a hand to her cheek, brushing away the rebellious curl.

"You worry about Jack, don't you?"

She knew she should step away and tell him not to touch her, but after what they had done last night it would have seemed disingenuous. "Yes. I think Jack's a good boy but I don't know that I can always nudge him in the right direction."

"If he comes to Somerton I will keep an eye on him," Sinclair said gently. He bent and brushed his lips against her skin, his arm slipping about her slender waist and drawing her against his side.

"You must stop this," Eugenie said, but she closed her eyes, unable to help losing herself in the pleasure.

She'd found it difficult to sleep last night. The memory of being held in the duke's arms, of the temptation that he represented, kept her tossing and turning until almost dawn, her body aching for his touch.

She knew it was her own fault for staying but still she was inclined to blame him for leading her astray. And as she knew only too well, Sinclair did not have marriage to her on his mind.

"You are deep in thought."

His intimate tones brought her back to the present.

Sinclair was watching her with an intensity that made her nervous. "You have a frown," he said, reaching with the tip of his finger to smooth the crease from her brow. "Something is making you unsettled. What is it?"

"Household matters." She dismissed it with a shake of her head.

"Tell me," he demanded.

Eugenie affected a laugh. "Oh Sinclair, I'm sure you don't want to hear about the twins' misdemeanors and our servant woes and the fact that we have no money to pay the butcher." It was meant to sound lighthearted but her annoyance colored the words so that they came out with a sting to them.

"And I don't have to remind you that I can solve all those concerns."

"Oh? With a wave of your magic wand?" she

retorted, but again it wasn't humor she heard in her voice but something almost waspish.

"If you accept my offer then you will be able to leave all your worries behind you."

Eugenie gave him a sharp look and there was a burn of temper in her cheeks. "What a pleasant opinion you must have of me, Your Grace. So you imagine I could ride off with you into some cozy nook, and leave my family to struggle on without me?"

In contrast to hers, his voice remained calm. "If you wish to help your family out of their financial troubles, if their current situation would interfere with your own desires, then I will see to it."

See to it? As if it were something so minor it was barely worth mentioning. Her family and her reputation and her future happiness! Well, if he thought she was going to allow him to solve all her woes with a stroke of his pen, then he was badly mistaken. Did he imagine she had no pride?

"Don't you think that sounds like asking them to sell their daughter for their own benefit? I've heard such things happen in the slums of London, but not in rural Gloucestershire. Besides, surely it is against the law?"

His lip curled in that way she loathed. Eugenie clenched her hands into fists.

"You are being overly emotional. This is a practical solution where all parties benefit."

"You make it all sound so simple," she burst out a little wildly.

"Because it is."

Eugenie looked up into his eyes and wondered how he could be so obtuse. Did he really imagine she could bear to have him "save" her like this, in payment for the use of her body? And yet he saw it all so differently from her, like a businessman coldly signing a mutually acceptable deal. A practical solution. Well, Eugenie refused to go along with it. She wasn't going to be his mistress. There was a man out there, somewhere, who would be her perfect husband and who would be every bit as handsome and appealing as Sinclair—she just had to find him.

"I want you, Eugenie," he said, his breath warm against her ear. "I'm willing to do anything I can to have you."

They had each been so engrossed in their contrary thoughts that they had not heard someone approaching, but now that person's querulous voice brought them to their senses.

"Sinclair? Who is this young lady?"

He muttered a curse beneath his breath but when he turned around he was perfectly composed. "Mother, I did not hear you."

"No, you were otherwise engaged," she retorted. Her dark eyes didn't leave Eugenie. "Please introduce me."

Eugenie looked back at the Dowager Duchess of Somerton and found herself surprised by what she saw. This wasn't a woman like her own mother, overwhelmed by life. The Dowager Duchess was dressed in a gray silk skirt and close-fitting jacket, decorated with fine lace, accentuating her still fine figure. Her graying hair was swept up in a flattering style, covered with a small confection of silk and ribbons.

There was a distinct resemblance to her son, perhaps more in her expression than her actual features—an air of haughtiness that characterized them both.

Sinclair had finished introducing them.

"Belmont?" the dowager duchess declared, as Eugenie made her careful curtsey. "Never heard the name. Do they live locally?"

"Sir Peter, my father, and Mrs. Belmont, my mother, live in Belmont Hall, in the village, Your Grace," Eugenie said evenly, determined to be polite even if Sinclair's mother wasn't. "Actually, it is my brother who His Grace invited to Somerton. I am here as his companion. He is ten, you see, and very good with His Grace's horses."

The dowager duchess was staring at her as if she was speaking a foreign language. "Indeed," she replied at last, cold as frost, and turned back to her son. "When you are done with Miss Belmont, Sinclair, I wish to speak to you in my rooms."

And with that she turned and was gone.

"My mother believes she lives in another age," Sinclair said apologetically.

"I really should be going home now anyway," Eugenie said, and began to walk a little shakily toward the stables to fetch Jack. She was angry, and upset, and she didn't want him to see either.

"There is no need . . ." he began.

"I think there is. Good-bye, Your Grace." The slight emphasis on the 'good-bye' was her way of letting him know this really was a last farewell. After last night's tender embraces she might have been able to convince herself that there was a slight chance of winning Sinclair, but not now. His mother's behavior had made up Eugenie's mind well and truly.

He didn't follow her. Eugenie expected he was keen to get back to his mother and be told he must not associate with the peasants. Insufferable woman! To speak to her so! Was she so above the rest of the world that she did not need to show good manners? It certainly explained a great deal about Sinclair.

Eugenie could not imagine how she ever thought it would be possible to marry him. She was someone to look down upon. How she could have believed for a moment she would fit into the life he lived and the world he occupied? Well, she knew the cold, hard truth now.

She refused to glance backward, even though this was the last time she would see him. How could she have let her silly tongue and her overactive imagination to get her into this scrape in the first place? Husband hunting, in her opinion, was a very overrated occupation! And as for the reaction of her friends. . .

She'd have to make up some tale. If worse came to worst, Eugenie told herself, she could always run away with a circus and become a bareback horse rider. It seemed preferable to telling them the truth.

Chapter 14

As Sinclair expected, his mother was waiting for him, back perfectly straight, hands clasped in her lap, chin high. Her dark eyes followed him to his chair opposite her and something perverse made him fling himself down into the soft leather, rather than seating himself fastidiously, as he usually did.

She winced. "Sinclair," she said, as if she was in pain. "Whatever is wrong with you? No, don't answer me. I believe I already know, and that is what I wish to speak to you about."

"Can you read my mind, Mother?" he said in mock surprise.

Her dark eyes bored into his and eventually she shamed him into the reaction she wished.

"My apologies, Mother. That was childish. Tell me what you wish to speak to me about."

"I will, but first I think I should mention the time you have been spending playing with your paints. I know my brother encouraged you but I thought we had dealt with that problem years ago. It is childish and pointless, Sinclair, and you must stop it. All those shameless hussies. If you had wanted to paint landscapes perhaps I could have accepted it, but naked females! Such things are not for gentlemen and particularly not for dukes. I simply will not allow you."

He was speechless, and then he was angry. "How do you know . . . ?"

"I always commanded loyalty from my servants, and they still tell me what is happening at Somerton."

She sounded smug, and that infuriated him even more. "How dare you set your spies on me!"

"Oh Sinclair, do calm down. I am your mother and it is my job to keep an eye on you. You were always inclined to stray from the path, although I admit that until recently you have been behaving exactly as your father and I would have wished. When I heard you had returned to your old ways I could not understand what it was that had caused it. Until now."

Sinclair didn't know what to say. There were so many words in his head it was as if a storm were roaring inside his brain. But he knew well enough that shouting and stamping would not work with his mother. She did not understand feelings with any heat in them and did not approve of such displays.

"Yes, I am the Duke of Somerton," he said with dangerous quiet, "and I am a grown man of twenty-seven. I do not take instruction from anyone. Not even you, Mother. You should know better than to try to organize my life."

"There is no need to be rude," she retorted. "I

have your best interests at heart, and that will not
change no matter how old you are. Need I remind
you that the Dukes of Somerton have a long and
proud tradition, and I do not want to see it tainted
by foolish behavior? You have always had an odd
kick in your stride, Sinclair. I feared for you when
you were young. You reminded me very much of
my father."

Her face grew pinched. His mother did not
speak of her father and suddenly he wondered
whether there was something unpleasant in her
past, something that made her the person she'd
become.

"Was your father an artist?"

Her eyes fixed on him. "A Bohemian, you
mean," she said icily. "He ruined my mother's life,
and mine. If he had not squandered our money
on—on . . . if he had not squandered our money I
would not have had to marry your father."

This was news indeed. "You did not want to
marry my father?" he ventured, knowing that at
any moment she would close up whatever doorway had opened to her past.

"He was my senior by forty years," she
whispered.

So old! Sinclair had known his father was an
old man when he was born but he hadn't considered it in relation to his mother, hadn't thought
how such a marriage must have affected her,
and whether or not she'd been agreeable to it.
She always seemed so very much the Duchess of
Somerton, as if she'd been born to the role.

"Speaking of marriage," she said, and he realized she had regained her poise. The angry, bitter woman he'd seen hiding behind her eyes was gone. "Perhaps it is time we spoke about a suitable wife for you, Sinclair. Of course she would need to have the correct background, suitable family ties, and a reasonable dowry. I have been giving it some thought and I believe I know just the young lady—"

"Mother, I am perfectly capable of finding my own wife when the time comes."

"And when exactly will 'the time come'?" she mocked.

"When I am ready." Were his teeth really gritted? He felt as if they were. His jaw was so tightly clenched it was aching.

"And this lack of enthusiasm for marriage has nothing to do with the young person I saw with you earlier?" His mother's voice had dropped several more degrees.

"Miss Belmont?" He forced out a disbelieving laugh. "Miss Belmont is hardly wife material. She is an acquaintance, that is all. I enjoy her company."

But he could see she was not fooled. Her eyes, fixed on him knowingly, made him want to squirm as he had when he was a little boy and had been caught in some misdemeanor. And that made him angrier still.

"I shouldn't have to remind you of this, Sinclair, but it seems I must. If you were to make a misalliance then I would refuse to see you or speak to you again. I would not be able to hold my head up if our great name was brought low by your actions. Your sister would suffer, too, by association, and would necessarily have to cut all ties with you. Your friends would snigger as you passed by and your wife would never be invited to their homes. You would be a pariah. So think very hard, Sinclair, before you do anything foolish."

He had a terrible urge to tell her he was marrying Eugenie, just to spite her. Just to see her expression. How dare she speak to him in this way? How dare she try to manage him at this stage of his life?

But Sinclair had been brought up too strictly to find rebellion a simple matter, and even as the urge rose up in him to throw aside the traces that had kept him in line all his life, he found he could not do it. Obedience had been fed to him with his childhood bread and butter, and was now part of his flesh and bones.

"There is no need for you to say anything," Sinclair said, wondering why he felt so dispirited. After all, he agreed with her assumptions in regard to Eugenia and her suitability as a wife. He had even listed them himself, when he explained why she could only ever be his mistress. These were facts, the harsh facts, of the society he lived in and were not to be disputed.

"Is there not?" The dowager duchess was watching him closely.

"I am fully aware of what is expected of me and I will marry accordingly. Now, I beg of you, can we leave the subject?"

But of course she could not. "So you will not see this Belmont woman again, Sinclair?"

It would have been a simple matter to tell her what she wanted to hear, but instead some devil made him say, "Of course I will see her again, Mother."

"Sinclair!"

"I have said I will not marry her. Isn't that enough for you?" He rose to his feet, telling himself he was in perfect control of his temper. "Now, please excuse me. I have letters to write."

He could see she was bursting to speak, but he didn't wait to hear her arguments. He closed the door on her, and took a relieved breath. The days when his mother could browbeat him into doing as she wished were over. If he wanted to paint, then he would. He would hang his pictures all over the house. But Sinclair was not naïve. He knew there were some rules he must not break.

He could not marry Eugenie.

But even his mother would have to admit a duke was allowed a mistress. Indeed, it was almost de rigueur.

So, Eugenie would be his mistress.

He smiled. Like his painting, Eugenie had brought color to his life and he was damned if he would let her go.

"What on earth have you done to Mother?"

Annabelle gave him a curious look as she stood in the open study door. Sinclair glanced up and then continued writing his letter.

"What makes you think I have done anything?"

"She is like an icicle. I am afraid to touch her in case I freeze my fingers. She only looks like that when someone has denied her something she set her heart on. And I know she was closeted with you earlier today."

"It was a private matter, Annabelle."

But if Annabelle heard the warning in his voice she ignored it.

"Did she see you with Miss Belmont? She would insist on going down to the stables to see who you were meeting. I don't know how she knows these things; I believe the servants spy for her." Annabelle shuddered. "When I have my own home I will insist on having complete loyalty. If anyone so much as tells Mother what I ate for breakfast they will be dismissed."

Sinclair smiled grimly. "I wish you luck."

"You like Miss Belmont, don't you, Sinclair?"

He gave her a sharp look but she seemed to be merely stating a fact, not making sly accusations. "Yes, I find her good company."

Annabelle walked to the window at his back and stared out. He heard her sigh.

Sinclair set down his pen and turned his chair to her. Her face was pale, her mouth down turned, and there were dark shadows under her eyes. "What is it?" he said gently.

But she wouldn't meet his eyes, continuing to stare out into the garden.

"Annabelle? You know you can speak to me. I may not always agree with you, but I will always listen."

She shrugged her shoulder, something her mother abhorred. "I was thinking about how unfair life is. With so many interesting things to do and people to meet you would think we wouldn't have a moment to feel lonely or bored or sad, but the trouble is we never get to do or meet most of them. We live in a—a made-up world."

"What do you mean?" ·

"Well, there are rules and regulations. We must not do that or this, or see that person or speak to this one. Sometimes I feel as if I cannot breathe, Sinclair. Do you ever feel that?"

"Yes," he said.

She looked at him in surprise.

"Why don't you fight them then? Break the rules? I don't understand how you can bear it."

"Being the Duke of Somerton is a great privilege," he reminded her, "but it comes with those rules you speak of. I knew that when I became duke."

"I wish I didn't have to marry Lucius," she said in a small voice.

"I thought you liked him when you first met?" Sinclair reminded her. "You said he was handsome and kind."

Annabelle moved restlessly. "I did. He is. It is the life I will lead that depresses me. I am not like Mother or you. I do not find it easy to obey rules."

If only she knew, he thought wryly.

She smoothed down her skirts, and he knew the discussion was over.

"I think you'd better spend some time making up to Mother before she leaves Somerton. Please."

"Very well."

She smiled, hesitated a moment, and then left the room, closing the door softly behind her.

Annabelle had something more on her mind than she'd disclosed to him, but he hoped she'd resigned herself to marriage with Lucius and the grand affair her wedding promised to be.

Now he turned back to his desk and tugged a second note out from under the letter, the one he had hidden as soon as Annabelle opened his door. It was brief and to the point and addressed to Eugenie. With a smile twitching his lips he folded it and slipped it into an envelope. He thought about ringing for one of the servants but changed his mind. He could not trust any of those in the house. He knew Barker would ride to Belmont Hall for him in the morning and never tell. He would walk down to the stables and find the man, then he could seek out his mother.

It would be easier to keep his temper with her knowing he had a pleasant interlude to look forward to. One she had no chance of putting a stop to.

Chapter 15

Jack brought the note to her, slipping it into her hand under the breakfast table. His eyes were bright and he put his finger to his lips when she would have asked what it was. So a reluctant Eugenie hid it away until she was able to read it in private.

But there seemed to be more problems to deal with than usual in the Belmont household. The twins were up to their usual mischief, causing her mother to retreat to her parlor with palpitations and leaving Eugenie to smooth matters over. Terry had gone to market with Mr. Belmont, and returned with a filly his father said had cost his son far too much blunt.

"You'll see," Terry retorted. "I'll double it and more."

It seemed unlike her brother to exert himself in such a way but Eugenie was pleased that at least he was doing something other than playing cards and drinking at the Five Bells. He and Jack were out with the new filly as soon as they'd finished luncheon, discussing how they were going to train it into a prize-winning champion.

With a sigh of relief, Eugenie retired to her room and closed the door. A moment later she'd broken the seal on the note and was seated on the bed, reading it with a growing sense of anger.

Eugenie, I have a new dare for you.
Let me see how fearless you are.
Come to the old Jobling house tonight and I will
be waiting.

Sinclair

The tap on her door startled her, and she quickly slipped the note under her skirts and sat on it. But it was only Jack.

"Barker brought it," he explained, when she asked how he'd come by the note. "He told me not to tell anyone but you. He'll come by later for a reply. Is it a secret, Genie? Is it from Somerton?"

"Yes," she said, cautiously, "but Barker is right. You mustn't tell anyone, Jack."

Jack nodded. "I wish I had a secret, like you and Terry," he said, a little wistfully.

Eugenie was about to ask him what Terry's secret was, but his next words drove all other thoughts from her mind.

"Are you and Somerton lovebirds?"

"Goodness no!" she burst out. "How could we be? He is a duke, Jack."

He looked so disappointed she relented.

"I suppose you could call us friends."

"Oh."

"But even friends have to be careful. Father wouldn't approve, and neither would Somerton's mother, so it's best if we keep it to ourselves, Jack."

"You don't have to remind me to stay quiet," he said, with a roll of his eyes. "Terry's already been on and on at me. Are you going out tonight, too?"

Too? What was Terry up to now?

"Better tell everyone you have a headache then or they'll be knocking on your door. In fact, if I was you, I'd tell them you were sick and bring up a bowl with you, and then you can be sure the twins won't be bothering you. They're terrified of vomit."

Eugenie giggled at his practical advice, despite her present state of emotional upheaval. "Thank you, Jack."

When he'd gone, she lay back on the bed and stared at her ceiling. She wasn't going to meet Sinclair. He could wait all night if he liked but it was over and done. She'd already told him so, and if, in his arrogance, he chose not to believe her then that was his problem.

As if to emphasize the fact, she rose determinedly from her bed and went to her dressing table drawer, where she kept paper and ink. Full of righteous zeal, she began to compose a letter to her friends from Miss Debenham's Finishing School. Soon she was so caught up in her comical tale of woe she barely noticed the time slipping by.

Alas, my friends, I will never be the Duchess of Somerton.

At first she decided to stick to the truth—more

or less—in saying that the dowager duchess would never approve. But soon she was embroidering the story to make them laugh. She giggled as she finished the letter and signed her name, setting it aside to be posted.

Her next chore was not quite so enjoyable.

Eugenie wrote a brief reply to the duke's note, telling him she would not be meeting him and it was over. Completely and utterly over.

I request you not to approach me again. We are unsuited in every way and you must see that yourself.

She signed her name and, suddenly remembering Erik, wrote a postscript that if there was ever any trouble with the goat she would prefer it if Barker contacted Jack.

It was done. Quickly, Eugenie addressed the letters and slipped them into their envelopes. The letter to her friends could go by post, but the one to the duke would return via Jack and the groom, Barker.

"Do you think it will work?" Annabelle asked anxiously, eyes big and dark in the twilight.

She had slipped out into the garden but said she couldn't stay long. Her mother would be looking for her and she seemed to have a sixth sense for mischief. Lizzie had promised to guard her bedchamber door like a little lioness, swearing Annabelle had a migraine if anyone asked, but Annabelle was dismissive of Lizzie's tale-telling abilities.

"It has to work. Then we will have enough money to get to Scotland."

For a duke's sister, Terry had discovered, Annabelle was always short of blunt. Everything was bought for her or sent from London. When she was married—so she told him—she would receive an allowance, but for now she had nothing.

"You just have to make him believe you are set on the filly and nothing else will do."

Annabelle nodded, although he could see she didn't like the idea of using her brother in this way. She probably saw it as underhand and dishonest. But what choice had they? To Terry's relief she seemed to realize that herself and asked no more questions.

"I long to be safe in Scotland," she murmured, with a glance over her shoulder. "I will live the life of an ordinary girl. I will call myself Miss St. John and—"

"Perhaps you should think of another name. Something less distinctive."

"Miss Penniless?" she teased.

"Miss Mysterious?"

She laughed, glancing over her shoulder again. "I'd better go back to the house. It would be awful if we were discovered now, just when our plans are going so well. Good-bye, Terry." She pressed his hand and was gone, her pale skirts drifting through the dark garden. Terry watched her go, until there was nothing left but the call of the night birds and the hum of the insects.

"Well, it is all arranged," Annabelle said, a tremor of excitement in her voice, as she flung herself onto her bed.

Lizzie watched her uneasily. "What is all arranged?"

"My future," Annabelle said mysteriously, and then laughed.

"Annabelle, you know that Terry Belmont is not suitable as a husband for you. Your brother would never allow it."

Annabelle gave her a knowing smile. "I'm not marrying him, Lizzie. No need to worry."

Lizzie closed her lips tightly. She was worried sick about her charge and yet she felt compelled to keep her secrets. If she went to the duke or the dowager duchess, Annabelle would deny everything and then insist she was sent home to the vicarage. Apart from the ignominy of it, Lizzie knew if she wasn't here then there would be no one to stop Annabelle's headstrong rush to destruction.

"You like him, don't you?"

Annabelle was watching her, a little gleam in her dark eyes, a curve to her lips. Lizzie pretended not to understand.

"Terry Belmont," Annabelle explained. "You like him, Lizzie, and don't pretend you don't."

"I don't like or dislike him. He is nothing to me."

"You're fibbing, Lizzie. I didn't think vicar's daughters were allowed to tell lies."

"Annabelle—"

"Do you want me to ask him if he wants to marry you?"

Lizzie felt light-headed at such a humiliating idea. "Don't you dare do such a thing! You are being cruel, Annabelle."

The other girl looked taken aback, as if something she had believed perfectly tame had suddenly bitten her. "Very well. It was just a thought. My apologies, Lizzie."

Lizzie took a deep breath, and then another, calming herself, reminding herself of her position.

"Besides, he would probably refuse," Annabelle went on. "He wants to join the army but his family can't afford a suitable regiment. You wouldn't want an army husband, would you, Lizzie? Always traveling about from town to town, living in foreign countries, sleeping in a tent!"

Lizzie said nothing, but her thoughts had taken flight. She imagined traveling through lands she had never seen before, living in close quarters with her husband, sleeping beside him in the cozy warmth of a canvas cave, darning his shirts while he sat beside her, feeling a warm sun on her face that was far from England.

She had never expected such a future. Life, for Lizzie, was plain and unadorned. But now she knew that if she had the chance to be an army wife, to be Terry Belmont's wife, then she would take it.

Chapter 16

Eugenie was helping Cook carry in the pudding—rice custard and cream—when Jack gave her a wink. Presumably that meant all was well and Barker had taken the reply for the duke. She refused to dwell upon what that meant. Yes, there had been pleasant moments between her and the duke—dangerously illicit moments!—but the risk was far too great.

She sat down and had taken up her spoon when a nasty thought occurred to her. She only hesitated a moment before she began to eat, because of course the idea that she could do something so stupid was impossible. She had been rushing and in a bit of a state, but . . . No, impossible! But a moment later the same thought occurred to her again, and this time she put down her spoon.

Knowing she wouldn't be able to relax until she'd made certain, Eugenie excused herself from the table and went into the hall. All letters to be posted were placed in a basket there, and she took out the letter she'd written earlier to her friends. The envelope was addressed correctly—to Marissa, who would pass it on to the others—and yet it felt thin. Surely her letter had been bulkier than that? It was Sinclair's letter that had been thin.

Fingers shaking now, heart thudding, Eugenie tore open the missive and stared at the paper inside.

Dear Sinclair. . .

Oh dear Lord! It could not be; and yet it was!

Her tale of woe had gone to the very man she'd written about. He would read it and know all she had said and planned. Her face was already scarlet at the very thought that he would see her as such a scheming hussy. She could not bear him to think so badly of her, she really couldn't, especially when she had been in such a high moral position when she broke off with him.

And it wasn't even as if she had ever intended to marry him. It had all been a terrible mistake.

With a whimper, she ran up the stairs to her room, clutching the crumpled paper in her hand. There was only one thing to be done. She must meet him at the old Jobling manor house. She must . . . she must . . . somehow she must get the letter back before he opened it. And if he had opened it then she would apologize and explain.

Because Eugenie knew in her heart she could not let things between them end in such a horrid fashion. She must at least try to smooth it over or she would never be able to think of him again without cringing in shame.

It was already dark when Eugenie set off determinedly on her mare, although the stars were bright enough to light her way. This journey was not one she wanted to make. She didn't know what she would say when she got there. No doubt something would occur to her—it always did. She could only hope she was in time to retrieve the letter and avert Sinclair's anger and her embarrassment. Remembering what she had written to amuse her friends made her quiver and groan aloud, as well as curse her wayward Belmont tongue.

When would she learn?

The old Jobling manor house was really a large farmhouse, once owned by a local squire, before his family died from illness and he sank into a depression. The house was set in a field and hidden by overgrown shrubs and rampant brambles, although the dark line of the roof and a crumbling pair of chimneys were visible against the night sky. No wonder it was known in the village as the haunted house. At night, lights were said to shine from the windows and ghostly figures were said to dance to long forgotten tunes. Eugenie told herself she didn't believe in ghosts; she found the house rather sad, abandoned, and tumbling down as it was.

Perhaps Sinclair had been expecting her to cling to him in terror? Well, in that case he'd be disappointed. Eugenie might be a hoyden but she was courageous when it came to the supernatural. It was the thought of that letter in Sinclair's hands that was frightening her.

When she reached the haunted house, her mare's wicker of recognition led her to Sinclair's horse, already tethered in the bushes and hidden from passing prying eyes. Eugenie dismounted and, with wobbling legs and a courageous determination she was far from feeling, set off toward the front door.

The bleak weather didn't help to make the place look any more inviting. Dark shadows filled the windows and the damp patches on the brickwork looked like misshapen faces.

"You took your time."

She jumped at the sound of his voice.

He was standing just inside the open door, looking impossibly elegant and completely out of place.

"I wasn't going to come," she said breathlessly. "I wouldn't have, only . . ." She stared up at him, trying to read his expression and failing. "I sent you a letter." The words were like stones down a well.

"A letter?"

"Yes. Jack gave it to Barker. Is it here?"

He eyed her curiously for a moment. "Barker put it down inside somewhere. I haven't had a chance to read it. Why, was it important?" His eyebrows rose. "What did it say?"

"Nothing," she said, relief washing through her so that she could hardly stand. "No, it wasn't important."

Surprisingly, he seemed to believe her.

He held out his hand to her. "Come in."

Now that she knew the letter was inside she had no choice. Eugenie put her fingers in his and stepped over the threshold, lifting her skirts so that they didn't trail in the dust.

"Why choose this place?" she asked.

"Your brother Jack happened to mention it to me."

"Jack is a mine of information, isn't he?" she said wryly.

"It seems this house has quite a reputation in the area. No one comes here; they believe it to be haunted. Ideal for my dare, wouldn't you say?"

"Because we don't want to be seen together?"

He gave her a predatory look over his shoulder. "No, Eugenia. Because we don't want to be disturbed."

She gave him a sharp look. "I don't think that's likely."

He smiled as if he had a secret and strode off down the gloomy corridor. Eugenie, wanting to turn and run the other way, again had no choice but to follow after him. There were probably spiders and creepy-crawlies lurking in the corners, she thought miserably, but it was thankfully too dark to see them. The air smelled musty, and it was cold. She folded her arms about herself, hoping he wasn't expecting her to linger too long.

She would find the letter, hide it in her clothing, and then she would leave. Although, now she'd destroyed the other letter, explaining to Sinclair their association was "utterly and completely over," she would need to tell him face-to-face. Well, she told herself briskly, she would do that and then she would most definitely leave.

Ahead of her, Sinclair paused and with a flourish flung open a door at the end of the passage. Light spilled out, and he gestured for her to enter.

Eugenie, not sure what to expect, glanced up into his face as she went by, and found it full of suppressed excitement. A smile was twitching at the corners of his lips and his eyes were glittering, as if he had some overwhelming secret and he was bursting to tell her.

And then she looked into the room and understood all.

Candles were everywhere, standing on the floor and windowsills and tables, their golden light illuminating the scene. The walls had been draped with silken cloth, and a divan took pride of place, weighed down with cushions and fabrics that looked as if they wouldn't be uncomfortable in a courtesan's boudoir. Underfoot were the softest, most luxurious carpets she had ever seen, swirling with exotic patterns. A table had been laid, with champagne in an ice bucket, and food arrayed like bright jewels on silver platters.

He gave a deep chuckle at her gasp.

"How . . . ?" she stammered in amazement.

"I have a faithful servant or two left, and I swore them to silence. They did rather well for outdoor servants," he added, looking pleased.

"I think you would need an army of servants for this," she said bluntly.

"Do you like it? I thought we could be private here while we discuss our future."

"I don't think a well-bred young lady would discuss anything in this room," she said nervously. "It screams seduction."

"I would like to make you scream, Eugenie,"

he said, his voice dropping low. "Scream with pleasure."

She understood him all too well. Looking about her again, she thought: *He has done all of this for me. He is trying his best to win me. I should be flattered.*

She was flattered, and touched, but she was frightened, too. This was not a place she should be—she did not trust herself to behave. Sinclair had a very bad influence on her.

"Where's my letter?" she burst out, and then wished she hadn't.

His expression grew suspicious. "Why are you so interested in this letter?"

"I wrote something in it that I . . ." She gazed up at him pleadingly. "Sinclair, I wish you would give me my letter back. If you were a gentleman, you would."

He considered her request. "I will give you your letter back if you stay here with me for a little while," he said evenly.

Eugenie gave a nervous glance at her surroundings. But as she dithered he made the decision for her, taking her hand gently but firmly in his, and leading her toward the divan.

"Please be seated, Eugenie."

With an uncertain little smile she sat down and promptly sank deep into the cushions. "Goodness," she said breathlessly, "there is only one way to tackle this piece of furniture and that is to lounge upon it."

"You lounge very nicely," he teased, and began to gather together a selection of foods onto a

fine china plate. He set the plate before her, then
poured her a glass of champagne, which bubbled
and sparkled as he placed it into her hand.

"To us," he said, holding up his own glass and
smiling over the rim, his eyes full of reflected
candlelight.

She drank, mesmerized, and then he sank
down beside her on the divan and began to feed
her from the plate. There were exotic fruits, bright
as jewels, and creamy cheeses and spicy meats. It
seemed to her, or perhaps she was imagining it,
that everything was sharper and more flavorsome
than it could possibly have been, while the feel of
the silken fabrics against her skin resembled the
gentle wash of the warm ocean.

"It's not every day I am fed by a duke," she said,
trying for levity, as he popped some pomegranate
seeds between her lips.

"It is entirely the duke's pleasure," he replied,
then bent closer to capture one of the seeds which
had landed on her chin. As she watched him, he
slipped it into his own mouth.

Something in her stomach dived. She was giddy.
Was it the champagne, or desire, or both? Whatever
it was it was too late to run away, because suddenly
his mouth was on hers and she was in his arms
and they were both sinking like drowning sailors
into the seductive depths of the divan.

Sinclair's senses were swimming in the warm,
sweet scent of her skin. The silky cloth of her
dress slid under his palm and he felt the firm
mounds of her breasts beneath. His body ached.

For a heartbeat he wondered if he was going to be able to control the urge to ravish her and make her his in the quickest time possible, but his training as a gentleman stood him in good stead.

Lightly, tenderly, he turned her over and pressed kisses to the pale skin of her back as he unbuttoned her bodice. Her hair was held up with pins and combs, and he slid them out, enjoying the rich color as it tumbled into his hands. He buried his face in her curls, breathing in their clean scent, and then pressing his mouth to the sensitive place on the nape of her neck.

She shivered and made a little sound of pleasure. Or perhaps she was asking about that damned letter.

He kissed her again, and slid her loosened sleeves down her arms, caressing her bare shoulders. She turned in his arms, her mouth finding his, wrapping herself close. He kissed her until she lay languid, her lashes veiling the shine of her eyes, her skin flushed with desire. The lacy edge of her chemise had caught on her bodice, and when he released it, he realized she wasn't wearing a corset. Her small, perfect breasts rose above the silk cloth and lace, her nipples pink and engorged, and he bent and took one in his mouth.

She moaned, arching toward him.

He rolled her nipple with his tongue, before bending to work on the other one. Her fingers shook as they crept through his hair, clinging, drawing him closer. She was slender and yet perfect, her skin like ivory and rose, and he wanted to sample every inch of it before he let her go.

Until now he hadn't been sure why he'd gone to so much trouble tonight. He'd simply wanted to see her. But of course it was all about seduction; making her his. Bringing her to the realization that there was only one outcome possible between them.

Giving her no choice but to be his mistress.

His touch, his caress, was sending little aches and thrills into all parts of her body. She wanted to squeeze her thighs together, as if to hold on to the pleasure building there, in her secret places. She felt abandoned, free, no longer bound by anyone's rules or regimen, and the wonder of it went to her head.

He'd taken off his jacket and she ran her hands up his arms, feeling the soft silk of his shirt and the firm muscles beneath. There was a knotted necktie to pick apart and open, and then buttons to undo so that she could finally place her palms against his bare skin. Dark hair grew on his chest, and she pressed her cheek to it, and then her nose, breathing him in, enjoying the roughness of his masculine body.

"So this is how a duke smells," she murmured, and heard his chuckle deep in his chest.

Her dress was about her waist, and as she leaned against him she felt him tug it down over her hips, and then the heat of his hands cupping her bottom through the thin cloth of her undergarments. He drew her closer and she could hear her breath loud and irregular against his skin, her heart rising to pound in her throat. His fingers slid down, finding the opening of her bloomers, and the warm, slick skin between her thighs.

Eugenie went very still. She felt as if she dare not move, that all her energy was devoted to feeling his gentle exploring touch. She felt swollen, and hot, as if her body was readying itself for something momentous. He continued to stroke her with his fingers while his lips were against her hair, whispering words into her ear that she hardly heard and yet seemed to increase her pleasure unbearably.

"Please." She was saying the word over and over again, her voice ragged, her pulse jumping.

Sinclair knew what he should do. He should give her the release she was asking him for. A few more strokes of his fingers, a little pressure on her eager little nub, and she would be there. She'd be grateful, too. But of course then she'd pull herself together and make her excuses and leave him sitting here, alone.

And that wasn't what he wanted. Selfish he may be, but he wanted to thrust his body into hers, claim her in the most primitive way. So he made a conscious decision. They would enjoy this moment together, even though he knew that once it was over there'd be no going back.

He lay her down on the divan, and rested on top of her, taking his weight with elbows and knees, kissing her mouth, his fingers stroking her breasts. "You are beautiful," he told her, "so beautiful."

She opened her clear green eyes and gazed up at him with passion and trust. Complete trust.

He almost changed his mind.

Almost.

But then his fingers were on the top of her stockings, then the warm skin of her bare thighs. She was ready for him; the damp heat of her made him groan. It was an easy matter to unbutton his trousers and free himself, and then press the head of his cock against her slick entrance. She wound her arms about his waist, rubbing against him, as if she couldn't wait for him to be inside her.

"Eugenie," he said, his voice hoarse with longing, "are you sure . . . ?"

He didn't know if she heard him. She seemed to be listening to something else, something inside, and he pressed the advantage, entering her a little before withdrawing, some distant part of his brain reminding him that she was more than likely a virgin.

She gasped.

In pain or pleasure? He didn't want to take the chance it was the former, and reached down to stroke her with his fingers, this time not stopping as he felt her body gathering itself for release, and when she arched upward with a soft, surprised cry of pleasure, he finally drove his body deep into hers.

Resistance was slight and then she was his.

She felt like velvet, squeezing him, tremors of ecstasy shaking her and him, until they both clung together in breathless abandon. He'd felt sexual pleasure before, but not like this. This was something beyond his experience and he was shaken by it. Changed by it.

But one thing he knew for certain—he'd been right to seduce her.

Eventually their breathing calmed, and he cuddled her in his arms, turning his face to kiss her cheek and nuzzle her skin. "Eugenie." Her name sounded different on his lips, and he heard the possessive note in his voice. She was his, and he wanted to lift his head and shout it.

"It isn't fair." Her voice was quiet with a tremble in it. "You know it isn't fair."

He gave a surprised chuckle. "I didn't want to play fair," he admitted. "I wanted you to give in and agree to everything. Be my mistress, Eugenie!"

Something warm and wet trickled down her cheek from the corner of her eye, and he was shocked to see it was a tear. Another one followed, and then she turned her head away quickly, as if she didn't want him to see. Suddenly he felt uncomfortable, remembering that moment when he might have stopped himself, when he could have kept control. And the guilt made him irritable.

"What is it?" he said. "Eugenie?"

She shook her head but he reached for her chin, his fingers rough in his need to see her expression, to read what she was feeling. If it was hatred, if it was regret . . . he didn't know what he'd do. She sighed and lifted her damp lashes to meet his gaze.

"Eugenie," he said again.

Because he saw no regret, no loathing for what they had done.

Only tenderness.

* * *

She didn't speak, but put her arms about his neck and pressed her lips to his, her heart aching, knowing she was jumping from the fire into the furnace and not caring. What did it matter now? What was done was done and she wasn't about to act like a wronged maiden. This was her fault as much as his.

He only hesitated for a moment and then he was kissing her deeply, and the trembling excitement was rising inside her again, unstoppable in its urgency.

"I need you, Eugenie," he whispered, bending to taste her breasts. "Why won't you believe that?"

"I do," she breathed, kissing his brow, his eyelids, tasting the salt on his skin. Right now, she knew, she would have believed any good thing of her duke.

Boldly, she reached between them, and felt his growing hardness. Her fingers stroked him as he had touched her, gently, curiously. He rested his head against hers, his breath ragged, prisoner to her touch.

A moment later he was sliding between her thighs, sending her into gasps of ecstasy. She closed her eyes against the candlelight, but she could still see the brilliance against her eyelids. This was pleasure as she'd always dreamed of it, all-consuming pleasure.

Eugenie struggled to shut out unwelcome thoughts, not wanting anything to interfere with her moment of physical joy, reminding her that this was not what she'd planned.

Chapter 17

It was very late. Eugenie could feel the perspiration cooling on her body. She was aching in places she hadn't known existed until now, but again she didn't care. She felt a wild, recklessness inside her, a throw-caution-to-the-wind type of mood that had gotten her into trouble more than once. But this was trouble of a new sort.

She sat up halfway and looked down at Sinclair. Her lover. Well, it was true, wasn't it? He was her lover, even if it was just for one night. His hair had tumbled over his face and she brushed it back, smoothing the lines about his mouth, the firm jaw and aristocratic nose, the deep-set eyes with their thick lashes.

He murmured his pleasure at her touch, and she went farther, trailing her fingertips down over his wide throat and broad shoulders. Breathless she lay on top of him, feeling his body molding to hers, more intimate than a man had ever been. She could feel every inch of him, the heat of his skin, the rough texture, the cooling sweat from their vigorous lovemaking. She felt the tingling urge to do it all over again.

"You planned this all along, didn't you?" she said, feeling her recklessness goading her to say things she would be better not saying.

"I'm a ruthless man. How else could I get what I want?"

"Oh Sinclair . . ."

He quirked an eyebrow. "What?"

She shook her head.

He probably expected her to ask for clothes or jewelry or a pretty barouche—all the accoutrements of being his mistress—that was the sort of world he lived in. She trailed a finger across his lips. "I cannot be your mistress. That was what I wrote in the letter . . . the other letter. I did not mean to come here at all. It would have been better if I had not. I want to end our association now and forever, Sinclair."

He froze. She could see the shock in his eyes, before she rolled onto her back beside him on the divan. His reaction was anything but encouraging, but she had spoken now.

"What about your reputation?" he said in his most chilly voice. "Doesn't that mean anything to you?"

"Of course it does. But becoming your mistress is hardly going to mend my reputation, is it? The only way in which you can repair my reputation now, Sinclair, is to marry me."

"Marry you?" he said, and laughed.

The words had just popped out but she instantly wished them back again.

"My dear girl," he drawled, in a hatefully superior tone, "let me explain the facts of life to you. The reason I asked you to be my mistress was because we deal so well together; we enjoy each other's company. If you wish me to be poetical, then you would be my sanctuary from the tedium of my everyday life. My—my bower of joy. That is what a mistress is, Eugenie. A wife—a duchess— is something else altogether."

His voice had gained strength and certainty now, and a core of steel.

"When I marry it will be for reasons other than my own personal gratification, although I would hope to find my wife at least moderately attractive."

"For breeding purposes," she said, and her voice was without emotion, although her feelings were such an angry jumble she felt as if she might choke on them. Her emotions confused her—she knew she could never have married him—and yet the way he was speaking to her upset her.

"Yes, I will need an heir and a spare," he drawled, and his lip curled. "I must marry someone with similar bloodlines to my own—and forgive me, Eugenie, but your family is hardly what I would call a suitable prospect. To be raised to such heights as Somerton would only cause them grief. No, my wife must be someone who has been brought up to put the name of my family and my position in society before any personal preference. She will do as she's told and make no difficulties and help me to run Somerton and my other estates."

"Make no difficulties?" Eugenie repeated, with a faint laugh. "Is there such a woman? I think you will find few of us able to subjugate our feelings to that extent, especially if we are unhappy. What if she meets someone she likes better than you? You say you will have a mistress. Can your wife have a lover?"

"If she is discrete—very discrete—and only after she has given me my heir and a spare."

"And will you be discrete?"

"I will not cause her any embarrassment, but it is different for men."

"Of course it is."

"Then you do understand!" he said, relieved.

She nodded her head, and then sighed. "You've answered my questions completely."

She sat up and swung her legs over the edge of the divan, reaching for her discarded clothing. Her hands weren't trembling, and yet she felt shaky. Was it anger or hurt or a combination of both? Despite all her declarations to the contrary had she wanted to marry him after all?

"You are no fool, Eugenie," his voice went on, reasonably. "You know the rules of the world we live in. I cannot believe you really expected me to agree to marry you. Being my mistress is the best offer I can make, and I do so with all my heart."

She turned to face him, eyes searching his face in the candlelight. If she was any other woman she might give in now and say yes to his offer, but Eugenie knew she would never be content. When she married she wanted to be the most important woman in her man's life, she wanted to share with him the highs and lows of marriage, to have his children and to stand beside him knowing he was entirely hers.

And if she couldn't have that then she'd rather have nothing.

"I should go," she said, and continued to dress, hastily now, wanting nothing more than to get away from this place. She'd been a fool, but she wouldn't blame Sinclair for seducing her. The blame was on her side, too. She could have stopped him.

The simple truth was she hadn't wanted to.

"Eugenie, for God's sake," he began, getting to his feet and coming toward her with his arms open. "Give me some hope."

She let him embrace her but stood unmoving in his arms, and eventually he heaved a sigh and let her go.

"Very well," he said gruffly. "But we will talk again."

She didn't answer him and after a moment she felt tidy enough to leave.

"May I have my letter now?" she said, holding out her hand.

He frowned, but went to a chair where he'd placed his coat and hat, and returned with the letter. Eugenie took it without looking, stuffing it hastily into her sleeve, simply relieved to have it back.

"Thank you," she said. "And for this evening . . . this glorious evening . . ."

The words caught in her throat and she turned away and hurried out into the dank passage-

way and through the front door into the night. It
did not occur to her to check the letter until she
reached home, and by then she was too tired and
shattered and fell upon her bed. So it was morning when she finally held the letter in her hands
and realized she had been tricked.

Sinclair had given her a letter from his tailor
and inside was a bill for a new waistcoat costing
fifty pounds.

Sinclair dressed and proceeded to snuff out
the candles, one by one. The fading of the light
felt somehow symbolic, as if . . . well, as if now
that Eugenie was gone so had the brilliance she
brought to his world.

Had she even for a moment expected him to
marry her? He found such an idea incredible.
Marriage for a duke was a business arrangement,
nothing to do with feelings of the heart, while a
mistress was someone he chose himself.

The last candle fluttered out.

He stood alone in the dark.

She was young, he reminded himself, and perhaps for all her grow-up ways she still had some
girlish dreams. She would come to understand
the impossibility of marriage and agree to what
was possible. And he would sweeten her surren-
der with an endless supply of presents and treats.

He smiled, imagining it. She was the one
woman in the world he both admired and was in-
trigued by. He doubted he'd ever understand her
completely, but that was part of her charm. Thinking of her now he felt his body tighten, wanting

her again with a combination of tenderness and primitiveness that astonished him.

Sinclair reached to put on his coat and remembered the letter Eugenie had been so keen to secure. Barker must have taken it to the house, and no doubt it would be waiting for him there. He hadn't told Eugenie that. She'd seemed so fidgety, as if she might run out into the night, and he'd wanted her to stay. No doubt she knew by now he'd fobbed her off with his tailor's bill.

He smiled to himself as he imagined her expression. She could take her feelings out on him the next time they met. He just hoped it would be soon.

Chapter 18

Eugenie had barely slept a wink all night. Sinclair must have read her letter by now and she didn't believe he would ignore it. She'd made such a fuss he'd be too curious to resist, and when he saw what she had written . . . Eugenie was under no illusions when it came to her duke; she had seen his ruthless streak.

It was still early when she heard a commotion outside and the overworked servant was sent up to her room to fetch her down. "Sir Peter says you have a visitor, miss, and to hurry."

"Who is this visitor?"

"He didn't say exactly, miss, but I think it's someone wanting to buy that mare o' his."

Eugenie would have preferred to stay in her bed, with the covers pulled over her head, but she reluctantly rose and dressed. She felt unlike herself, despite the familiar clothing and the familiar face that stared back at her from her mirror. She was no longer the girl she'd been. Sinclair had changed her; last evening in his arms had made her someone else. Certainly she would never be able to look at the world in the same way.

How he must despise her! Even if she was able to explain to him why she had written such a letter, and why she had entered into such a plan, he would never understand. She could only hope he decided she was now beneath his contempt and would avoid her from this day forward.

Sir Peter met her at the door of his study, face beaming with smiles. "Eugenie, good, good. Look who has come to take a second look at our mare?"

Eugenie had already seen and her feet took root. Her father had to grasp her arm and tug her into the room.

"Good morning, Miss Belmont."

His voice was even, his mouth smiled, but his eyes were full of fury.

Feeling sick, Eugenie looked away. "Your Grace."

"The duke wants you to ride the mare for him, so that he can assess her suitability as a mount for his sister. I said you'd be only too pleased," her father warbled on.

"I don't think—"

Sir Peter leaned close to her, lowering his voice for her alone. "And I don't want any excuses from you, my girl," he warned. "You'll do as you're told."

"I thought Miss Belmont and I could ride out on the lane," Sinclair was saying in a pleasant voice, totally at odds with the expression Eugenie knew was in his eyes. "If I have your permission, Sir Peter?"

"Certainly, certainly."

Dizzy from lack of sleep and too much emotion, Eugenie found herself out at the stables and tossed up onto the mare's back. Behind her Sinclair was listening to her father pushing up the price, and she rode off a little way, hoping that they would fall out and she may not have to be alone with him. But the next moment Sinclair had mounted his own horse and set off through the gate and down the lane, away from the village.

Reluctantly she followed.

The lane was empty, with only a few farm workers busy in the fields either side. Eugenie's stomach felt hollow and she remembered she'd had no breakfast. Last night's meal of exotic fare seemed a long time in the past. Sinclair had fed her with tenderness, his smile warm, his eyes glowing with desire. The man she was riding with this morning might have been a stranger, with his face chiseled from marble and his black eyes blazing.

She'd been dawdling along the verge, hoping to turn back before he could accost her and spill his venom all over her, but now he had stopped his own progress and turned back to her, waiting for her to catch him up.

Coward that she was, Eugenie also stopped, leaving a good distance between them. Too far for conversation, at any rate. She didn't see the puddle, but the mare did. As soon as she caught sight of her reflection, the creature started violently and jumped to one side. Eugenie, taken by surprise, was almost unseated. She screamed and clung on. Her hair, which she had tied back simply in a long braid, now came lose, hampering her efforts to regain control of the terrified animal.

He appeared at her side—the last man in the world she wanted to rescue her.

"What do you mean by such madness?" Sinclair roared. He looked furious, the icy arrogance she was used to completely vanished. Sinclair was out of control, and she had never seen him out of control.

"The puddle," she gasped. "She's afraid of them."

He glared at her, his black eyes narrowed and savage.

"You read the letter then?" she said, her voice husky with dread.

"Oh yes. I read the letter."

She flinched, as though he'd struck her, but Sinclair wasn't fooled by her act. She'd played him all along and he'd been taken in by her, but no longer would he act the besotted fool. Her written words were burned into his mind, into his soul, and he meant to pay her back a hundredfold for humiliating him.

"Perhaps you would allow me to explain . . ." she began, but her voice trailed off when she met his gaze.

"I'd like to hear your explanation," he bit out. "Why would you write to your friends and make me a laughingstock? Tear apart my character and mock my pride and my position? Turn me into a game for your amusement!"

His voice was growing louder. He couldn't

remember ever being so angry in his life. She'd
done all the things he'd accused her of, but there
was something he wouldn't say aloud. She had
hurt him. Struck him to the heart. He'd trusted
her as he'd trusted few women and she had betrayed him.

"I'm sorry if I made you a laughingstock," she
said, tears filling her green eyes. "I didn't mean
to. It's all been an awful mistake. My wretched
tongue ran away with itself and I was trapped and
when I'm trapped I tend to make things worse . . .
well, I'm not making excuses. I accept it was all
my fault. I should have told them straightaway
that I didn't even know you, let alone expect to
marry you. Your name just sprang into my head! I
could just as easily have chosen an earl or a lord or
someone else. It didn't mean anything."

"I'm glad my pursuit of you didn't mean anything," he said between his teeth. "I'm glad you
were indifferent to me last night when I took your
maidenhead."

She jumped as if scalded by his anger, and it
took all her courage to meet the heat in his dark
eyes. "I wasn't indifferent," she said. "You know I
wasn't."

He stared her down. "I thought I wanted to
know why you acted as you did. I even thought I
might receive an apology."

She tried to interrupt but he held up his hand.

"Now I find I don't care after all. You are beneath my contempt, Eugenie. I am glad I discovered what sort of woman you were before we went
any further. I have had a lucky escape."

A blessed wave of anger washed over her.

"A lucky escape? I had no intention of becoming your mistress. I told you so from the beginning but you did not want to hear. You are so used to getting your own way you thought you could force me to your will. But I do not want to be kept like a nasty little secret. I want to share the life of the man I choose, Sinclair. I want to walk at his side and sit at his breakfast table. In short, I want to marry him."

His lip curled in that way she loathed. "I pity the man you finally trap."

Eugenie swallowed back more hasty words. This was not the time nor the place, and perhaps there never would be a right moment. But she could apologize, and then at least she may be able to put it behind her.

"The letter was very wrong and I'm sorry for it. Most of it I made up."

"*Most* of it?" he growled. "It was a pack of lies from start to finish."

Her wretched bluntness made her say, "Apart from your mother being so rude to me, that was true. And the way you sneer at those you consider beneath you—unless they can be of use to you, like Jack. And the way you curl your lip when you feel superior. Yes, just like that!" she burst out, as he obliged her.

For a moment he said nothing, his face white, his jaw bunching.

"So it is all right for you to insult me, but I am not allowed to insult you?" he said in a deadly tone. "Miss Eugenie Belmont can splatter her poison about without a thought for the damage she may do. And it is all my fault for curling my lip?"

"That isn't what I meant at all!" she cried.

"Good-bye, Miss Belmont. Tell your father I have decided against his mare. She is far too tricky for my liking."

She might have said more but her voice failed her. With a sob, she turned and kicked the mare into a gallop, her curls flying behind her, her skirts tucked up about her bare legs.

Anger was Sinclair's companion on the way home to Somerton. He had business to attend to, important affairs he'd left to come here and see Eugenie. Luckily his mother had already set out to her friends in the west, but Annabelle wanted him to look at some filly she had her eye on, and he'd promised.

He needed to get himself under control before then.

Although his anger was justifiable, he told himself, it was aimed at himself just as much as Eugenie. Somehow he'd allowed himself to be drawn into her net, to the extent of believing she would be his. He'd even made plans as to where he would install her in London, he realized, with a savage bark of laughter.

How deluded he had been!

He lifted his head and looked up at the sky. Eugenie Belmont was nothing more than a devious, conniving slut who wanted to be a duchess and believed she could inveigle him into setting aside his principles for another taste of her body. Well, he would never marry her. There were plenty of other far more compliant girls out there who would be forever grateful for the chance to be his mistress. He could have any of them.

All of them!

Eugenie rode through the village, almost knocking over the postman's wife. The woman shook a fist after her, but Eugenie didn't stop. Everyone thought her a hoyden, even Sinclair. Suddenly their opinions of her seemed justified. She thoroughly deserved their approbation.

For several miles she rode on without easing her pace, and it was only when the tears had dried on her cheeks and her sobs quieted, that she finally stopped. She'd cried herself out but her heart was leaden in her breast.

Eugenie knew she'd learned a lesson she'd never forget. This silly scrape had changed her, made her more aware of her actions and how they might affect herself and others.

She'd been foolish and selfish and she told herself that from now on she would be neither.

Chapter 19

Once again Belmont Hall was in an uproar.

"Send for the doctor!" Mrs. Belmont wailed. "The twins are worse. I told your father it wasn't a simple fever. The twins can never do anything simple!"

Eugenie put her palm on Benny's and then on Bertie's brow. They looked at her with listless eyes and flushed cheeks, lacking their usual mischievous grins.

The doctor, when he arrived, ordered the boys to bed until their fevers had broken, and wrote out a script for the apothecary in Torrisham. "Until we know what it is, I think we should keep the twins away from Jack and any other young children, Mrs. Belmont. Just a precaution. There has been a case of scarlet fever in the village."

"Scarlet fever! Oh doctor, I don't think I could bear to lose my dear, dear boys."

By this time Eugenie's mother had worked herself into a state of hysterics, which the doctor—with familiar impatience for her ways—treated with firm language and a sedative. Mr. Belmont escaped to his study and closed the door, and Terry vanished to the stables with Jack. That left Eugenie and two wide-eyed servants, one of them the new cook, who was yet to serve any meal that wasn't slightly singed.

"Do you think you will be able to cope with nursing these two young rascals?" the doctor asked, with a sympathetic smile.

"I usually do. Cope, I mean," Eugenie said wryly.

The doctor, who had known her since she was born, rested his gaze on her pale face for a thoughtful moment. "You do not look well yourself, my dear."

"A lingering headache, that's all," she reassured him.

"You should take care of your own health, Eugenie. Your family depends upon you a great deal. Too much, perhaps."

When the doctor had gone, reminding her to send a message to him if anything further developed, Eugenie set about her tasks. She didn't really mind. Besides, keeping busy took her mind off her own troubles, and she was certainly busy with two sick little boys. They, and the running of the household and the instructing of the new cook, took up most of her days. Several times she was also called up in the night to give out doses of the doctor's medicine and comfort the children back to sleep. Finally the twins' fevers broke, and when no rashes or other symptoms developed, the doctor declared them on the mend.

This didn't mean Eugenie could escape her

duties. The twins were still inside, kept warm and as quiet as possible, and she spent lots of time playing games and putting together jigsaws and making up silly stories that had them in fits of giggles.

"You have done a remarkable job, Eugenie," the doctor complimented her, when he visited for a final time. "The boys are fully recovered and it is all down to your care and competence."

Eugenie couldn't help but wish Sinclair were here to hear the compliment. Perhaps he would think better of her then. Although, she reminded herself, she was not supposed to care what he thought of her.

It seemed incredible that a fortnight had passed since her night of passion and the horrors of the following morning. Most of the time she managed to put those memories out of her head, but occasionally a word or a scene would pop into her head before she could stop it. She could only hope that soon she would be so recovered that she would cease to think of him altogether.

One afternoon Terry found her in the garden and informed her that he'd sold the filly he and Jack had been training. "Don't tell Father," he warned her. "I'm using the blunt for a surprise for someone."

"A surprise for whom?" Eugenie said, putting down the book she'd been reading.

He dug his hands into his pockets and looked away. "I can't say. But don't worry," he added quickly. "It's for something good, Genie."

Normally she would have teased him into telling her the whole story but she didn't feel like making the effort.

"Do you think any deed is acceptable, even a bad one, if it is done for a good reason?" Terry asked her, his face serious, as if she held all the answers to such tricky questions.

"I suppose," she said doubtfully. "Sometimes. But if you do something bad, even if it's for a good reason, then it usually comes home to roost."

She was thinking of her own situation. She'd begun to make a list of suitable husbands, but so far it was rather sparse. She didn't know many and those she did know did not compare to Sinclair.

When Eugenie glanced up at last, she saw that Terry had left her and she was all alone again in the garden. She'd been so caught up in her own thoughts that she hadn't asked him what deed he was speaking of.

I'll ask him later, she told herself.

But she never did.

Sinclair had planned to break his latest canvas in two. He'd begun the painting the night after he made love to Eugenie—and before he read the letter—representing her as she had looked when she lay on the divan, her hair wild about her, her green eyes full of passion and trust, as if all that was good in her shone out. But after one glance into her eyes, at her smiling lips, the strength to destroy her image deserted him.

Angrily he strode from the attic room and locked the door, telling himself he would never paint again. And that was her fault, too. Everything was her fault.

But the next evening he was back up there again. A prisoner to his own desires. Without a word he began work on the portrait, losing himself in the world of color and texture, and it wasn't until the dawn light made him blink that he realized he'd been there all night. It was a madness that would have to stop, but he didn't know how else to drive her from his mind. He told himself that the painting was a form of exorcism, and he was certain that when it was finished he would have rid himself of her once and for all.

And then there was Annabelle and the filly.

He blamed his lack of sleep—and ultimately Eugenie—for that as well. His sister had been pestering him for days to look at the animal and finally he gave in. He hadn't realized it was owned by the elder Belmont boy until he reached the stables and found them waiting, Jack and Terry, the filly between them, and Annabelle in raptures over the creature.

Sinclair wouldn't put it past that particular family to trick his sister into buying a horse that was lame, but after looking thoroughly over the filly he found no fault with her. The price was exorbitant, but with Annabelle looking at him with tears in her eyes, as if she sensed his current weakness. . .

"Please, Sinclair? I want something of my own to love. Perhaps I might even race her one day."

"You don't like horses, Annabelle."

"I do, I do. Please, Sinclair."

Well, in his present gloomy state of mind he found it impossible to deny her. So he paid Terry Belmont the money and his sister thanked him in a shaky little voice.

But there was something about the whole incident that made him suspicious and later that night, sitting up over a decanter of brandy, he stared into the firelight and replayed it over to himself. What was the catch? The scene almost felt as if it had been cleverly contrived. And yet he couldn't find a reason, other than the typical Belmont scheme designed to do him out of more of his blunt.

He shrugged.

What did it matter? He had plenty, and at least Annabelle was happy for the moment. Their mother had written, reminding her daughter to have her trunks and boxes packed, ready for when she came to collect her and take her to London. Then would begin the whirlwind of final arrangements for the wedding and Annabelle's new life as a married woman in the society she had been brought up to inhabit.

With surprise Sinclair realized that when she was gone he'd be alone here at Somerton. Despite the difficulties he'd had with his sister he knew he'd miss her. It was such a large house and he was but one man.

Perhaps his mother was right. Perhaps it was time for him to marry. He should begin to look about, find someone suitable. Someone obedient and willing to set aside her own wishes and feelings to be the Duchess of Somerton. Certainly no one with curly hair with a hint of red to it, or green eyes, or a blunt way of saying exactly what she thought. No, a person like that would never do.

Sinclair sipped his brandy and sighed.

Chapter 20

Eugenie found herself slipping back into her life as it used to be. At night she might dream of Sinclair's kisses, with his body warm on hers, but she refused to remember him during the day. Once she woke with a start, thinking she heard the scatter of gravel against her window pane, but when she rose to look outside there was no one there.

The household and the twins took up most of her time, and her mother seemed grateful to leave most matters to her. "I don't know what I'd do without you," she took to saying. One morning Mrs. Belmont informed her with a beaming smile that as a special treat she had accepted an invitation to a supper party on her behalf.

Eugenie didn't want to go. She found she no longer trusted herself in social situations.

"I really think I should stay home with the twins, Mother. You and Father go to Major Banks's supper party. No one will miss me."

"The twins are perfectly well, and the major asked for you particularly, Eugenie. You know how he admires you. If you are not there we will never hear the end of it."

Eugenie was well aware that the major had a tender for her, but the fact that her admirer was fat and forty and happily married meant it was most unlikely anything romantic would come of it, even had she wanted it to.

"Your father is hoping to sell him a horse," her mother added the clincher.

"And he wants me to butter him up first?" Eugenie said wryly.

"Well, a few words from you might help." Her mother fixed her with a sharp look. "Are you well, Eugenie? You have been so unlike yourself lately I am beginning to wonder if you are lovelorn."

"And who would I be lovelorn with, Mother?"

"Well, there has been talk in the village about one of the Duke of Somerton's grooms. Of course I dismissed it immediately. I would hope you could do a lot better than a groom."

She eyed her daughter, awaiting confirmation that the whole thing was nonsense. Eugenie did her best to supply it. "There is no one I am lovelorn about, Mother. Maybe I'm out of practice when it comes to supper parties."

"All the more reason to go."

Satisfied she'd made her point, Mrs. Belmont went to peruse her limited wardrobe in search of something to wear to Major Banks's supper party. Eugenie, with a growing sense of trepidation, did the same.

In the end she chose her pink taffeta, which was old-fashioned and rather too short and had faded over the years to a dusty color. But then it was only the major, she reassured herself, and he wouldn't notice.

It wasn't until they arrived that she found there were a lot more guests than she'd expected from her mother's blithe description. The major had outdone himself this time, and there were a large number of well-to-do families as well as business-men and merchants from Torrisham. Eugenie, re-gretting now she hadn't made more of an effort with her appearance, accepted the major's effu-sive greeting.

To her surprise she found herself enjoying the company. Her experience with Sinclair had dinted her confidence but she soon regained it, chatting with the guests. As long as she kept a tight rein on her unruly tongue she could manage very well, and she'd learned her lesson there. Never again, Eugenie vowed to herself, would she do some-thing so reckless.

After a time she wandered into Major Banks's library. She knew the major was an enthusiastic collector of travel memoirs, and that she'd find plenty of fascinating tales about jungles and des-erts and snowy mountains to peruse. Eugenie had opened the door and was heading toward the tall bookshelves before she heard footsteps behind her and realized that someone else had followed her in.

Turning with a smile she began to make some comment to the tall, broad-shouldered gentleman in evening dress silhouetted against the brighter lights outside the door. And then he came farther into the room and with a paralyzing shock she recognized him.

"What are you doing here?" she burst out rudely.

"Miss Belmont," he said in a cold, clipped voice. "As charming as ever."

"I . . . Your Grace," she said hastily, and dipped a curtsey, although her knees felt weak. "I'm sorry. I did not expect you here this evening. No one said." She didn't need to add the unspoken, *I would not have come if I had known*.

Typically Sinclair took her words as a slight upon his character.

"It is part of my responsibility as the largest landholder in the county to be on good terms with my neighbors," he said haughtily. "I hope I'm not too proud to sit down with farmers and shopkeepers."

"I did not mean—"

"Your opinion of me has never been high, has it, Miss Belmont?"

"You're wrong. It is your opinion of me that is low. It would not matter if I had the patronage of the queen herself, you would still curl your lip at me."

He frowned. Perhaps she had been too blunt?

"But I am interrupting," she said, edging around him toward the door. "I will leave you to your reading."

He looked around him, as if surprised to see he was in a library. "I was late arriving. Just as I was apologizing to the major I looked across the room and saw you creeping in here."

"I wasn't 'creeping,'" she retorted, blushing. "I enjoy reading."

"Melodramas, no doubt."

Eugenie ignored his snide remark. "Why did you follow me? I would have thought I was the last person you wished to see here tonight."

He gave her his arrogant stare. "I am not so mean-spirited as you think, Miss Belmont. Jack mentioned that the twins had been unwell and I merely wished to ask you if they were recovered."

Her eyebrows rose at the unlikeliness of his concern. "They are fully recovered, thank you, Your Grace."

"I am glad to hear it."

It was a very odd conversation. So polite and yet Eugenie could not help but recall the last time they spoke together, and the anger and bitterness in his voice. Perhaps it was a good thing that they were meeting here like this among others. Eugenie could put the past behind her and move on. But despite her determination to forget, her memories were still unpleasantly fresh. Should she apologize again? Would that give her the peace of mind she craved?

She took a deep breath. "Your Grace—"

"Miss Belmont—"

Their eyes met in shock and then slid away, but in that moment of surprising contact Eugenie was certain she saw lingering in his gaze his previous hot passion. It occurred to her that it would not be very difficult to stir the coals to their former intensity, if she should wish to try.

What should have been a terrifying thought was actually extremely tempting.

"I must go back to the supper room," she said, sounding breathless.

"Don't go, Eugenie." His voice was gruff, unwilling, as if he was speaking words he'd rather not speak.

"I think I had better." She forced a shaky laugh. "You know me. I am liable to do something scandalous."

His dark gaze was piercing. "You are a thoughtless little minx, I'll give you that."

"And you are an arrogant . . ."

He bent his head as if to kiss her. She was certain that was what he meant to do.

Would she kiss him back? Had she learned so little that she would fling herself once more into the chaos of his arms?

Luckily they were interrupted.

Someone cleared their throat.

Sinclair spun around, his face white, and found Major Banks standing in the doorway with a servant goggling behind him. Eugenie put a hand to her face, wondering if Scarlet Woman was written there in flaming letters. She began to slip around the duke, hoping to make her escape without anyone noticing, but the major's next words brought her to a stop.

"My apologies, Your Grace," he said stiffly, his face perfectly composed. If he was wondering what he had just interrupted then he hid it well. "An urgent message has just come for you."

He nodded to the servant, who held out a sealed paper on a silver salver as if it was an entrée.

Impatiently Sinclair snatched it up and tore it open without a word. Eugenie, watching his face change as he scanned the words, knew at once that something dreadful had happened. All her personal doubts melted away as her generous spirit compelled her to help him in any way she could.

"What is it?" she said. "What does it say?"

He looked at her as if he didn't know her. "Leave us," he said icily, jerking his head at the major and his servant. His rudeness was evidently to be excused on this occasion, because a moment later the library door closed and they were again alone.

"Sinclair, please, what is the matter?" she tried. If she hadn't known better she might think this was another of her mistakes. She even searched her consciousness in case some new piece of reckless behavior had slipped her mind.

Sinclair was speaking in a clipped, precise voice that was as cold as winter.

"My mother arrived at Somerton this evening to accompany my sister to London in preparation for her wedding."

"The wedding. Of course. Wish her well from me, won't you?"

His look was baleful. "My sister was not there. She has left a written note saying she has run away to Scotland with your brother."

Eugenie opened her mouth to refute his accusation utterly. "Terry would never . . . !" she squeaked, and then stopped. Certain conversations jumbled into her head, snippets of things Terry had said, secrets half disclosed, and suddenly she knew with a sinking heart that it was indeed possible. In fact it was more than likely Terry had run off with Lady Annabelle.

"Never fear I will bring them back," Sinclair said with cold fury. "The rascal will not benefit from his base act."

"I'm sure if Terry has taken your sister to Scotland then it wasn't his idea alone," Eugenie dared to argue.

"We both know who is the villain in this tale."

He stared at her a moment more, as if there was more he wanted to say but could not, and then he walked out.

Eugenie stood as if turned to stone. She wanted to slump down into one of the leather chairs and cover her face with her hands. She wanted to lose herself in a storm of wailing. But it wasn't possible. She had to tell her parents what their son had done, and then they must go home. Perhaps he had left an explaining letter for them; perhaps it was all a mistake.

Hope buoyed her up as she hurried from the room.

Sinclair sat slumped in the corner of his coach, seething with such a mass of contradicting emotions that he lurched from fury to rage to self-recriminations and back again. Of course he blamed himself. He should have seen what was happening and taken action to remove Terry Belmont from his sister's orbit. His mother, in the brief and bitter note she'd sent to Major Banks, had informed him that Annabelle's maid had known all about it. Of course the poor chit was no match for the dowager duchess, and soon told tearful tales of Annabelle's evening meetings in the garden and the woods, of plans made and secrets kept, and finally, this evening, the flight north to Scotland with her lover.

As for Miss Gamboni, where was she in all this? Her part was, as yet, a mystery because they could not find her. She had disappeared. Perhaps, too afraid to face her charge's family, she had fled to the safety of her home.

I blame you, Sinclair.

His mother had only written what he believed to be the truth. If he had never pursued Eugenie, if he had not become so obsessed with having her, to the exclusion of everything and everyone else, then the warning signals would have jolted him into seeing what was happening long ago. Instead, whenever he had felt a faint niggling unease, he had chosen to ignore it and continue on his merry way.

Bleakly, he stared ahead.

There was Somerton, windows ablaze, as though by lighting every candle and lamp in the house his mother could bring Annabelle home. The coach circled the drive and came to a stop. Grimly Sinclair prepared himself for what was ahead.

He would find her. He would redeem himself. No matter how long it took, he would bring his sister home.

Chapter 21

Eugenie was surprised her nerves weren't shredded by the time they reached Belmont Hall. Her mother was already in a terrible state and when they found a letter awaiting them from Terry, she insisted Eugenie read it.

By now all the family were gathered about, uncharacteristically silent, wide-eyed and waiting.

"My dear mother and father, forgive me for my haste in leaving. I was not planning to go for several days, but Annabelle's mother sent word she was returning early and we had no choice. We are traveling to Scotland. Loving her as I do, I have no option but to help her. Your fond son, Terry."

The silence was broken by a shriek from Mrs. Belmont, who promptly threw herself upon the sofa, prostrate. Her husband hovered over her, useless in an emergency, while Jack stared on. Even the twins were subdued, huddled together near the door, ready to bolt to safety.

"He's eloped!" she sobbed.

Mr. Belmont gave a nervous chuckle. "I didn't

think the boy had it in him. A duke's sister, eh? That should raise our family's fortunes."

"How can you?" His wife turned on him. "The duke will go after him and then what will happen to our son? He will be gaoled, I know it! Locked up for the rest of his life! Or—or challenged to a duel and killed. Oh dear Lord, my son, my son . . ."

Eugenie let their histrionics roll over her. Her last hope was gone. It was all true. Terry really had run off with Annabelle to Scotland. There was no doubt that Sinclair would go after them. With his position and his power he would be able to cover up his sister's situation, quash the gossip, and marry her off to the man they had already chosen for her.

And what of Terry?

Would he really be thrown into prison, as her mother said? Or would Sinclair shoot him and leave his cold body to be buried somewhere far away from home? Eugenie knew she was becoming hysterical herself, but she couldn't help it. She kept remembering the duke's expression as he stood in Major Banks's library and she wouldn't put it past him to revenge himself upon Terry. And, possibly, through him her? Was he still so angry with Eugenie that he would use Annabelle's elopement as an excuse to punish her in so awful a way?

Don't be ridiculous, a calming voice warned her. But the emotion was building inside her, panic and a desperate need to do something. Anything!

To save her brother from Sinclair's wrath. And as usual Eugenie felt that this was probably all her fault. If she hadn't been distracted by her own problems she would have realized what was happening. She could have put a stop to it before the situation reached these catastrophic proportions.

The fault was hers; it was up to her to put things right.

"Don't worry, Mama," she said in a voice that betrayed little of her inner turmoil. "I won't let the duke hurt Terry. I will go with him and bring Terry home."

"Such a terrible calamity to befall my family," Mrs. Belmont moaned. "I will never recover from it."

But Eugenie's quick mind was already busy, putting plans in place. She looked about her, fixing each member of her family with a serious look. "None of you must mention this, not to anyone. Do you understand? If no one knows and we can get them back home again then there need not be a scandal. As long as no one knows."

They all nodded and gave their promises in somber voices, even the twins. Eugenie tucked Terry's letter into her pocket. "Good. I'll go and quickly pack a bag. I must hurry to Somerton before the duke sets off."

It said something for their shocked condition that no one thought to protest or point out that Eugenie's own reputation would be ruined beyond repair by setting off on such an adventure, alone, with the duke. They had simply accepted that Eugenie would step in and make everything all right.

Just as she always did.

Only Jack followed her out of the room to the foot of the stairs. "Do you want me to come with you, Genie?"

Eugènie didn't want to linger, but he looked so worried. She gave him a reassuring smile. "No, Jack, I'll be fine. The duke is likely to be cross and you won't like that."

"Somerton won't be cross with you," Jack assured her confidently. "He likes you. Are you riding the mare? You know what she's like, and it's been raining. I'd better come, too."

Practical as always, Eugenie thought, as she hastily threw a few belongings into her bag, hardly knowing what she was doing. Wrapping her warm wool cloak about her, she hurried back downstairs and followed Jack to the stables.

"You knew about Terry and Lady Annabelle, didn't you, Jack?" she said, as he saddled the mare.

"He told me not to tell." He gave her an anxious sideways glance. "I didn't know he meant to run off with her. He said they were friends, that was all, and he was going to help her out of her pre-predicament."

"What was her predicament?"

But he just shrugged.

"Didn't he mention it at all?"

"Well, he asked me once if it was right to do something to help someone even if it meant you'd get into trouble."

"He asked me something similar."

So Terry must have had his doubts but he'd gone ahead anyway. Run off with the duke's sister! Eugenie sighed. Terry really had set a new Belmont standard for harebrained behavior.

On the ride to Somerton she clung to Jack and tried to be calm despite the maelstrom of panic in the pit of her stomach. Jack, misreading her tension, assured her they'd reach the estate before Sinclair left. "And if we don't then I'll follow on until we catch up with him."

Eugenie's angst was more about coming face-to-face with the duke. The thought of being on the receiving end of his icy anger yet again was making her feel nauseous.

He'd refuse to take her. Of course he would. He would leave her standing on the road while he drove away and there wasn't a thing she could do about it.

When they reached Somerton the house was brilliantly lit, bizarrely, as if the St. Johns were about to host a grand gala. They cantered up the side of the driveway, keeping to the few shadows thrown by shrubs and a trellis of vines, and Eugenie saw the duke's coach waiting outside. A pair of burly servants were busy strapping luggage to the back, while a coachman in a great coat, an old tricorn hat over his grizzled gray hair, held steady the four horses.

Behind them were the doors to the house, wide open, light spilling over the curve of the stairs. As if daring her to climb them.

Her heart began to thump harder than ever. She knew what would happen if she climbed those stairs and demanded to speak to Sinclair. He would refuse to have any conversation with her. And if she insisted, then he would refuse to take her with him. She couldn't win, not on his terms. And she had to win, for Terry's sake.

Eugenie needed a better plan; she needed to hand Sinclair a fait accompli.

"Jack," she whispered, "will you do something for me?"

While she explained her idea he nodded seriously, but there was a twinkle in his eye. He was only a boy, after all, and to him this was probably a great adventure. Eugenie slipped from her mare, taking her bag with her, and made her way as close as she could to the coach without revealing her presence. Jack waited until she was in position, and then dug his heels into the mare's flanks. The silly creature darted forward, kicking up gravel, and flew past the coach, servants, and the waiting coachman.

The sudden commotion made them all jump and shout. The burly servants started after Jack, waving their arms, while the coachman followed a short way, then seemed to remember that it was his job to look after the duke's horses and turned back. But the distraction gave Eugenie time enough to reach the coach, quietly open the door and slip inside.

Creeping into the farthest corner, she curled up and made herself as small as possible. There was a neatly folded travel rug which she spread over herself, hoping she resembled some lumpy piece of luggage that had not fitted onto the back of the coach. She could not hide here for long, she knew that with a stark sense of inevitability, but perhaps it would be long enough for her to persuade him it was easier to let her stay than to waste time turning back.

Sinclair drew on his gloves as he strode down the steps. He didn't feel cold, although his breath was white in the night air. The urgency of the situation was keeping him warm. Behind him in the doorway his mother stood with a stiff back and a white face, watching him go. As he'd expected she blamed him for the entire dire situation, and because he felt it was justified, he'd bowed his head and accepted her anger.

"I will bring her back," he swore, when she was spent.

"I never did trust that Gamboni woman. She is behind all this, you can be sure of it. Annabelle would never do such a thing without encouragement. She is at heart a sensible girl, Sinclair."

They had still not found Miss Gamboni, although the clothing in her bedchamber was untouched and her luggage was still in the box room.

"What of the scandal?" His mother's eyes were red-rimmed with grief. "How can that be dealt with?"

"The scandal can be managed. Once she is married to Lucius and living in London all will be forgotten. You will see, Mother. We will get through this without too much tarnish attached to our name."

"You do not understand, Sinclair. Her life will be ruined. She may think she wants to be free of all this," she waved a hand about her at the pomp of her home, "but she will soon come to realize her mistake. When it is too late." She took a deep breath, trying to quell what she would see as too much emotion. In his mother's world one did not display one's feelings in front of others, not even one's son.

"I promise you it will not come to that."

"And what of this boy? His family will crow from the rooftops when they know he has secured himself such a prize."

"They may well crow but no one of any importance will listen to them. I will make sure the boy never speaks of what he has done and we never set eyes on him again."

His mother opened her mouth and then closed it again. Perhaps something in his voice, his face, made her think it was wiser not to ask how he was going to achieve that.

"Very well," she said instead. "Remember who you are and what you represent, Sinclair. The family is relying upon you to set this matter to rights."

He kissed the cold cheek she turned to him, and hurried down the steps. The coach was ready and waiting and he climbed in, calling for Robert the coachman. He'd decided against any other servants or outriders, thinking the less people who knew what was happening the better. And then there was a question of speed. A large retinue would slow him down and he needed to catch the runaways as soon as possible.

Sinclair had barely settled back against the leather seat when the vehicle lurched forward and then began to roll across the gravel, swinging around the circular drive and heading out between Somerton's grand gateposts and their stone lions.

Deep in thought he did not notice the shape in the corner, or if he did, it did not strike him as anything to be concerned about. He knew that time was of the essence and according to Annabelle's maid the eloping couple was heading northward, so they should be easy to trace. Sinclair had the advantage. He kept horses at some of the inns along the way, to enable his mother to visit her family in the north whenever she wished. He could travel with speed and would not have to deal with inferior horseflesh. No, this nightmare would soon be over and Annabelle would be back, safe in the dowager duchess's care.

A question niggled at him. How could his sister have done such an insane thing? He knew she was unhappy and anxious about her coming marriage—she had spoken with him about it—but he never for one moment imagined she would behave with such deceit. Such wanton recklessness. He'd believed that she was simply betraying her youth and inexperience, and once she married Lucius all would be well. That was the way of their world and in time she would come to accept it.

Just as he had.

He'd underestimated her willfulness and her determination to throw aside the traces of privilege for the sake of that wretched boy.

Restlessly, Sinclair stretched out his legs and knocked against something tucked by his seat.

He gave it a kick and when it remained in his way, reached down. He found himself in the possession of a luridly flowery carpetbag. Confused, he stared at it, and then with growing suspicion he unfastened the straps and peered inside.

Women's clothes, badly packed. Curiously he lifted up a well-worn chemise and then a pair of darned stockings. A nightgown with a line of lace about the throat drew his eye, and before he knew it he was holding it to his face. Breathing in the scent.

He knew the scent well; he'd even dreamed of it. He did not need to see the hairbrush with a few strands of curly hair still caught in the bristles— brown with more than a hint of red—to know who it belonged to.

Sinclair thrust the carpetbag aside, reaching for the traveling rug that covered the lump occupying the seat in the far corner. He tugged it hard. As he'd suspected his stowaway was none other than Eugenie Belmont.

Chapter 22

Lizzie closed her eyes and tried not to panic.

It had never been her intention to join Annabelle and Terry on their insane journey north. When she finally discovered what they were up to, it was too late to stop them. One moment she was standing beside Annabelle, arguing with her, begging her to see sense, and the next she was inside the coach with the pair of them.

It was a momentary madness, her decision to accompany them. At the time it made more sense to stay with her charge. At least then she could watch over and perhaps persuade her to turn back. Now she wondered what she could have been thinking. Would the duke commend her for such ramshackle behavior? More likely he would dismiss her without references and send her packing, if he didn't send her to gaol instead!

What would her father say about that? This was no way for a vicar's daughter to conduct herself. In every direction she looked Lizzie saw nothing but disgrace.

Perhaps that was the reason she didn't want to

open her eyes. What was the point in facing the situation she was in? No, she would keep them closed. Just a little longer. That way she could pretend she was still at Somerton, tucked up in bed, and everything else was a bad dream.

She reminded him of a cornered vixen, all huge green eyes and tangled curls, with her lips slightly parted. At any moment, he thought, she would take flight, escaping into the night. But she didn't. Probably because she couldn't.

"What are you doing here?" he said, his voice surprisingly calm.

She licked her lips like the wild and frightened creature he'd likened her to. He leaned forward, hands clasped between his knees, so that he could better see her in the gloom. She had a cloak on over the same dress she'd worn at the major's house, but she looked windswept and her hem was muddied, as if she'd been running about the countryside. Perhaps she had. He wouldn't put anything past her.

"Are you going to answer me, or will I stop the coach and throw you out?"

The threat worked. Her voice came in a breathless rush.

"Terry spoke to me about doing a bad deed for the sake of something good, for the sake of helping someone in need of help. I didn't understand at the time. I should have. I see that now. I wish I had understood because I could have stopped him before this!"

"Yes," he said grimly, preferring not to remember his own sense of guilt.

She bowed her head a moment as if she was accepting all the blame. "I want to come with you. I want to be there when you find them."

Words failed him. He curled his lip.

"I know Terry has behaved foolishly but he doesn't deserve to be . . . to be hurt."

"Do you think I'll hurt him?"

"I know you're very angry with—with me. I don't want you to take it out on him."

"So because you have made a fool of me you expect me to revenge myself upon your brother?" he said. "What a pleasant opinion you have of me, Eugenie. Thank you very much."

But she rushed ahead, refusing to apologize. "Whatever Terry's done he's still my brother, and he has not acted alone. He would never kidnap your sister against her will."

Sinclair supposed she was right regarding his sister, although he preferred to imagine Annabelle as the injured party and Terry the villain. But if she imagined he was so lacking in self-control that he would take out his frustrations with her on her brother then she was . . . He paused. Well, perhaps she was partly right, but he wasn't going to admit it to her. And he wouldn't harm the boy, beyond perhaps a bloodied nose and a black eye, if it came to a punch-up when they were caught. Nothing like a bit of bare-knuckle fighting to clear the head.

"I'll set you down in Torrisham and arrange for you to be taken home," he said coolly.

She leaned forward until her face was only inches away from his, her eyes feverish and wild.

"If you do then I'll follow you. I'll follow you all the way to Scotland if I have to. And I'll tell everyone along the way what I'm doing and why I'm doing it."

"You wouldn't dare!" Even as he said it he knew he wouldn't put it past her to pursue him across the length and breadth of Britain.

"Wouldn't I? You forget, I have my father's ability to tell a good tale. By the time I'm finished the scandal will have spread from here to the border."

He wanted to dismiss her words as bravado, but he remembered all too well the letter she wrote to her friends.

He had an insane urge to laugh. Last night at Major Banks's supper he'd found himself drawn to her again, that insane need in him overcoming all that had happened between them. The intensity of his feelings had worried him. The last thing he wanted now was to be in her company day and night.

"What of your reputation, Eugenie? My sister's is quite possibly tainted forever. Do you want to join her in ruination?"

Her green eyes gazed frankly into his. "My reputation did not concern you before. You were more than happy to lead me into ruination, as you call it. Why should you care now?"

"This is different," he muttered grumpily, and threw himself back into his seat, feeling uncomfortable.

"Well, I don't care about my reputation," she said impatiently. "What matters is finding Terry and your sister and bringing them safely home. I want to help, Sinclair. You need not speak to me, if you prefer it. You can pretend I am not here. But I want to join you in this search. I could not bear to sit at home waiting—I am not that sort of girl."

He sighed. "No, you are not."

She opened her mouth to say more, then closed it again. Perhaps she'd said all there was to say.

Sinclair knew he should refuse. He must refuse. She would be an added complication on what was already going to be a difficult journey. Who knew what they might encounter along the way? And what if he could not find the runaway pair and they had to come home and admit failure?

There were plenty of reasons he shouldn't agree to her accompanying him, and yet he found himself wavering.

The baggage sensed it and took advantage.

"Please, Sinclair," she said in a soft, wheedling voice. "I could not live with myself if I did not try to bring them home. I know my brother; I know he is at heart a good boy. I don't want the rest of his life to be blighted because of one silly mistake. I know you feel the same about your sister. We should be working together. As a—a team."

She sounded honest and sincere. He believed her—another concern because he well knew her propensity to lie. With a groan, Sinclair shook his head. "Eugenie, I don't think you realize what you would be letting yourself in for. I will not be stopping for hot soup and a nap at every inn we pass. I will be driving myself to extremes to catch them before they reach the border. No concessions will be given for the weaker sex."

"I do not ask for any." She tilted her head proudly.

He looked away from her, noticing her bag, where he'd tossed it on the seat. "Is this all you've brought with you?"

"Yes. Apart from the big box of teacups and crockery and my mother's best dinner setting—"

"This is no time for levity," he growled. By this time he knew her well.

"I'm sorry." She looked down, repentant, or pretending to be. "It is a bad habit of mine to make jokes during moments of stress."

"Then you should curb it while we are together."

A smile hovered about her lips, although she tried to hide it. She knew she had won, the minx.

He said no more, allowing the silence to grow. One thing about Eugenie, she didn't chatter. He heard her moving about, snuggling into her corner of the coach and getting comfortable. After a time, when he couldn't resist a glance at her, he found that her eyes were closed and she was resting her cheek against her arm.

Sinclair watched her through his lashes, enjoying the wash of shadows across her face as the coach raced through the night. He still didn't know what had come over him to agree to let her stay. Had her arguments been that persuasive? Perhaps. Or perhaps in his heart he'd wanted to lose.

Eugenie found that it was best if she said as little as possible to her companion. Then he couldn't glare at her, or worse, curl his lip at her in that appallingly arrogant manner. She knew, she just knew, that there would come a moment when she would no longer be able to control herself. He would curl his lip and she would slap it right off his mouth. And then where would she be? Tipped out of the ducal coach and onto her tail, most probably.

They had stopped to change their horses two or three times since they set out, and once they sat in a chilly parlor while a wide-eyed maidservant—clearly overawed by Sinclair's consequence—served them cold ham and warm bread and butter. There was hardly time to gulp it down before Sinclair was on his feet again, marching up and down like a Sergeant Major on parade, impatient to be gone. Eugenie had only just managed to stuff some bread and ham into her pocket, before she was out the door and back in the coach.

Not that the coach wasn't far better than anything she had ever ridden in before. It was well sprung and comfortable, with soft leather seats and padded squabs to rest one's head on. But despite the luxury the endless hours of travel grew tedious and her stomach churned from the constant rocking movement, as well as anxiety about her brother. She had had no time to pen even a brief note to her family, although she fully intended to do so as soon as possible. She also longed to wash her face and change her clothes and brush some of the dust out of her hair, but Sinclair did not offer to wait while she did so, and Eugenie had the feeling he'd probably take advantage of the opportunity by driving off and leaving her behind.

She was still bemused by the fact she was here at all.

Not that she was sorry to have won, but the question niggled at her: Why had he agreed? She could only imagine that he was planning some dreadful punishment and no doubt she would discover what that was in due course. She might have asked him straight out, but she didn't think he'd tell her. He'd probably just curl his lip at her. So for now most of their journey was spent in silence.

When they reached their next horse changing station, Sinclair spent more time than usual conversing with the woman whose inn it was, and then his coachman, Robert. Gratefully, Eugenie used the opportunity to walk about the yard and stretch her legs, at the same time taking deep lungfuls of fresh air. It had been raining and water dripped from the eaves and ran between the cobbles in the stable yard. A mother duck and her brood were making use of a small pond, and Eugenie couldn't help but smile as she watched them splashing about.

Sinclair's hand closing on her arm caused her to jump.

He ignored her nerves. His serious expression told her, even if he didn't, that he had no time for such female nonsense.

"Your brother and my sister passed through here last night. I gather their horses are inferior to mine so we cannot be far behind them."

"Then . . . we should catch up with them soon?" Eugenie's relief turned to anxiety. "But what if they know we're getting close? This is a busy road. Some other travelers might tell them we are following them. What if they change direction . . . take another road?"

"They won't know we're getting close—I haven't told anyone, have you?—so they have no reason to deviate from their route. They are no doubt blissfully unaware that we are on their trail. Don't indulge yourself with useless speculation, Eugenie. We will hunt them down before any real damage is done."

How many days and nights had Terry and Annabelle been alone with no chaperone? No, he was wrong, real damage had already been done. The facts would have to be covered up, money would have to be paid for the silence of those who knew too much, but she knew Sinclair would do all of that for the sake of his family. He would have planned for every eventuality.

Now he was smiling in grim satisfaction. "I calculate we will have our hands on them before nightfall."

Eugenie wasn't sure she liked the sound of that, but at least she was here to make sure there was no violence done when the moment of capture came. A wave of relief spread through her when she realized her adventure was nearly over. One more day in the coach and Terry would be safe. She could take him home and scold him—and hug him—as she longed to do.

And if she had any regrets about never seeing

Sinclair again, then she would keep them to herself.

"Do you wish to wash and change?" His voice startled her. Deep in her thoughts she'd forgotten he was standing so close beside her. Now he leaned down, his breath warm against her cheek. "Eugenie, did you hear me?"

"I heard you, I'm just not sure I believe you," she retorted, made nervous by his presence, and even more so by the fact he was being nice to her.

He gave a chuckle. His good humor appeared to have returned.

"Will you wait?" she added suspiciously. "Or is this a trick to be rid of me so that you can challenge Terry to a duel?"

His smile turned into a frown, because of course he considered her words a slight upon his character. "Of course I will wait," he said. "And I have no intention of challenging your brother to a duel. I am a crack shot and he wouldn't stand a chance."

"Unless you fired into the air."

"If I did that he'd probably aim at my heart."

"I'm relieved to hear you have one."

"Have one what?"

"A heart."

"Eugenie, go and tidy yourself," he said irritably. "You are frightening the horses."

Hardly the words of a gentleman, let alone a duke, she thought crossly. It was only when she reached the room she was directed to and looked into the mirror that she understood what he meant.

Her hair was dull from dust and riotous from

the rain, making her wild curls even more irrepressible. There was a dusty smudge on her chin and her dress was wrinkled and creased, with mud dried in patches on the skirt from her ride to Somerton with Jack, and the hastily eaten bread and butter had caused greasy stains.

With the help of warm water and soap she quickly set herself to rights, grimacing as she dragged her comb through her hair. When she was clean and neat again, she went downstairs and found Sinclair in a private parlor with his boots on the hearth before a roaring fire and a tankard of the inn's best ale in his hand. He looked up at her, quirking his eyebrows.

"Ah, I see you have put the hoyden to flight."

Eugenie could see that Sinclair had taken the time to tidy up, too—his boots were shiny again and his dark blue coat had been brushed—but he seemed in a good mood and she didn't want to spoil it by making a similar joke at his expense, no matter how sorely she was tempted.

The table in the room was set with a platter of food and a jug of strong, hot coffee, to which she added cream and sugar, before sitting opposite Sinclair, and sipping greedily. The heat from the fire was just as delicious and she felt it seeping into her tired bones. Once she'd set aside her empty cup she leaned her head back against the chair, suddenly very sleepy.

Sinclair was dozing, she noticed with a smile, his mouth partly open as he softly snored, while a lock of his dark hair had fallen artistically across his brow.

Anyone seeing him now wouldn't believe him to be the most eligible man in England, she told herself, and yet somehow, to Eugenie, he still was. He always would be. The truth was she much preferred this man, human and fallible as he was, to the chilly and arrogant duke he displayed to the rest of the world.

Eugenie yawned. She really was very, very tired.

With a little wriggle of contentment, she closed her eyes and slept.

Chapter 23

She awoke to someone shaking her. Blinking, bleary-eyed, she looked up into Sinclair's flushed and angry face.

"You were asleep!" he roared accusingly.

"W-what?"

He was already striding from the room. "We won't catch up with them before dark if we don't hurry!"

Eugenie stumbled after him, tripping on her hem. "But you were asleep . . ." she began, only to fall forward into his arms as he turned. He caught her, holding with his hands firmly about her slender waist. " . . . too," she finished hoarsely.

For a moment he seemed to have nothing to say, his chest rising and falling heavily, as he looked into her upturned face. Then the passion between them sparked and flared into life. She saw the heat and longing in his dark eyes a moment before he swooped and took her mouth with his.

Pleasure curled ribbons in her stomach. She stood on her toes, and wrapped her arms about his neck, losing herself in the warmth of his lips and tongue, the rough feel of his cheek against hers. A great wave of emotion washed over her, a painful longing, and with it came memories of the wonderful sense of rightness she had felt in his arms.

Was this love?

Then where were all the flowers and butterflies? Why did it hurt so?

Sinclair's embrace was desperate, his kisses forceful. Could he have missed her as much as she'd missed him? Was it possible that he loved her, too?

"Yer Grace?"

The voice had been repeating itself for some time. Diffident, embarrassed, and perhaps even slightly amused. Finally it penetrated the cocoon about them. Abruptly Sinclair let her go and she blinked over his shoulder at Robert, the coachman, his broad shoulders filling the doorway, his tricorn hat held between his gloved hands.

"Yer Grace, we need to be going."

Sinclair ran a hand over his face as if to wipe away the distraction she'd become. "Very well, thank you, Robert. We'll be there in a moment."

He turned to her as the coachman strode away, and there was a frown line between his dark brows. "I apologize for taking advantage of you. I thought all that was behind me."

"For heaven's sake, Sinclair," she said in frustration, "there's no need to apologize."

But he wasn't about to be interrupted. "After we bring my sister and your brother home, all of this will finally be over."

"Will it?" Tears were shining in her eyes and she couldn't stop them. "What if I . . . what if we don't want it to be over?"

His eyes grew icy as they looked into hers. "This isn't a matter of choice. It's a matter of proper and sensible behavior. The less I have to do with you or your family the better. You have a bad effect on me, Eugenie."

She gave a laugh that was almost a sob.

"After this is over I never want to see you again."

He said it like a promise, or a vow—as if he really meant it with all his heart and soul. Eugenie straightened her back, pride coming to her rescue.

"That makes two of us!"

She pushed past him, hurrying out of the inn and into the stable yard. The ducks were still in the pond but she no longer saw them or paused to smile at their antics. She was determined he would not see how much he'd worked his way into her silly heart. Climbing into the coach, while Robert sat waiting, his long whip poised over the four horses, she flung herself into what had become her corner.

Blast the man! Why did he blow hot and cold like this? It was almost as if he were determined to deny his own feelings. One moment he was kissing her passionately, the next he was telling her he couldn't see her again. It was like being on a seesaw. If she wasn't so closely involved in it, Eugenie might have laughed at the ridiculousness of the situation.

* * *

They'd lost precious hours and Sinclair blamed Eugenie, despite the niggling sense of fairness that told him it wasn't her fault. Her being with him meant he'd wasted time changing and washing, and then falling asleep in front of the fire. If she hadn't been there he'd never have stayed so long. She was a distraction, a bad influence, and he wanted to be rid of her.

Just as well she isn't my mistress, he told himself, *or I'd have strangled her by now.*

He looked up sharply as she made a movement, and found her eyes questioning him, although she quickly glanced away. Her profile was proud and irreproachable. Had he spoken aloud? He hoped not. Well, soon it would be over and he could go back to being the Duke of Somerton. No more of this painting nonsense. He'd make a bonfire of his canvasses and then find himself a pretty, biddable blue-blooded girl and marry her.

I shouldn't have kissed her.

Well, that was her fault, of course it was. She'd looked up at him, her pink lips parted, her green eyes so . . . so green, and he'd lost all control. Again. And now he had the taste of her in his mouth, on his skin, and it was turning his thoughts dangerously carnal.

He'd sworn to himself all those feelings were behind him, he'd been certain they were. After the way she'd treated him his pride should have been in tatters. And now with one kiss she'd stirred it all up again.

No.

Sinclair bit back a groan. That wasn't true; none

of it was true. He'd been indulging in wishful thinking. His feelings weren't behind him—they'd been traveling with him all along. He'd wanted her then and he wanted her now. He could rant at her all he wished, punishing her for making him feel this way, but it hadn't changed anything.

She had wormed her way inside his skin and he had no idea how to be rid of her forever. Unless . . . would one more night in her arms do the trick? All very well but what of Eugenie? Sinclair knew that as a man of principle he could not do such a thing to her. Only a cad would use her and then discard her. He wouldn't be able to live with himself if he harmed her.

Unless she wanted him to make love to her once more?

There was a thought. What if he pulled her across the coach and onto his lap? She'd protest and struggle but he sensed a rebelliousness in her that matched his own when it came to their physical attraction for each other. *One last time,* he would promise her. *Just one more night together, you and I, and then never again.* She would sigh and nod her agreement. Yes, yes, he thought feverishly. She would sit astride him, her arms about his neck, her mouth hot on his. It would only take a moment for him to flip up her skirts and run his hands up the soft, silky skin of her thighs, and then he would slide himself deep inside her. Her body would ripple around him, welcoming him, and she would make those little gasps of pleasure he remembered so well. He would gaze into her eyes, just as he . . . as he. . .

The sensation was so damned real that for a moment he was lost in this fantasy of his own making and he had no idea of what was happening in the real world.

The coach seemed to be tilting, falling, spinning through space. And suddenly Eugenie was in his arms, really in his arms, her cries shrill and frightened. All the same, the warmth of her soft body against his, the brush of her hair against his face, was too much like his daydream and he groaned and began to kiss her. His body was hard and aching with need and he was holding Eugenie, the real Eugenie, not a fantasy woman. He wasn't sure how his dream had turned into reality but he was certainly going to make the most of it.

The sharp sting of her palm against his cheek cleared his head with a jolt.

Sinclair's eyes sprung open.

"What . . . ?" he began, finally realizing that there was something very wrong with the coach, and he was lying on the floor between the seats with Eugenie on top of him.

The vehicle was still moving, slowing, with one corner of the body dragging along the ground. Robert Coachman was doing his best—they could hear his voice hoarse with shouting at the horses, words of encouragement interspersed with curses. A moment later the coach came to a halt, and if Sinclair hadn't been wedged so tightly between the seats he might have been flung into the air. Eugenie, clinging to him like a limpet, her cheek pressed to his, was breathing in his ear.

He no longer felt like kissing her.

His back was aching and one of his legs seemed to be twisted beneath him. As if sensing his urge to tumble her off him, Eugenie clung even more tightly to him.

"You're choking me," he muttered. "Dash it, Eugenie, let me go."

Reluctantly, it seemed to him, she withdrew her arms and pulled herself up onto the seat, kneeling there and peering down at him.

"Are you hurt?" he added. There was a red mark on her cheekbone that looked as if it might turn into a bruise. His reached up to brush her skin with his fingers and she flinched, refusing to meet his gaze.

"I'm fine," she said. "I'm sorry I slapped you. You seemed to be about to kiss me, and I didn't want you to blame me for it."

Her voice was stiff and he didn't understand what she meant, although he had a feeling it was to do with what he'd said to her earlier, at the inn. He supposed it was odd, one moment insisting he never wanted to see her again, and the next kissing her. But then again he felt strange when he was around her—completely unlike himself. Not that he intended explaining that to her right now.

He sat up, then clambered to his feet, and reached for the door. The coach was on a dangerous lean, and when he looked out he saw why. One of the wheels had indeed come off. Robert was still settling the horses, and Sinclair jumped down to the ground and turned back to help Eugenie down, too. She seemed reluctant to allow him to touch her but he did so anyway, swinging her out of the crooked doorway and placing her gently on the ground.

She stepped away at once, turning her back on him.

Leaving her to her sulks, Sinclair went to speak to Robert, who was eyeing the broken coach and shaking his grizzled head.

"My fault, Yer Grace. Went through a puddle and it were deeper than it looked."

"You should have known better." Sinclair, normally a fair master, was feeling off kilter after his run-in with Eugenie, and not considering his words. He frowned at the damage. The wheel shaft seemed to have splintered and the axle was bent. The coach would probably be out of action for some time, and they didn't have that long to wait if they were to catch the eloping pair before they reached their destination and were irrevocably wed.

"It is not your fault if the highway needs repairing," Eugenie said loudly. "And if you were not such a good driver we could have overturned completely. We could have been killed."

Robert shuffled a bit and was clearly embarrassed by her championing of him. "I should've known."

"Nonsense, how could you?"

Sinclair gave her an impatient look. "I am not blaming Robert for our accident, Miss Belmont."

"You are not blaming me, either."

They glared at each other and then Sinclair sighed, giving up on winning this battle, and turned back to concentrate on his coachman. "Take one of the horses back to the inn and get the staff to help."

"And what of you, Yer Grace? You don't want to be waiting here with the lady. Lord knows how long I'll be. Rumor has it the woods up ahead are full of thieves and highwaymen. Won't yer come with me and wait at the inn?"

Sinclair shook his head. "I want to go on. Miss Belmont and I will take two of the horses and ride on. You can take the other two with you, and then at least they will be safe from any thieves. Once the coach is repaired, or you can get hold of another one, follow on after us. I'll make certain we leave directions for you, and by then—with luck— we may even have caught up with the runaways."

Robert Coachman knew to obey his master's instructions, whatever they might be, and he obeyed them now. "Aye, Yer Grace. What of your luggage?"

"Miss Belmont only has one bag, and I will put what I need into another."

Eugenie waited, huddled into her cloak and stamping her feet to keep warm, as Sinclair collected such items of clothing as he considered necessary. She saw him reach into the coach and take a pistol from a pocket between the seat and the door, adding it to his saddlebag. The bags were then attached to his horses.

Robert Coachman set off, and without him it seemed very still and quiet, because of course Eugenie could not speak to Sinclair.

The coach horses had no saddles, and the traces

were unwieldy, but Eugenie was an experienced horsewoman and had no trouble riding bareback. He took a moment to admire her seat. Much as he disliked Sir Peter, he knew he was right when it came to his daughter's riding abilities. Eugenie would have made a fine addition to the local hunt.

They set off at a comfortable pace.

"It can't be far to the next village," Sinclair called to her over his shoulder.

Eugenie had allowed him to go first, so that she didn't have to speak to him. She didn't answer him now. She had a great deal to think about, and it suited her to remain at a distance from the duke while she did so.

There was the problem of him trying to kiss her in the coach, after he had insulted her so thoroughly at the inn. She'd slapped his face and enjoyed doing it. It had certainly soothed her hurt feelings, but it didn't seem to have affected him greatly. Instead he had continued to treat her with scrupulous politeness. Why couldn't he be rude and arrogant again, so that she could hate him as he deserved?

If Eugenie hadn't felt so confused herself she may have realized Sinclair was feeling no better. That he kept glancing over his shoulder at her made her uneasy, and his treatment of her after the coach collapsed, as if she was as fragile as a porcelain doll, made her want to slap him again. Honestly, she didn't know what to think anymore.

Chapter 24

The woods were as dark and villainous-looking as Robert had warned. Sinclair, who had taken his pistol from his bag and slipped it into the waistband of his breeches, could imagine every sort of rascal hiding among the trees, watching them pass. The rain grew heavier, which didn't help. Whenever he glanced back to see if Eugenie was still following him, she had the hood of her cloak pulled low over her head and he couldn't see her face.

She was sulking about something, although he didn't know what. Women had always confounded him. As a boy of seventeen he'd loved drawing their bodies but what went on inside their heads was a complete mystery. It didn't help that she wouldn't ride beside him, so that he could speak to her or at least keep a watch on her. No, she had to keep back, too far for him to converse with unless he wanted to shout. He told himself for the hundredth time how lucky he was not to have done anything irrevocable, like making her his mistress.

Although, of course, the fact that he'd wanted to and it had been Eugenie who denied him, was something he preferred not to remember. Better to believe the decision had been entirely his; certainly more soothing to his self-esteem. And right now his self-esteem needed all the soothing it could get.

By the time they reached a tavern in a small village in the forest, Sinclair was soaked to the skin. Which certainly didn't improve his temper. But like the gentleman he told himself he was he waited for Eugenie and helped her down to the cobbled yard beside him. She swayed a little, stiff from riding, and he held her longer than necessary, worried she might fall, worried she might be ill.

"I should never have agreed to you coming on this mad journey," he said.

Her head came up, her green eyes narrowed in her white face. "You've already made your feelings perfectly clear, Your Grace," she said in a voice as icy as the weather. Tugging herself free she whirled around and began to make her way toward the door leading into the low, smoky-looking and rather dismal establishment.

Sinclair ground his teeth. Once again she'd misunderstood him—deliberately he was sure. Maybe she was right in not speaking at all. Yes, they would proceed in deathly silence; it was the only way they could manage to be together without arguing.

But as he went to follow her he saw that she'd stopped and was standing perfectly still. Puzzled, he drew closer. Something had caught her attention and a moment later he saw what it was.

A child of about seven or eight with a pale, peaked face and dirty dark hair. It was standing by what looked like a pile of old straw and stable rakings. Wide, suspicious eyes flicked between Eugenie and the duke, and the child took a step back. His—Sinclair thought it was a boy—feet were bare and he was wearing clothes that had been roughly cut down to fit his skinny frame.

Forgetting they were not speaking to each other, Eugenie reached out to grasp Sinclair's arm. "Oh," she whispered. "The poor thing must be frozen."

The sight of such children gave Sinclair no pleasure, but London was full of them, and he was currently busy trying to catch up with his sister, as well as getting his coach repaired or arranging for a new one, and more important getting Eugenie out of the rain and into whatever comfort this poor hostelry could offer.

"Come on," he said gruffly, and brushed past her, leading the way into the building, confident she would follow.

But she didn't follow. After waiting impatiently and stamping his feet, he was forced to retrace his steps. As he expected she was still with the child, only now she was kneeling at the boy's feet, holding his hands, her skirts dragging in the muddy water of the yard while droplets of rain ran down her cheeks from her sodden curls.

The first emotion he was aware of was shock. And then the gentle compassion of her face, in her eyes, caught his heart and squeezed so tight he reached out to grasp the doorjamb, to steady himself. No woman he knew would act with such wholehearted love and compassion; no woman he knew would behave in such a way without worrying what her fellows might think. Would they laugh at her, snigger at her, tell her that she was behaving in a manner that ladies did not behave in?

One does not allow oneself to show emotion in public.

It was his family's mantra. And yet here was Eugenie, completely unaware that she was breaking all of society's rules. They simply did not matter to her as much as the plight of this child.

He didn't know what to feel. A part of him knew he should drag her roughly to her feet and tell her she was disgracing herself, and him, by kneeling in the dirt before the urchin. That was what he should do. But the other part, the part that had been closed off for so long, wanted to wrap his arms about her and hold her. Eugenie was a woman completely oblivious to the petty rules of his world, and if she had known them then she wouldn't have cared.

He was confused. Until now it seemed as if everything had been clear and precise, laid out before him so that he knew exactly how he was supposed to act and what he was meant to do. And now . . . Eugenie had shown him that those rules were like paper in the wind.

Feeling naked and vulnerable, Sinclair became even more the arrogant duke. In this role, at least, he felt ironclad.

"Miss Belmont, what *do* you think you are doing?"

She looked up at him, her green eyes wide and startled, as if she'd forgotten he was here. "His name is Georgie and he has no one, Your Grace. His family are all dead and he has been left here in the hope that someone will take him in. They give him some work, but he sleeps in the barn and makes do with scraps of food."

If he wasn't so agitated, Sinclair might have retorted that this sounded like a melodrama. But such cruel things did happen in his England, and he could see that Eugenie was deeply affected by the child's predicament.

He searched her face and tried not to groan. A look of determination had firmed her chin, giving it a defiant tilt, and she didn't have to tell him what she was thinking. The child was in need and Eugenie was not one to abandon anyone or anything in need. Look at all the trouble she'd caused herself—and him—over her brother Terry! Sinclair knew that arguing with her would waste time and he really didn't have time to waste.

"Bring him in and I'll get the landlord to feed him," he ordered brusquely, and turned his back on her, knowing that this time she would follow.

He could hear her murmuring encouragement to the boy.

An unbidden thought crept into his head. Eugenie would never refuse her own child the joy of painting because it was "not done." She would love him for what he was and not what others might think of him.

Angrily he shook his head and told himself he had no time for such nonsensical notions. If Eugenie was in charge of the world then there would be complete anarchy! Besides, he had Annabelle to find and bring home. He needed to focus on his task and forget about Eugenie Belmont.

The suspicious-eyed landlord turned into an obsequious fellow when he discovered who Sinclair was, at the same time giving the child a frown as if he were a stray cur. He even waved a hand at the boy, as if to shoo him away. It was only when Sinclair announced he would pay for the boy's food and lodgings that his manner changed.

"Poor little lad," he said, patting the boy's head. "But we can't feed every orphan who comes along, can we? We have to make a living. You understand that, don't you, sir?"

The child ducked away from the hand, not taken in by the landlord's sudden change of manner.

"Perhaps you have some clothes that would fit him?" Eugenie gave the landlord a look there was no arguing with. "And some shoes. He cannot go about with bare feet in this weather."

"He's used to it," the man muttered, and then made a hasty retreat as Eugenie's eyes narrowed.

Sinclair began to remove his coat and hat, both sodden, while Eugenie settled the child down in a chair she'd drawn nearer to the fire before kneeling down once more, this time to inspect his feet. The boy didn't object, just stared at her as if she was something completely unknown to him—a gentlewoman who cared about his predicament and was willing to do more than hand him a coin as she walked away.

Perhaps, Sinclair thought, the two of them were both coming to terms with the shocked realization. Eugenie had probably never seen a child like this, living all her life in the village apart from her stay at the finishing school, and the child had probably never known a respectable young woman who was willing to fight for him.

"You are as wet as he is," Sinclair reminded her almost gently. "Take off your cloak at least, so it can be dried before we resume our journey."

She began to fumble with the ties, but her fingers were too numb to manage the knot. Sinclair brushed her hands away, bending to unpick the tangle with a frown. He bent even lower, his voice quiet in her ear, the words for her alone.

"You cannot save every abandoned child."

She looked up at him, her eyes clear green, her damp curls clinging to her temples and water dripping down her neck. "But I can save this one," she replied, and she didn't bother to whisper.

Sinclair finally released the ties and her cloak fell from her shoulders. Beneath it, Eugenie's dress was wet, clinging to her body so that he could see the rounded shape of her breasts. He tried not to groan. A moment before he'd been in awe of her goodness and now he was lusting after her.

Clearly he was suffering from some kind of mental illness.

He busied himself laying her cloak out, in an effort to distract his disordered thoughts, while

Eugenie went back to her inspection of the boy's feet.

"Is he really a duke?" the child said with a note of cynicism that belonged to someone much older.

"Yes, he is."

"What's his name then?"

"He is the Duke of Somerton, but my brother Jack calls him Somerton."

"Are you his duchess then?"

"No, I'm not," Eugenie said, with a nervous glance in Sinclair's direction he decided it best not to see.

"Are you his baggage then?"

A pause. Sinclair gave a bark of laughter. She probably didn't know what a baggage was, or was he once more underestimating her?

"No, I'm not his—his baggage, either. We are just traveling together, Georgie."

"A lot of ladies and gents travel this road, but most of 'em don't stop here. Can't blame 'em, really."

Sinclair leaped at this information. "Have you seen any of the other travelers along this road, boy? Did a young man and a woman, a very pretty woman with dark hair, stop recently?"

The boy thought a moment. "Might o' done," he said cautiously. "This morning, early. Stopped for a bit. The lady said she felt sick."

"This morning," Sinclair repeated, relieved.

"They didn't stay on the highway though," Georgie went on, scratching his hair in a way Sinclair was sure meant he had fleas. Or worse.

"They took the road up ahead that runs through the forest."

"Why would they do that?" Eugenie asked, looking between the two of them.

"They must know we're close after all," Sinclair replied. "Perhaps we'd be better riding the horses rather than waiting for the coach. We can move more freely then if we have to travel on narrow roads and lanes. They won't be expecting us to do that. We can catch them up."

"They was arguing," Georgie said, his eyes sliding away in a manner Sinclair could not help but think was suspiciously sly. "Havin' a real barney, they was."

"Arguing? Arguing about what?"

The urchin shrugged one shoulder. "Dunno. The lady said something about wishin' she'd never trusted him to do it right, and why couldn't he have found a coach that didn't rock about so."

"I knew this was your brother's fault," Sinclair growled. "He has forced this upon my sister."

Eugenie glared. "If anyone is to blame then it is you, Sinclair! If you had not tried to force your sister into a marriage she did not want then my brother would not have been obliged to rescue her! Surely you know that young girls look to marry for love in these modern times? Even our queen has married for love."

His lip curled. "You are showing your lack of breeding again, Eugenie. My sister's situation is very different from your imaginings. She is not a poor put-upon heroine. Lucius does love her and if she would give herself a chance, she would soon return his affection. They are perfectly suited in every way."

"Oh? Then why has she eloped with my brother?"

He leaned closer, his manner almost threatening. "Do I really need to tell you why? Because he inveigled her into it, telling her lies and persuading her against her better judgment. She is young, impulsive, and he played on that. She is also rich. Are you saying *that* had nothing to do with it? Your family have a reputation for getting hold of money in any way they can. It wouldn't surprise me if your father didn't plan the whole thing."

Eugenie looked furious enough to slap his face again, but before she could do anything a small figure wriggled between them and gave Sinclair a hard shove.

"Hey, mister duke, you leave her alone!"

Surprised, Sinclair looked down into Georgie's angry face. The boy had his fists clenched, as if he was prepared to do battle for his benefactress. For a child with such a delicate form, he was full of courage. Sinclair felt inclined to laugh. Knowing that would make Georgie even angrier, he settled his face into a sober mask. "I wouldn't hurt her," he said in a mild voice, "no matter how infuriating she is."

"I'm not infuriating," Eugenie said, more mildly. "At least no more than you."

"I have never offered you any violence."

She flushed at his reminder of her own behavior. "It was a very light slap."

"Did you slap the duke then?" Georgie butted in, eyes wide with admiration.

"She did," said Sinclair. "What do you think of her now?"

Georgie considered for a moment. "I think you must have deserved it."

Eugenie bit her lip, but her eyes were dancing.

Sinclair raised his eyebrows at her. "It seems you have a champion."

"Yes, it does." She smiled at Georgie.

Sinclair found himself wishing she'd smile at him like that, and then it occurred to him that he, a duke, was jealous of an urchin.

Could the day get any worse?

Chapter 25

⌒◯◯⌒

The landlord came bearing food and drink, and announced that their bags had been taken to a room upstairs. Eugenie was relieved when Sinclair suggested she make use of it first. Georgie watched her go with an appearance of unease, but she assured him that the duke would not harm him and despite appearances was really quite nice. As she closed the door she saw Sinclair's expression at being described in such a way, and it made her giggle to herself as she climbed the stairs.

Sinclair was certainly not used to the treatment he was receiving from Georgie. Although perhaps it would do him good. He was too used to getting his own way and being fawned upon. Such deference couldn't be good for him—well, not all the time.

Her smile faded when she opened her carpetbag. There was only her pink dress left to change into, and that was none too clean. But at least, she comforted herself, it was dry, so she made the best of it. The room looked as if it was used as a storeroom, with boxes stacked against the walls and the window filthy with disuse. As Georgie had hinted, this was clearly not a place where people stayed for long, and she was glad to return downstairs.

She paused outside the parlor. It was very quiet. With a feeling of growing concern she cracked open the door to see what was happening. Had Sinclair tied Georgie up and gagged him? Or were they glaring at each other warily, like two dogs with one bone, as they had been when she left?

But the scene before her was actually very domestic.

Sinclair was sitting at the table, busy putting himself on the outside of a plate of stew and potatoes, while Georgie was seated opposite him, just finishing his helping. He set down his spoon and eyed the serving dish longingly.

"More, brat?" Sinclair said, before Eugenie could utter a word. He reached over and spooned more stew into the boy's bowl and then added a huge serving of the mashed potatoes. "Enough?" he asked dryly.

Georgie nodded happily and applied himself to the meal.

Only then did Sinclair look up and see Eugenie watching them from the doorway. A flush colored his lean cheeks and he looked almost shame-faced, as if he'd been caught doing something he shouldn't. Being kind to an urchin, she supposed, wasn't the done thing for a duke, although he would probably be more than happy to hand out a few coins. Close contact with the masses, that was something Sinclair wasn't used to, but in Eugenie's opinion it was very good for him.

"You'll make the child ill," she said mildly, making her way across the room, to where her cloak lay spread out before the fire. To her relief it was almost dry, the woolen cloth steaming.

"Impossible," Sinclair retorted. "He has the stomach of a grown man."

She was surprised to hear Georgie chuckle in response. Evidently while she'd been away upstairs the two of them had formed some strange sort of masculine bonding.

Eugenie joined them at the table and spooned some of the food onto her own plate.

"Our host found Georgie some clothes and a pair of boots. They look rather large but he can always stuff the toes with cloth," Sinclair went on blithely, as if he discussed such things every day. He gestured to a pile of clothing and the boots, which had been placed on the sideboard.

"The duke used to stuff his boots when he went to boarding school 'cause they was too big for him," Georgie explained, his mouth full of potato.

"Did he?" Eugenie gave Sinclair a puzzled look. "Didn't you mention to your mother or your father that they were too big?"

"My parents were away somewhere or other on the Continent when I was sent off to my first public school. I was seven. I suppose I could have written a letter to them but by the time they received it and sent me new boots I would have grown into the old ones."

He sounded matter-of-fact but to Eugenie,

who'd been hemmed about with her family most of her life, his childhood appeared lonely and bizarre. It gave her an entirely new slant on his character. Who would have thought she could ever feel sorry for the Duke of Somerton?

They ate in silence.

"Will you be happy to stay here, do you think?" Eugenie asked brightly, smiling determinedly at Georgie.

The boy gave her a sideways look. "Dunno."

"You will have work and food and a warm place to sleep," she reminded him.

"Paid for with my blunt," Sinclair added dryly.

"He won't keep me after you're gone," the boy said with the certainty of the old at heart. "He'll pocket the blunt and send me off down the highway. Probably make me give back the boots, too."

Eugenie gave a gasp. "Oh no, we won't let him, Georgie!"

"Once you're gone how will you know?" Georgie replied calmly.

"I'll see about that," Sinclair declared angrily, rising to his feet, but Eugenie put her hand on his arm to stop him.

"He's right. How will we know? And how can you force the landlord to do what you want?" she said. "You cannot be keeping an eye on him after we've gone." Her eyes widened, a glint in them he knew well. "Sinclair! There's only one thing to be done. We'll have to take Georgie with us."

"Definitely not," Sinclair said in his chilliest voice. "I knew this would happen, Eugenie. I knew you would want to take the child with us, and I utterly refuse. We are not taking Georgie and that is final."

The rain had stopped, although it was still overcast and cool for the time of year, but English weather was never to be relied on. The road through the woods was gloomy, rather like one of those horrible children's fairy tales Eugenie read to her younger brothers—the more horrible the better they liked them. Stories full of trolls and wolves and wicked witches. When a bird flew up from the bushes with a shriek, she jumped, and Georgie's arms tightened about her.

"All right?" She glanced back at him and smiled.

He nodded, but she noticed his eyes were flickering nervously about them and every now and then he'd give a shiver, despite his new warm coat.

"The duke will look after us," she tried to reassure him. And herself. "You do like him, don't you, Georgie? He has been kind to you?"

Georgie's gaze turned sly. "He's only doing it because he wants to please you, miss."

"What do you mean?"

"He's sweet on you, miss."

Eugenie tried to think of something to say but Georgie's cheeky grin was unsquashable. In the end she shook her head at him and turned again to face Sinclair's back, her face fiery and no doubt her freckles standing out.

It was a ridiculous suggestion.

She would rather have said Sinclair was cross with her. He certainly hadn't been very happy when she insisted on bringing Georgie with them, but eventually he'd given way to her on the condition that once somewhere suitable was found they would leave Georgie behind. Of course Eugenie and Sinclair had different opinions of what "somewhere suitable" might look like.

She considered the duke as they rode. His bark really was worse than his bite. That gruff manner he affected when he was actually being kind, and the haughtiness that hid his uncertainties about himself. It was as if he believed his generosity was a weakness to be hidden. She felt as if she was beginning to know him rather well. Strange to think they had been so intimate, that she had touched him and kissed him and . . . well, she knew things about him she'd never tell—and yet it was only now that she felt she understood the way he felt and thought.

At first Sinclair didn't see the men. They were up ahead, lurking in the shadows of the dripping trees. Waiting, as he later found out, for him. It was only as Sinclair and Eugenie drew closer that the two men rode out of the forest, hard-eyed, roughly dressed, and placed themselves directly in front of the little party. Blocking their path through the woods.

Every instinct warned Sinclair they were dangerous.

If he'd been on his own he would have ridden straight at them. Usually that ensured that anything in his way soon moved out of it. But there was Eugenie to consider and there was no way he could leave her to the mercies of these bandits—he knew instantly that was what they were. Thieves, ruffians, lawless highwaymen. No, he would have to stay and bluff his way out of trouble. As a duke he was used to being obeyed, and most people were used to obeying him. It came in handy.

"You are in our way," he said loudly. "Move aside."

They didn't answer, their eyes watchful and wary.

Time to show these ruffians who was in charge, he thought grimly. Reaching into his saddlebag, Sinclair expected to place his hand on his pistol, which he'd placed in there during their stay at the tavern.

It wasn't there.

Disbelievingly he began to search, and then search again, more desperately, but he found no familiar comforting shape to place his hand on. The pistol had gone.

He saw one of the ruffians nudge the other with a grin and his heart sank. They knew he was unarmed. That meant that this meeting wasn't an unfortunate coincidence but a calculated assault. Someone had taken his pistol and sent word of it to their companions.

With no weapon there was nothing he could do but continue to play the duke, using his authority as a threat. Some people found that more frightening than a gun.

"Move aside at once," Sinclair demanded loudly.

"I don't think so."

"We've come to relieve you of your savings,"

the other man retorted, the one with the scrappy beard. "You was flashing it about in the tavern back there, so we heard. I reckon we have more need of it than you."

"I am the Duke of Somerton, a peer of the realm," Sinclair said angrily, "and you will regret it if you molest me."

The two men looked at each other and snorted with laughter. "We heard you was a duke. Some of the other travelers seen you in your pretty coach with your pretty horses."

"My man will be here soon. He's following behind us."

"You haven't got no man," scrappy beard sneered.

His glance moved toward Eugenie and Georgie, and Sinclair's stomach twisted. They would not harm Eugenie and the child, not if he had to fight them with his bare fists. But who had taken the weapon? He knew there was only one way to find out.

"I have a pistol and I will use it," he said and waited to be proved right.

"No, you ain't."

Was it the slippery landlord? But then a new solution came to him, one that sank his spirits even further. As if to confirm his guess, Georgie leaped nimbly off Eugenie's horse and scampered toward the two outlaws. The grin he gave Sinclair was pure mischief. "I relieved the duke of his pistol," he informed his friends, and reaching into the pocket of his new coat, he took out the weapon and carefully handed it up to scrappy beard. "Here you go, Seth."

Seth weighed the pistol in his hand, grinned back, and then slipped it into his own belt. Suddenly his eyes narrowed as he spied Georgie's new clothes. "Where'd you get them boots, Georgie? You been thieving again?"

"The lady there, she got them for me," Georgie said, looking uncomfortable. "And the clothes, too. I was that cold. She's been kind to me. They both have," he added in a mumble.

"Maybe you'd rather stay with them then, Georgie. What do you think of that?"

"Yeah, maybe you'd get better pickings with them, eh, little brother?"

Georgie looked from one to the other, his thin face anxious. "Course not," he said, with an attempt at a sneer. "I want to stay with you and Seth. You're me brothers. I wouldn't go off and leave you, now would I?"

"We'd miss you if you did," Seth said, and there was a threat implicit in his voice that Georgie seemed to understand.

"I said I wouldn't." Georgie shuffled his feet and edged away a little. When the other brother lifted a hand as if to strike him, the boy ducked, and both men laughed.

"All right then. So tell us, where's this duke of yours keep his blunt?"

Sinclair glanced back at Eugenie, still and white-faced, shocked into silence by the revelations. He could see she felt betrayed, her kind heart broken, and he wanted to hold her in his arms. But this was not the time for maudlin sentiment, he told himself.

Their very lives were at stake.

Georgie swaggered up to Sinclair. "Where's the blunt?" Georgie said, mimicking his brothers' menacing growl. "We won't hurt you if you give us your blunt."

But there was something in the boy's eyes, a plea to do as he was told. Georgie may have betrayed them but suddenly Sinclair knew he was as much a prisoner of circumstance as they were. Slowly Sinclair reached down and untied his bag and tossed it to the ground. Georgie ran to where it fell, opening it and rummaging through it. He held up a couple of items to show his brothers, and they greedily snatched them from him, slipping them into their pockets. The money wallet was at the bottom and he fumbled with it a moment before finally holding it up with a triumphant grin.

They grabbed that from him, too, emptying it and sharing the notes between them. Sinclair knew, with an impotent sense of rage, that the loss of his money meant he would have difficulty continuing his journey. Not everyone knew him and he could not rely upon the goodwill of those who didn't. How would he find Annabelle now? How would he save the family honor?

"Did you really see my sister come this way?" he said harshly. "Or was that a lie, too?"

Georgie looked hurt. " 'Course I saw her. She and the bloke and the other girl, the yellow-haired one."

The yellow-haired one? Then Miss Gamboni was with them. Well, at least that was one piece of good news. A chaperone would help still the wagging of scandalous tongues.

"Get down off your horses." Seth was waving his pistol, keen to regain control. "You won't be wanting them. I reckon that thieving bastard at the tavern will give us a good price for horses like this."

It went against the grain for Sinclair to give up his horse so easily, but once again he knew he had no choice. He jumped down and went to help Eugenie. Her hand was cold through her glove and he squeezed it in his, trying to give her courage.

"I won't let them hurt you," he said quietly.

Her eyes fixed on his and she managed a shaky smile. "I know you won't. But, Sinclair, who will stop them from hurting you?"

"Hey, are you listening?" Seth blustered. "Your ring and your pocket watch, Your Dukeship." He chuckled at his own joke.

The signet ring was a present from his mother when he'd turned eighteen, and the pocket watch had belonged to his father. Sinclair wavered. As items they were not worth much monetarily, but emotionally they meant a great deal to Sinclair.

Suddenly he knew this was the time to make a stand. He had to show these villains he wouldn't be pushed about. No matter how foolish and reckless his knew it was, he couldn't give up his signet ring and his watch without a fight.

Eugenie was watching him nervously.

He stepped away from her.

"No," he said. "You can't have them. What are you going to do about it?"

Chapter 26

Eugenie was jumping out of her skin. "Sinclair," she hissed, tugging at his hand. "Don't argue with them. Give them what they want."

"Some things mean more than money," he told her coolly, watching the two ruffians.

"Sinclair, please . . ." she began.

Sinclair raised his voice and drowned her out. "You have my money. Now go on your way and leave us alone. And make certain you keep looking over your shoulders, because one day I promise you I will be there."

His words, or perhaps the threatening tone of his voice, seemed to give them pause, but a moment later they were nudging each other and chuckling, reconstructing their tattered courage.

"Sinclair, please give them what they want." Eugenie's voice was urgent.

"No."

Seeing he meant to make a stand, Seth ordered Georgie to hold the horses, while he and his brother climbed down. They swaggered toward Sinclair, making a show of tensing their arm muscles and squeezing their fists. He realized with a sense of fatalism that they were as keen for physical combat as he.

"How are you in a fight, Your Dukeship?" Seth smirked. "I expect you only fight in them toff places where the gents always win, eh?"

"I am rather good in a fight, if I do say so myself," Sinclair replied, readying himself for the onslaught. "And no one has ever allowed me to win."

"So you say, so you say . . ."

"You may test my words . . . if you dare," he goaded them.

It had the desired effect. They both rushed him.

The unequal struggle was short and unedifying, but Sinclair got in one good punch to Seth's jaw and another into his brother's soft middle. Before he could congratulate himself, he received a blow in return that stretched him out on the ground. He lay there, his head spinning, while the two men, favoring their own hurts, hurriedly tugged off his signet ring and removed his pocket watch.

So much for making a stand.

He could hear shouting and screaming. Feeling the brush of Eugenie's skirts he realized she was trying to push them away from him. He tried to sit up, but one good shove sent her to the ground beside him. He managed to stretch out a hand and hold her down.

"Stay there. You'll hurt yourself," he growled, wincing as the movement sent pain ricocheting through his aching jaw.

She crawled closer to where he lay, wriggling up his shoulders so that his head was resting gently on her lap. Her curls tickled his face. He saw the warning in her green eyes as she leaned over him, and didn't need the press of her finger against his lips, warning him to silence.

"You've killed him!" she wailed. "He's dead!"

Seth looked startled. There was blood on his lip from Sinclair's blow. His brother backed toward his horse. "You've killed him, Seth," he said. "That's hanging, that is."

Sinclair supposed Eugenie's plan was to save him from more pain and drive the villains away. He was content to allow her to go ahead, but he tensed his muscles, ready to spring back into the fray if it became necessary.

"What about her?" Seth said, nodding toward Eugenie, who was keening to herself like a banshee. Rather overdoing it in Sinclair's opinion.

Then Georgie spoke up, something which must have taken a great deal of courage. "The lady's been kind to me," he said, shuffling from foot to foot. "I don't want her hurt, all right? Please, Seth."

The brothers stood either side of him, nudging each other, working on regaining some of their bravado. "And how are you going to stop us, eh, little brother?"

At that Georgie lifted his head, eyes defiant. "I won't help you no more. I won't bring you no more toffs to rob."

They were no longer laughing.

"Maybe the duke's man *is* coming," Georgie went on, with a conspiratorial glance at Sinclair.

"I don't want to end up in gaol. Do you? Can't spend our blunt there, can we?"

He must have known his brothers well, because the threat of losing their money did the trick. They both sprang into action. One of them grabbed Georgie by the scruff of his new coat and tossed him up onto Eugenie's horse. A moment later they were all mounted, with Sinclair's horse tethered behind them.

Georgie followed as they wheeled around and into the woods, vanishing as quickly as they'd come. The last Sinclair saw of the boy's face was a pale blur before the trees swallowed him up.

He blinked, wiping a hand over his face. It was raining again and he hadn't even noticed. He groaned and started to get dizzily to his feet, only to have Eugenie grasp his shoulders and push him back down to the ground. Her face was above him, frightened and angry, her cheeks streaked with rain and tears.

"What were you *thinking*, Sinclair? They could have killed you!"

Sinclair grinned at her, strangely buoyant despite everything that had happened, then winced when his bruised jaw protested again. "I couldn't give up my watch and ring without a fight, Eugenie. What sort of man would I be if I did that?"

She shook her head at him in despair, and gently brushed the bruised skin where Seth's fist had connected. "Why are men such fools?" she said, clearly not expecting an answer.

"At least we're in one piece."

Eugenie had been brave up until now, but now

her emotions overwhelmed her. Her lips trembled and then she pulled away from him, crumpling onto the ground in the damp leaves, her head in her arms.

She was weeping. Sinclair watched her shoulders shaking. His limited experience of women told him she'd be better off when she got whatever was bothering her out of her system.

He waited.

But when her sobs began to grow louder and more violent, he was worried enough to kneel over her. "They didn't take anything that mattered," he insisted untruthfully. "We're alive, that's all that counts, isn't it? Eugenie, please be calm. You'll make yourself ill."

He rested his hand on her hair and after that it seemed natural to stroke her soft, damp curls. That seemed to do the trick because her sobs stopped and eventually she lifted her head. She was a mess, he thought pragmatically. Her green eyes were swollen and pink, her skin was red and blotchy, and she seemed to be very damp about the bodice of her dress.

She seemed so vulnerable. His protective instinct urged him to gather her up in his arms; he resisted.

"I'm sorry," she gasped.

"Why on earth are you sorry?"

"This is all my fault. I shouldn't have trusted Georgie. I thought—I thought—" The tears began to spill over her lashes again.

Sinclair gave in and wrapped his arms about her and held her close. Yes, it was her fault, but only because she was too honest and trusting, too good at heart, and she could not see there might be wickedness in a child's heart.

"He fooled me, too," he said. "And if it makes you feel any better, I don't think he enjoyed robbing us."

"Did you see that, too?" she asked hopefully, wiping her eyes with her sleeve.

"Yes, I did," he said, and found his handkerchief—at least they'd left him that—using it to mop at her tearstained face. After she'd blown her nose and restored herself a little, she looked around at the woods and the gathering darkness.

It wasn't late, but the rainy weather and the thick forest reduced the light so that they could have been in a twilight world.

Eugenie shuddered. "This is a horrible place," she said.

Her wet lashes were spiky against her flushed cheeks, her lips still turned down at the corners, and slowly, but with increasing heat, it occurred to him that he wanted to make love to her.

"It will be all right," he said, knowing he was babbling and not caring. "I promise it will be all right." He leaned closer to her and his lips brushed the soft skin of her cheek. "I promise, Eugenie."

She turned her face, and he was gazing into her remarkable eyes, telling himself there was no one else in the world who looked at him like that. He kissed her damp eyelids, gently. He knew that if she opened her eyes again he would probably have to stop, but she didn't. She lay in his arms, snuggled against his chest, as if she was sleeping, except that her breasts were rising and falling very quickly. There was a telltale flush of desire on her cheeks.

He knew, with a sense of triumph, that she wasn't going to deny him.

Eugenie felt his warm breath against her cheek, and then the feather light brush of his lips. If she kept her eyes closed then she could pretend this was a dream, one of her very best dreams. It felt right that this should happen now, after their brush with death.

With a happy sigh she surrendered herself to his kisses.

He began to undo the fastenings on her bodice, his mouth warm against her chilled skin as each inch was exposed. She shivered. She heard him get up and spread out her cloak, and then he was lifting her, cradling her close, and laying her down in a warm nest he'd made. The rain was still falling but the heavily leafed branches above them gave them protection.

His body was heavy on hers, but she welcomed his weight and his strength, her arms slipping about his waist. His mouth was on her breast, closing on the rigid peak. Pleasure shimmied through her and she wriggled against him, wanting to get closer, wanting to feel his naked flesh pressed to hers until she couldn't tell which of them was who.

The emotion and trauma of the past days was replaced with the need to be held and loved, to feel alive, and she reveled in Sinclair's touch.

Feeling her way, Eugenie discovered the ties to his shirt and began to undo them. His flesh was masculine and warm, and when she pressed her face to his chest she tasted salt and sweat and man.

Her hands moved lower, finding the hard rod in his breeches, and she set about freeing him. He groaned against her, pushing into her palm as she held him. And then he was kneeling, drawing up her skirts and petticoats, his fingers exploring her darned stockings and closing on her bare thighs.

"You are so beautiful," he said, or perhaps the words were in her head. It was the sort of thing he always said in her dreams.

His mouth closed over her most intimate place, his tongue caressing her, and she arched upward, pleasure spiraling through her. Her body readied itself for climax, but then he was lying over her again, easing himself inside her, taking her.

As she moved to the rhythm of pleasure, her body gripped by the fever of need, she no longer felt as if they were duke and commoner. There was no gulf between them. They were Sinclair and Eugenie.

Just man and woman.

He could hardly breathe, the pleasure was so strong, so all-consuming. Sinclair held her as the world came back into focus and knew he didn't want to let her go, no matter what he had said to her and to himself.

For the first time he thought of marriage without instantly dismissing it.

Would it be fair to her, to raise her up so high

and bring her to the attention of the gossips and the subtle cruelties of his class? And what of him? Could he bear the laughter of his friends and the mockery of his peers? His mother had threatened to turn her back on him . . . never to speak to him again. Could he live with that?

Right now, as he lay with the sweat cooling on him from loving her, he felt as if he could put up with anything. But later, what of later? Would he still feel the same in a month, a year, ten years? And then there was the letter she had written. Was he prepared to forgive her for humiliating him like that? Could he trust her not to do so again?

She stirred, rubbing her cheek against his chest, her tongue warm and wet against his flesh.

"This has been a very strange day," she said, her voice soft and fuzzy. She yawned. "Perhaps it has all been a dream. Perhaps I'll wake up on that divan covered in pomegranate seeds."

He laughed. She always had the ability to make him laugh when he'd thought it impossible. Or was it just that she made him happy?

He sat up and looked down at her. She was still a mess. He tucked her unruly curls back and smoothed a truant eyelash from her cheek. "If this really is a dream then I would like to wake up at home in my bed."

She gave him a temptress smile. "Would I be there?"

"Oh yes," he said. "Most definitely, minx."

Her gaze tangled with his a moment more, enjoying the connection, and then she raised her arms and stretched. He looked about them. The rain had stopped for now, but it was decidedly gloomy and growing colder. Time to start moving out of this wretched wood, although where they would go after that he had no idea. Certainly not back to the tavern; it wasn't safe there.

The problem of Annabelle and her beau jumped into his head, but he pushed it away. No use in worrying about them now. The thing was to find civilization and a warm room, and then he could begin to decide what to do.

He took Eugenie's hand in his and tugged her to her feet. She leaned against him, her head on his shoulder, his arm about her waist. For a moment they stood together, as if neither of them wanted to be apart ever again.

Chapter 27

The road they'd followed through the woods no longer seemed as clearly defined, and several times Sinclair stopped and pondered their direction before continuing on. Eugenie was so tired that she let him make the decisions. She would have been just as happy to lie down and sleep the night away and start off again in the morning, but she supposed it was safer to leave these trees far behind them, in case Georgie and his brothers changed their minds about letting them go free.

Her heart ached still when she remembered Georgie's perfidy, but she could understand why he'd done it—why he felt he had no choice but to obey his older brothers. How could he know that if he'd confided in her and Sinclair they would have done everything in their power to help him escape their clutches? The child was obviously used to shifting for himself and didn't trust anyone else. Life was risky business if you were an orphaned child reliant upon a brother like Seth.

The sound of galloping horses came at the end of this thought and Eugenie, fearing the worst, grabbed Sinclair's hand. "Who is it?" she whispered.

Sinclair, peering through the darkness, wrapped his arms tight about her and did not answer.

There was a light.

Someone was carrying a lantern, its pallid glow valiant against the permanent night of the woods. And then a voice cried out, a voice they both knew.

"Yer Grace? Is it you?"

"Robert? Here, we are over here!"

"Yer Grace, thank God I've found ye. Are you or the lady hurt?"

"No, Robert. Apart from our dignity," Sinclair replied, relief making him light-headed.

The coachman jumped down from his mount and was hurrying toward them, the lantern held high. Light sent strange shadows flickering through the branches of the trees.

"How on earth did you find us?" Sinclair said, grasping his servant's hand in a firm, grateful grip.

Robert grimaced and gave a glance over his shoulder. "Boy! Come on over here and face the music!"

They followed his gaze. Someone else was with the horses, someone small like a child. He shuffled toward them, his boots too big, every step getting slower, as if he'd rather be going in the opposite direction.

"Georgie!" Eugenie cried, and a moment later she was holding his hands, just as she'd done outside the tavern. "Oh Georgie, I was so worried about you. Are those awful men really your brothers?"

Georgie bowed his head. "Stepbrothers," he said in his gruff little voice. "I didn't want to do it, truly I didn't, but I knew if I didn't they'd belt me. They've belted me before, miss."

"Oh no, poor Georgie."

Sinclair came over and rested a hand on Eugenie's shoulder. "I think Georgie needs to tell us everything before we absolve him of his crimes," he warned her.

She glanced at him beseechingly. "But Sinclair, surely—"

"No excuses, Eugenie." He fixed a serious gaze on the boy. "Well, Georgie? What is the whole story? And make sure you leave nothing out because I will know if you do."

Georgie glanced nervously at Eugenie and then swallowed and straightened his back and lifted a brave face to Sinclair. "I expect you'll belt when me I'm done, Duke."

"I expect I will."

Robert gave a snort of laughter, turning it into a cough under his master's baleful look.

The boy began to speak. "My stepbrothers make me hang around the tavern, keeping an eye on whoever passes through, and if there's someone with blunt—like you, Duke—then I send them word. I get them to travel into the woods, tell them some tale or other. It was easy with you and the lady, because you were looking for someone and I could pretend I knew they went that way."

"Yes, very clever," Sinclair said sternly. "And you took my pistol, Georgie, didn't you?"

"Yes, sir." He swallowed audibly. "I had to take it. I didn't want no one shot. I knew once Seth and Harry had your blunt and your horses they'd be happy. The landlord always buys the horses from them. He pretends he doesn't know where they come from but he knows, course he does. He pays for the horses and everyone is happy."

"I found your horses at this tavern the lad talks about," Robert put in. "The landlord was trying to sell them to me, but to buy time I said I'd have to consider it. Then this brave lad came up to me and told me the whole tale, including his part in it. I shook the truth out of the landlord and promptly sent for a constable. I don't know if the constable'll find the other two, Georgie's stepbrothers. Georgie won't tell me where they're hiding out, will you, son?"

Georgie lifted his chin as three pairs of eyes fixed on him. "They're still me brothers," he said. "I can't see 'em hang, can I?"

"Might be the best thing for them," Robert muttered, but at the same time he gave the boy a pat on the shoulder as if to commend his loyalty.

Sinclair found himself glad to see his horses, and in a strange way he was glad to see Georgie, too, although what they were going to do with the boy now he had no idea. He was certain of one thing, Eugenie would not want him to go to gaol. The boy had showed courage when it was needed and he deserved to be rewarded.

"So your stepbrothers have my money. Where does that leave us?"

"I took some of it out and left it in your bag," Georgie said quickly. "Didn't you see it? I didn't give it all to them, Duke, I promise you. I wouldn't have given them any but they knew you were a toff and toffs always have blunt on 'em."

Sinclair believed the boy about the money. "Still I doubt it will get us very far."

"They was surprised you fought for your ring and your watch. They thought you was a right 'un."

"Does that mean they admired you?" Eugenie said in amazement.

"He stood up for himself," Georgie explained. "Not many toffs do."

"He risked his life for a ring," Eugenie retorted.

"It weren't the ring, it were the principle of the thing," Georgie said.

"Very true, Georgie," Sinclair agreed. "One should always stand up for principles."

"What about Framlingbury, Yer Grace?" Robert interrupted. "We could go there. Wouldn't your uncle help you?"

Sinclair turned to him in surprise. "Good God, is Framlingbury so close? I didn't realize."

"About twenty mile, Yer Grace. You'd be welcome there."

"I would indeed. Thank you, Robert." And he clapped his coachman heartily on the shoulder, nearly toppling him over. It was only when Robert shot him a startled look that he knew he wasn't behaving like his usual level-headed self.

But he couldn't help it. He didn't feel like his usual level-headed self. He hadn't done so since he met Eugenie.

"What is Framlingbury?" the lady in question asked warily.

"It is my uncle's house. My mother's brother." His Bohemian uncle, whom his mother blamed for his interest in painting naked women. He'd always got on well with his uncle, but his mother had avoided such contact for many years now, claiming he was a bad influence.

"Do you think Annabelle might go there?" said Eugenie.

It was a clever idea but regretfully he shook his head. "I doubt it. My uncle would send her home if she did. He knows my mother has set her heart on a society wedding for Annabelle and he's learned to his cost what it means to cross her." He looked to Robert. "Is the coach mended?"

"It's being mended, but it will take some time. I have arranged for another vehicle in the meantime, Yer Grace. That was what I was coming to tell you when I ran into young Georgie here."

"Then I think we should go to Framlingbury and consider our options. If Annabelle is heading for the border we will still find her in time."

And even if they didn't, he thought grimly, they could drag her back to Somerton. He could not imagine the Belmonts refusing cash for silence.

"I have never felt so *sick* in my *entire* life."

Terry had heard Annabelle say those words, or

remarkably similar ones, so many times he'd lost count. Now he just clenched his jaws and tried to ignore her. Who would have thought his heroic journey would come to this? They couldn't reach Scotland soon enough for his liking.

"We will have to stop at the next village."

He opened his mouth to inform her they weren't stopping again, but she had her handkerchief to her own mouth and her eyes were begging him over the top of it. Her skin was certainly an interesting shade of green.

At her side, Lizzie gave him a pleading grimace. "She is very ill, Mr. Belmont. I know you are worried about slowing our journey but would a few moments hurt . . . ?"

"We will never reach our destination if we keep stopping," he said, attempting to stand firm against them. "The duke will catch us and that will be the end of it. The end of me at any rate."

"And me," Lizzie added, to his surprise. "I will lose my position and he will send me back to my father in disgrace. I shall never ever hear the end of it. I shall never escape the vicarage again."

"Then why did you come with us?"

Her blue eyes met his almost shyly. "It just seemed to—to happen! One moment I was standing on the ground arguing with you and the next I was here, in the coach. I suppose I considered it my duty as Annabelle's chaperone to remain by her side."

Terry found himself smiling at the sheer ridiculousness of the situation. Lizzie's soft mouth curved, too, as if she was on the verge of bursting into laughter. It occurred to him that he had never heard her laugh. Perhaps she didn't have much to laugh about. He was beginning to feel responsible for her.

"We could set you down at the next town."

But Lizzie shook her head, her fair hair a bright beacon in the gloomy interior. "I'm rather afraid I have burned my bridges."

"We have all done that," he murmured.

"I expect I will find employment in the north," she went on. "Somewhere."

Annabelle, feeling the lack of attention, groaned and flopped back against the seat. "I think I will die before we reach Scotland, and I think I will be glad of it."

"Stop being so melodramatic," Terry said. "I thought you were courageous? You told me you wanted to live like an ordinary girl."

"Well, I don't. I want to live like a duke's sister."

They glared at each other.

Terry had only been in the coach a day before he knew that contrary to his hopes and dreams, he could never marry Annabelle. Not even if she'd have him. And a day after that he was sure he would murder her long before they reached the border. She was demanding and selfish and ungrateful. In fact she seemed to blame him for all their misfortunes, even the fact that the coach made her sick.

Was it his fault he only had money enough for a vehicle whose standard was far beneath her? He'd done his best. He could go to prison for what he'd done, or worse, Botany Bay, and all she did was moan about her stomach.

Two pieces of good luck kept him going.

One, Lizzie was here, with her gentle and sympathetic influence. Without her he really might have murdered Annabelle.

And two, the duke hadn't caught up to them yet. Terry could hardly close his eyes for fear of seeing Sinclair stalking him, like the monster in some nursery story. His hope was that he'd get Annabelle safely to her friend. After that his plan was to join the army. He no longer cared which regiment he was in, nor did he care if he was a simple soldier of the line. As long as he was sent far from England and far from the Duke of Somerton then he'd be happy.

Perhaps, he thought sourly, when he was shot by renegades or speared by savages or—or eaten by wild animals, then Annabelle would be a little bit sorry she'd been so nasty to him. Then she'd regret she hadn't admired him as he deserved for his sacrifice on her behalf.

Terry had just reached the part of his fantasy where Annabelle was throwing herself, sobbing, upon his grave, when he was rudely interrupted.

"Terry!" Annabelle gurgled, and lurching forward, she vomited.

Into his lap.

"I told you I was going to be sick," she said smugly. "Now see what you've done."

* * *

"She can't help it, you know," Lizzie said. "The movement of the coach makes her sick."

They had found an inn and Annabelle was upstairs, sleeping. Terry had stripped off his clothing and washed and changed. Lizzie, as always, was trying to make peace.

"At least you have a change of clothing," she said, casting an envious look over him. "I don't even have that."

Guiltily, he realized that was true. He hadn't taken it into consideration before, or perhaps he'd imagined Annabelle would share, unlikely as that was. They'd taken Lizzie with them in the coach with nothing more than the clothes she stood up in and until now she hadn't complained. Not once.

"You have a loose button."

Looking down he saw that one of the buttons on his shirt was dangling by a thread. He opened his mouth to tell her it didn't matter, that Eugenie always fixed his buttons, until he remembered Eugenie wasn't here. But Lizzie was already asking the servant for needle and thread.

"Do you want me to . . . ?" he began, miming removing his shirt.

"No, it's all right. I can repair it without you needing to undress," she assured him, and then blushed.

He watched her as she thanked the returning servant, and then drew her stool closer to his chair, leaning forward to begin her work. Her hair brushed his chin as she bent her head, and he wondered whether she was hiding her blushes from him. Why had she blushed? Was the thought of a man half-naked so embarrassing to her? Or was it the thought of *him* half-naked?

His cogitations were abruptly halted by the needle pricking his flesh. He jumped; he couldn't help it.

"Ooh! I am so—so . . . Forgive me, please."

She looked up at him, wide-eyed, appalled.

He touched her cheek with the back of his fingers, at first to reassure her and then because her skin was so soft and smooth, and at this moment he wanted to touch her more than anything in the world.

"It was nothing."

She shook her head and he saw the beginnings of tears in her eyes. "You will be glad to be rid of the pair of us. Annabelle is ill on you and then I stick you with a needle."

He smiled. "If I am to join the army and be a soldier I will face worse than a sewing needle, Lizzie."

She blinked up at him. Her lashes were long and curling. He wondered if the reason she had leaned so close to him was because she needed glasses. There was something endearingly unfocussed about her gaze.

"Are you really going to be a soldier?"

"Yes." His smile grew wry. "I will have to do something to escape the duke and joining the army seems the best option."

She nodded. "He is rather intimidating, isn't he?"

"I think I need the English Channel between us, Lizzie."

She smiled and then looked away. "Do you trust me to finish sewing on your button?"

"Completely," he said gallantly.

With a determined breath, Lizzie set to work again. When she was done she broke the thread and examined her handiwork. "There," she said. "You look every bit the gentleman."

He thanked her gravely. She was avoiding his eyes now, as if she had revealed too much or their intimate moment had unsettled her. Terry admitted to himself that it had unsettled him, too. What was happening to him that he suddenly found Lizzie Gamboni so fascinating? Wasn't he in enough trouble as it was, without seeking more?

"Why don't you rest for a while? Until Annabelle feels able to continue?"

Lizzie shook her head. "I can't sleep. I keep seeing the duke in my dreams and he's very angry with me."

Terry grimaced. "My sister seems to get on quite well with him," he said. "Jack whispers to horses and mends magpies, but my sister has a way of soothing even the most savage beasts."

Lizzie giggled.

A tap on the door heralded the servant. "The lady upstairs is calling for you, miss. Says she ain't well."

Lizzie rose hastily to her feet. "I'd better go," she said, only to hesitate, as if she wanted to stay.

"Yes," he said. "Thank you for the button."

When she was gone Terry sat alone and tried to tell himself that everything would work out. Annabelle would reach her friend in Scotland and Lizzie would find work with a kind family who appreciated her and Terry would . . . would. . .

He frowned, because the thought that had popped into his head wasn't the one he'd expected.

Terry would never see Lizzie again.

Chapter 28

"Are you sure Annabelle has eloped? I thought she had more sense than to act so impulsively, Sinclair. Wasn't she marrying that Salturn chap? Worth a mint."

Lord Ridley, Sinclair's maternal uncle, was fifty and a bachelor. Sinclair's mother always said he was far too selfish to think of settling down and giving up his freedom. He'd been injured in the Peninsula during the Napoleonic Wars and walked with a limp, but other than that he was in good health, and the injury gave him a certain cache among the ladies.

"She's young," Sinclair answered now, "and the man she's run off with is very persuasive."

"Ah yes. Miss Belmont's brother." Lord Ridley smiled, more inclined to be amused than shocked by the revelation that his nephew was traveling with the sister of the villain of the piece.

"I assure you she is very different from him," Sinclair said stiffly.

"Of course, of course," Lord Ridley agreed, but there was a twinkle in his eye Sinclair found slightly offensive. "Tell me again how a slip of a girl managed to persuade you to carry her off into the night?"

Sinclair's mood had plummeted since they left the woods and traveled in the coach Robert had provided for them to Framlingbury. It was truly the worst contraption he had ever been in. There were so many things wrong with it he ran out of fingers to count them, and when he began yet another rant, Eugenie had turned to him with sparkling eyes and said, "Enough! It is not nearly so bad as you make out."

"How can you say that?" he'd retorted. "It is so ancient it must have been built for Elizabeth Tudor, and I'm willing to bet it hasn't been resprung since."

Georgie, who was riding up on top with Robert—who seemed to have become his new hero, another reason for Sinclair to feel out of sorts—laughed loudly at something the coachman said. Robert cracked his whip and the coach began to jolt alarmingly as their pace increased. The coachman was showing off, Sinclair was certain of it, and in a moment they would be smashed to pieces in a ditch.

He reached up and pounded his fist angrily on the wall. "Slow down, you damn fool!" he roared.

Eugenie leaned toward him. "Stop it. You are behaving like a spoiled child."

"Like Georgie you mean? He is certainly spoiled. He robs me, holds me to ransom, and now he's treated like a prince."

"You know he had no choice. You said so yourself."

The coach went around a corner, rocking so violently Eugenie clutched the strap with both hands, her face blanching.

"Not too fast for you?" Sinclair mocked her with a savage smile.

"M-maybe just a—a little," she agreed.

He thumped his fist on the wall again, roaring at his coachman. There was a sharp crack and the wooden paneling under his hand broke off, leaving a gap between the inside of the coach and the cold air outside. He could see the folds of Robert's coat and then Georgie's face appeared in the gap, cheeks pink, eyes shining, grinning at them.

"You've broken it, Duke," he said.

"Slow down, will you," Sinclair ordered through gritted teeth.

"Robert was just showing me how fast we can go. If we ever needed to outrun highwaymen."

"I'm glad we've got that sorted. Now slow down."

Georgie sighed, as if Sinclair had spoiled his fun, and his face disappeared. But at least the coach had begun to slow to a more reasonable pace.

"When we reach Framlingbury I am going to make a bonfire of this pile of rubbish," Sinclair announced. "And I will probably dance around it."

Eugenie wasn't amused. "This is exactly like the Belmont coach. In fact it is probably nicer. Just because you have always had the very best does not give you the right to whine when you are forced to make do. It shows a distinct lack of character, Sinclair."

Whine! He had never whined in his life. But her words gave him pause. Was he such a snob? He hadn't thought so but perhaps he was a little bit spoiled by everything always being exactly as he wanted it. He remembered seeing the Belmont coach but apart from noting it was rather shabby he hadn't given it much thought. He hadn't had to ride in it, of course—if he had then things might have been different. Would he have complained? Probably. Eugenie was right, he *was* used to the best, but that was hardly his fault, was it?

"Am I supposed to go about in rags just to show my compassion for others less fortunate?" he asked gruffly. "I can't help being a duke. That's what I am."

Her mouth twitched, as if she might be about to smile. "I know that's what you are, but you could spare a thought now and again for those of us who aren't dukes and are never likely to be."

"I'm sorry," he said stiffly.

"Apology accepted."

A silence fell and it remained for most of the journey. The pleasures and terrors of the woods now seemed a long way behind them, even if they were not forgotten. Not by Sinclair, anyway.

"She sounds very like your mother." Lord Ridley's voice interrupted his memories and brought him back to the comforts of Framlingbury.

"Eugenie?"

His uncle raised his eyebrows. "Lord, no! I meant Annabelle. She sounds very like your mother when she was that age. Did you know she rebelled against marrying your father?"

Sinclair felt uncomfortable, remembering his mother's anger and her tears after Annabelle ran off, and her confidences when she feared he might be going to make his own misalliance.

"Our father had more or less run through the family fortune. I was supposed to find an heiress but there never seemed to be one about when I wanted one. Thing is I always went for the disreputable sort of girl, just like our father. He was a Bohemian, Sinclair, which is why your mother is so down on them. He was only a gentleman by name; at heart he was a ruffian and didn't care who knew it. Anyway, the time came when we were about to be evicted from Framlingbury and the family clubbed together and told your mother she had to marry your father, the duke. He was the only one who'd come up to the mark at that point, though there was another chap she was keen on. Handsome and penniless, that sort of thing, no good at all in the circumstances."

"I didn't realize," Sinclair said quietly. "Poor mother."

"Yes, well," his uncle looked uncomfortable, "she didn't like being forced into marriage. Your father was a lot older than her, very staid in his ways, but he was a duke, damn it. There was no other solution to our problems and your mother knew it."

"So she was the sacrificial lamb."

"I suppose she was. The experience made her bitter, though, Sinclair. She never forgave us, and especially not our father. If he hadn't spent all his money on his own pleasures, running with the

Bohemian set, she might have married for love. You know she still has a horror of such things? Well, of course you do. Remember the way she went after you when you took to painting your ladies?"

"I remember."

"You don't know the half of it, though. She came up here, so cross there was no reasoning with her. I tried to explain you were nothing like our father but she wouldn't have it. And it was my fault, of course, for leading you astray." He shook his head. "She had changed, Sinclair, and not for the better. We might have saved Framlingbury but I lost my sister."

It was horrible to think his mother could lose all warmth and humanity, could turn from being as warmhearted and reckless as Annabelle into a woman who no longer cared for anything but appearances. But at least Sinclair could understand why she was as she was, even if he didn't agree with her.

"I like your lady friend."

Lord Ridley's words reminded him that as long as he had Eugenie he would never turn into ice, like his mother. But he shook his head rather regretfully.

"She's not my lady friend. Not that I haven't tried. But she informs me she will be no man's mistress. She values herself far too highly."

"Hmm. I like the sound of that. A woman like that should be treasured and pampered and thoroughly loved."

"That's as may be, uncle," he said bitterly, "but

the Belmonts are rather low on the social scale."

Lord Ridley eyed him curiously. "Good God, Sinclair, are you thinking of marrying her? Your mother really would throw a pink fit." He paused, stroking his chin. "Might be worth seeing."

"Uncle, I hardly think this is any of your business—"

Lord Ridley waved a hand. "You're very touchy on the subject. Is she really so very ineligible? Her manners and deportment are ladylike. Indeed she could pass for an aristocrat, if she wished."

Why was it that one's relations thought they had the right to discuss personal matters with one? Sinclair thought irritably.

"If you must know then yes! She is completely ineligible. Her father is a baronet but he is penniless and sells horses at the local horse fair. Her mother seems to be permanently locked in her bedchamber with hysterics and she has four brothers . . . Well, one of them is acceptable. One of them has eloped with my sister. The other two are the devil's twins."

"No relatives who can be called upon to raise the tone?"

"Her aunt is married to a soap manufacturer."

"Oh dear, it gets worse." He eyed Sinclair sympathetically.

"And her great-grandmother was a chambermaid at the palace who became a mistress of George the Second."

Lord Ridley laughed. "Capital!" he said. "You genuinely admire this girl, don't you?"

The St. Johns weren't a close family, but his

maternal uncle had always been fond of him and
Sinclair had reciprocated the feeling. When he
was young Lord Ridley was the only one he felt
he could open his heart to, and he had done so,
much to his mother's anger. It was true, his uncle
had encouraged him in his artistic talents, advis-
ing him to follow his heart and be damned to the
rest. It had been good advice, although at that age
Sinclair hadn't been strong enough to defy his
mother and follow it.

"Perhaps I may be able to help," Lord Ridley
said. "I know a bit about females, you know. I'm
in the market for a wife myself."

Sinclair swallowed his spleen and gave a sickly
smile. "You've been in the market for a wife for
twenty years, uncle."

Lord Ridley looked surprised, and then he
laughed. "So I have, so I have. Well, take warning
from that. You don't want to still be a bachelor at
my age."

Sinclair couldn't be bothered arguing. His uncle
might play at matchmaker but he was afraid of his
sister, the dowager duchess. He wouldn't do anything to bring her raging down upon him. Lord
Ridley enjoyed the quiet life.

Framlingbury was small by Somerton's stan-
dards but Eugenie found the golden stone and
airy rooms far more pleasant than Somerton's
stilted glory. This was a house one could live in,
where one could be one's self. She doubted the
same could be said for the duke's residence, where
everything was designed for show, to display the

grandeur of the St. John family and remind one of their importance and, in the Belmont's case, one's own inferiority.

How could anyone be happy living in a house like that? Certainly not warmhearted Eugenie. Not that she'd ever have the chance! She'd long ago come to accept that.

Lord Ridley, too, was a great deal less stiff and proud than his sister and nephew. Unlike the dowager duchess's rude stare, he had greeted Eugenie amiably. He'd asked her polite questions and then listened intently to her answers, genuinely interested in what she had to say. He had an easy way of laughing, too, and there was a certain gleam to his eye she found rather flattering. Although it left her wondering why middle-aged men like Lord Ridley and Major Banks found her so enticing while younger men wanted to be her friends.

Apart from Sinclair, of course.

She smiled to herself and lifted her face to the sun. The weather had returned to some semblance of summer since they'd arrived, as if the incident in the woods had never been. That was how she thought of it now. "The incident." Although in her dreams she went over every word, every touch, every glorious moment, until her body was flushed and feverish and she longed for Sinclair to burst into her bedchamber and claim her.

She was fairly sure he wouldn't. He was too much the duke for that, too steeped in proper manners and proper ways of behavior. And of course that was what had drawn her to him in the first place, she reminded herself. He was so much more respectable than her own family. Was it wrong of her to wish that he would behave with just a little less propriety?

When they had begun to play their game of dares he'd been quite reckless, deliciously so, but she'd never felt as if she might be hurt by him, at least not intentionally. He made her feel safe. She knew that was something she'd been lacking all her life, that sense of stability and security. At Belmont Hall anything could happen and frequently did.

Now they were here at Framlingbury, it seemed that Sinclair had turned back into the cold and arrogant duke he'd been before. Eugenie felt as if he was growing far too distant, far too lofty for her. Oh yes, he'd changed. But had he done so on purpose? Was he withdrawing himself from her, hiding behind an icy wall of privilege?

If only . . . But she stopped that thought before it could form. It was no use wishing for what could never be. She was here to save Terry and bring him home. Anything else was unimportant.

Lord Ridley sent out spies to try to discover which way Annabelle and Terry had gone, but as yet there had been no word. The northern highways were empty of anyone resembling the couple and their chaperone, so they must have taken a lesser route. Eugenie hoped Terry knew what he was doing, that whatever the outcome he might be happy living with his decision.

Meanwhile Robert and Georgie had become

quite a team, and Robert had asked Eugenie's opinion on whether it would be possible for him and his wife to take on the boy. They had no children of their own and they'd always longed for one.

"He can be a little rascal, miss, but I don't mind that. I can steer him in the right direction, just like I did the duke, many years ago."

Eugenie had looked at him in surprise. "Have you known the duke that long, Robert?"

"Yes, miss, since he was a little nipper."

"I always think of him as the perfectly behaved child."

Robert had eyed her cautiously. "Well . . . I can say he weren't no angel, miss. They sent him off to school and he hated that, but I suppose every boy in his high position has to bear the bad with the good. Then he got that painting lark into his head . . ."

"What painting lark?"

Again Robert considered his words. "I could be speaking out of turn here, miss."

"I promise I won't repeat anything you say, Robert."

He nodded, accepting her at her word. "He wanted to be an artist, miss. A painter. You can imagine how well that went down with the duchess, as she was then. If he'd gambled his inheritance away on the cards they would have been upset, but at least that was what gentlemen do. Artists, according to the duchess, are Bohemians, not respectable at all. She made sure the tutor who'd encouraged him was sent packing and

Sinclair was told to pack up his paints and never put brush to canvas again, unless he wanted to be disowned."

Eugenie felt herself trembling with righteous anger on Sinclair's behalf.

Robert saw her feelings clearly enough and tried to sooth them. "He recovered," he assured her. "Went on to find other hobbies, more fitting for a gentleman."

"Well, they have certainly done a good job of turning him into the perfect duke," she said. "More's the shame."

Robert's eyes sparkled. "Don't you believe it, miss. He still has his days . . . and nights, when he's off painting away. No one to stop him now, see. He hasn't changed that much, not underneath."

Sinclair the Bohemian? Eugenie tried to imagine what sort of pictures he'd painted. They must have been risqué if they caused such consternation in his family. Perhaps, if she asked him nicely, he would paint her?

She thought she'd like that.

She'd like it very much.

Chapter 29

Sinclair had spent the morning riding one of his uncle's horses, enjoying the exercise after being cooped up in the coach for so long. As he took a shortcut past the formal garden back to the stables, he noticed Eugenie walking there with a young man.

Their heads were bent close together and they seemed so intent on each other that neither looked up at his passing.

"That is young Nicholas," his uncle said, when Sinclair asked him. "His father farms a good deal of land he leases from me. Nicholas will take over one day. They are a respectable family, well off, too."

Sinclair found himself uncomfortable with the notion of "Young Nicholas" walking in the garden alone with Eugenie, and said so.

"Good God, nephew, are you suddenly becoming all namby-pamby? After you've been racketing about the countryside with the girl?"

"That's different."

"I don't see why. Young Nicholas seems to have

developed quite an interest in Miss Belmont." He fixed Sinclair with a serious look. "You've said yourself that she's rejected your less than respectable offer."

"It was a perfectly respectable offer! Well," he muttered, "you know what I mean."

"Oh I know what you mean, dear boy! Swish apartment and all that. Strange she rejected you." His eyes twinkled. "And of course you can't marry her, can you? So what's left for the poor girl? You should be thinking of getting her comfortably settled. I think you could do a lot worse than to put her in the way of Nicholas and see what transpires."

Sinclair found he did not wish to see Eugenie comfortably settled. All very well for his uncle to place the practical solution before him but Sinclair was not feeling practical.

Not where Eugenie was concerned.

Eugenie was surprised to see Sinclair in his riding clothes striding toward her through the perennial borders. Mr. Fenton had just left her after a lengthy conversation about the butcher's daughter and how he longed to marry her, if only his family would come round to the idea. Eugenie wasn't surprised to be the recipient of a discussion of Nicholas Fenton's personal problems; it was something that happened to her often.

"Your Grace," she said, with a little curtsey and a smile.

"Miss Belmont." He glanced about. "Your companion is gone then?"

"You mean Mr. Fenton? Yes, he's gone home. Did you wish to speak to him?"

As she was conversing she noticed he looked a little ragged—not his clothes, they were impeccable as always, but his demeanor. Had something occurred? Bad news regarding Terry and Annabelle? But before she could ask Sinclair spoke again.

"I believe Mr. Fenton has been calling rather often?"

That was when the idea struck her that he might be jealous. That he imagined Nicholas was pursuing her and might win her and she would be happily married to another man.

Eugenie knew she shouldn't be pleased at the idea of the duke being so possessive of her, but she couldn't help it. She *was* pleased. And she was wicked enough to want to tease him into showing his feelings.

"Yes, he has come here every day. Twice yesterday. Do you know he has the bluest eyes I have ever seen?"

Sinclair gave her a sharp glance. "Indeed. From what I saw of him they looked a little too close together for him to be trustworthy."

"Oh no, I am sure Mr. Fenton is extremely trustworthy."

He grunted, and she decided to postpone her game.

"Have you heard anything about the runaways?" she said anxiously.

"No."

"Where could they have got to?" Eugenie sighed, downcast.

He reached for her hand. As he touched her she felt the tingle of attraction between them, and her blood grew warm. She tried to withdraw from his grip, but he held on, stepping closer, so that she had to tilt her head to meet his eyes.

"I wish . . ." he began, but didn't finish. His mouth closed tightly on whatever wishes he'd been about to share with her.

His fingers brushed across her cheek, lingering on her lips, and then he was gone.

Eugenie watched him walk away, longing for him to take her in his arms and make her body sing. It was the first time since they'd arrived that the Sinclair she knew and loved had shown himself. Yes, she loved him, she admitted bleakly. It was a love that could never have a happy ending but that did not stop her from feeling it.

He'd meant to stay away. He'd sworn he would not go near her again. But here he was, in only his breeches and stocking feet, outside her bedchamber looking down at the pale glow from under the door, like some lovesick hero in a Byronic poem.

His body trembled with need. He wanted her in his arms, his body inside hers. He couldn't bear the thought of her with someone else—he'd been tormented by visions of her kissing that Fenton boy. His thoughts were chaotic.

He thought about knocking but it seemed ridiculous, so he simply opened the door and took a step inside her room.

She was reading, propped up with pillows, her hair loose about her shoulders and curling wildly, catching fiery light from the candles. Her skin had a soft warm hue, the shawl about her shoulders slipping to disclose a nightdress of plain white cambric.

If she was Helen of Troy he couldn't have thought her more beautiful.

Her eyes were wide and dark. She didn't speak and neither did he. They knew each other's desires too well and with a need so desperate and raw there was only one way to assuage it.

He lay down beside her and blew out the candle. A moment later her hand touched his hair, fingers sliding through the thick wave at his temple, and the next moment her lips pressed to his skin.

"Sinclair . . ."

Blindly he lifted his face and found her mouth. "Don't speak," he muttered against her lips. "Pretend this is a dream."

"Yes, a dream," she breathed.

Their lips clung. He heard himself groan. Felt her arms slip about his neck as she pressed closer, the soft curves of her body melding itself to his harder angles. He curved his arm about her hips and his hand splayed over her bottom; she was so accessible without stays and petticoats. He hardly knew where to begin.

He lowered his face to her breasts, nuzzling against her, drawing up her voluminous nightgown so that he could press his skin to hers, breathe in her scent, taste her with his lips and tongue.

She was quivering with desire, and he could hear her heartbeat thundering in his ear as he held her close. He slid his hands up her thighs, reveling in her warm skin.

"I can't sleep," she said, a catch in her voice.

"Nor can I."

He drew her closer, and she cupped his face with her palms to kiss his mouth, his cheeks, his eyelids, as if she would know each inch of him. His hands closed on her hips, urging her. He was so hard. He knew if she touched him he'd explode and yet he wanted her to touch him.

"If this is really a dream . . ." she began softly. "I can do whatever I want and it won't matter."

"Yes."

She reached to stroke the ridge of him through his breeches.

He groaned, dropping his brow to her shoulder.

"Should I stop?"

"No, don't stop . . ."

When she undid his fastenings and began to explore he did not demur, giving himself into her power. She stroked the velvet length of him, her fingers curious, eager.

Her breathing was ragged. Touching him was arousing her. He cupped her mound in his palm, feeling the moist heat of her, and then used his fingers to tease her swollen, slick flesh.

It was time.

Slowly, he eased his way inside her. She was so ready there was no resistance, but the sheer joy of being within her, of knowing her desire for him, was urging him to drive wildly into her body and finish it.

He restrained himself with difficulty.

He rose again, until he was almost completely free of her, and then slid down into her. Slowly, with excruciating care. Using his powers to increase her pleasure. And his.

Her passion was building. Soon she was panting, the muscles of her thighs trembling, her breasts rising and falling, as she moved more quickly upon him. He caught her hips in his hands and thrust hard inside her, meeting her, pushing her.

And then it happened, the wild insane moment when their bodies merged and melded. He covered her mouth with his to stop her cries of ecstasy and his own groans.

For a long time they were quiet, allowing their breaths to slow and their hearts to stop racing. The perspiration cooled on their bodies. Then at last Eugenie shivered and sat up. Her white nightgown enclosed her, her hair was loose about her shoulders. She looked virginal, but he knew she was his own personal succubus, who came to him every night in the darkness and tormented him until dawn.

"Sinclair . . ." she began. "We cannot go on like this."

"I know."

He kissed her again, tenderly now, sated, and rose from her bed. The door closed behind him.

Eugenie lay back and closed her eyes. She knew she should be full of anxiety but she couldn't feel anything but the dull throb of pleasure. If she really did love him then she suspected he was close to loving her. Not that it made any difference to their future.

Half asleep now, she decided on a new epitaph for her gravestone:

Eugenie Belmont, who loved a duke, and died of a broken heart. . .

"They were in Stoke-on-Trent on Monday," Sinclair announced, looking up with a glitter in his eyes as Eugenie entered the drawing room. "Finally some news." He paced toward the windows and then back again, too wound up with excitement to stay still.

In the meantime Lord Ridley had risen to his feet and set about making Eugenie comfortable in a green silk-covered chair. "We have heard back from my spies," he said, with a wink. "The runaway pair has been spotted. They were on the Manchester road."

"Will we be able to catch them before they reach the border?" she asked anxiously.

"Perhaps you should stay here at Framlingbury," Lord Ridley said. "Let my nephew chase after them."

There was a pause. Sinclair looked irritated and distinctly uncomfortable. "No one is forcing Miss Belmont to go."

"My brother will need me," Eugenie said cautiously. She knew then they had been discussing her predicament, as if she was something untidy to be sorted and tucked away.

"There, you see," Sinclair declared triumphantly. "Miss Belmont wants to come with me."

His uncle frowned. "She hasn't exactly said that, Sinclair. Is that what you really want, Miss Belmont?"

Suddenly Eugenie felt as if she was at a cross-roads. He was asking her if she wanted to remain here and pursue her friendship with Nicholas. She was not silly enough not to realize Lord Ridley had been blatantly throwing them together over the past days. And it wasn't as if she didn't enjoy his company, but he was in love with someone else. Just as Eugenie was.

Well, there was her answer. She'd give up the Nicholases of the world any day to go off with the duke to who knew where and get into all sorts of trouble. If she was honest it wasn't only the need to help Terry that was driving her but the need to be with Sinclair.

"I want to go with the duke," she said firmly.

Lord Ridley sighed and shook his head. "Dear me, you are as bad as each other. Very well then. Now that is settled . . . With the roads in the state they are it will be quicker if you go by canal."

Eugenie saw that he had set out a map on the table before her, evidently he and Sinclair had been examining it before she arrived. She could see that it displayed the north of the country with its growing industrial towns and vast tracks of moorland and mountains. There were blue lines crisscrossing the land, some wide and some narrow. They passed through the towns and cities, intersecting and then traveling in all directions, to the ports on the coast as well as on to smaller towns and villages. For some reason there seemed to be a great many blue lines.

"Canals," Lord Ridley explained, tapping his finger on the intricate network. "They cut across

the countryside, using water as a means of trans-
port as opposed to badly maintained roads. The
larger canals are used for barges carrying raw
materials to the mills from the ports, for instance
from Liverpool to Manchester, and then when
the cotton has been spun or the wool woven, it
is returned to Liverpool to be shipped out. But
there are many smaller canals used for transport-
ing local produce from town to village and back
again, or carrying passengers."

He'd grown enthusiastic, and Eugenie could
see that the canals were a passion with him.

"And one of these barges will take us on
board?" Sinclair said doubtfully.

"Oh there's no need for that. I have a narrow
boat of my own, a vessel built especially for traveling the canals. I find it very restful on the water,
once I leave behind the busier commercial routes.
And I always have horses stabled at the end of my
journey, in Wexham. Once there all you'd have to
do is head for the border and stop the lovelorn
pair from plighting their troth." He raised his eyebrows. "So to speak."

Sinclair shifted restlessly. "I don't know, Uncle.
A narrow boat seems a peculiar way to follow
someone."

"Nonsense, my boy! It is the perfect way to
follow someone and I won't hear any more objections. I consider the matter settled."

Sinclair was wearing his haughty look but he
didn't offer any further arguments.

"I must write to my family before we leave,"

Eugenie said, hastily getting to her feet again. "They must be dreadfully worried."

At least she hoped so, she thought, avoiding Sinclair's cynical eyes. Her father would be disappointed if the elopement didn't come off, but the rest of the family would be relieved to have gotten out of yet another scrape.

"Be ready to leave in an hour," Sinclair called after her curtly.

"Give the poor girl two," Lord Ridley retorted. "What woman could be ready in one hour?"

"Eugenie can," Sinclair said with a note of pride in his voice.

"Oh-ho," his uncle murmured, with a wink at Eugenie, "then she is a unique specimen of her sex."

"She is matchless, Uncle."

Eugenie closed the door, her heart thumping. Matchless? Did he really mean that or was he teasing her? She didn't have time to consider the question now, she told herself, as she hurried toward the stairs. She had to pack and pen a brief note. Perhaps it was just as well she had so few clothes to worry about, although Lord Ridley's servants had cleaned and pressed what she did have so she was fit to be seen.

It occurred to her to wonder what Annabelle must be feeling. From what Sinclair had said his sister had taken very little with her, too, almost as if she was intent on leaving the past behind. But Annabelle was not Eugenie. All her life she had been used to having the best of everything.

Eugenie could not help but wonder how much the duke's sister was enjoying being out in the world, cut off from her family, reliant upon her own wits and Terry.

Remembering the way Sinclair had behaved when his comfortable coach was taken from him, she did not think Annabelle would be enjoying it at all.

Chapter 30

Terry had reluctantly let the coach go and taken to horseback. Annabelle insisted that was the only way she could continue the journey north and he was willing to believe her. But Annabelle was no horsewoman, and he should have remembered that. After only a day of riding she declared her back broken and could not rise from her bed at the inn. Lizzie, herself stiff and sore from the unfamiliar motion of the horse, eventually coaxed her into eating some toast and then they went out for a stroll, to stretch her "poor aching legs."

Manchester was one of the larger and smokier northern cities, and the noise from the mills, running day and night, was not something any of them was used to. Annabelle held her handkerchief to her nose and mouth and gasped and groaned, while Lizzie gazed about wide-eyed. Finally they succumbed to Annabelle's complaints and returned to the inn, where Annabelle shook out her skirts and pointed out the soot she found upon them, as well as the reek of smoke in her hair.

"How can people live like this?" she wondered.

"I suppose they have no choice," Terry said wearily.

"How can they have no choice? Everyone has a choice."

He looked at her in amazement. He shouldn't have been surprised at her lack of worldliness, not after the past few days, and yet he was.

Lizzie watched them uneasily, aware another argument was brewing.

"What have I said?" Annabelle demanded haughtily. When he didn't answer her eyes grew wary and a little anxious. "Terry, have I said something stupid again?"

He shook his head. "No, of course not, only . . . Annabelle, if a man, or a woman, has little or no money, how do you think they have a choice about how they earn their living? They will take any job offered them. I believe mill jobs pay well, so I suppose they will take them over laboring in a field or washing clothing for gentlefolk. With the money they can buy food and clothing, they may even buy a house—or rent one. If there are children, then more money needs to be made. Do you see? Not everyone is as fortunate as you, who does not need to work to buy things, because your family already has money."

"I am sure my ancestors worked very hard for their money," she reminded him coolly.

"I'm sure they did," he agreed, although he wasn't at all sure about that. He remembered his father saying the St. Johns had got rich from fleecing their tenants and enclosing their fields.

For a moment Annabelle was unusually quiet and then she sighed. "I am being stupid, aren't I? You have done all of this for me and I have been very ungrateful. I've never stopped complaining. I've even been ill on you, poor Terry."

She reached out to touch his hand and smiled. She was so beautiful that for a moment Terry thought he might be able to love her after all.

But then she spoiled it.

Her gaze went beyond him and her eyes narrowed. "I loathe the color of the walls in this room," she said. "Why on earth would anyone choose such a sour shade of yellow?"

Terry stood up. "I think I might go for a walk before dinner," he said, and closed the door as she began to complain about being left alone. He knew if he spent another hour with her, another minute, he would leap from the window.

He didn't realize at first that Lizzie had followed him out, and when he did he turned to face her, to tell her to return to the room, that he was not very good company just now. Instead to his surprise he found himself holding out his arm. With a shy glance at him, she slipped her hand through his elbow.

"She has been very spoiled, you know."

"Don't make excuses for her, Lizzie."

"I'm not excusing her. Annabelle is what she is. Perhaps you saw her differently, Terry. She is a beautiful girl. Could you have been wearing rose-tinted glasses?"

He smiled without humor. "You mean, was I blinded by her pretty face?"

"I am not blaming you for that," she said earnestly. "Annabelle has a great many admirers. She does not mean to break hearts and disappoint, it is just that she has been brought up to think only of herself."

"You need not make excuses for her, Lizzie. Or for me. And you needn't fear I will run away and leave you both. I won't do that. I have been brought up as a gentleman, even if the duke does not consider me one. I started this madness and I will see it through, at least until you and Annabelle are safe."

"I know you will," she said gently.

They wandered listlessly through the grubby streets and smoky alleys.

"Do you know I have never been farther north than Gloucester?" she said. "This is a great adventure for me, and I am determined to look upon it in that way. My life so far has been very boring."

Terry wondered what she would think of his family, his scheming father and Jack with his menagerie and the wild twins. Her blue eyes would grow very round. And yet he had the sense she would not judge them, but she would enjoy them and accept them for what they were.

However it was unlikely he would see his family for some time and possibly never again if he did not sort out his current problems. The riding on horseback idea hadn't worked. Could he afford to hire another coach? He knew he could not. He could probably afford a two-wheeled dog cart. Pity Erik the goat was back at home, he was always good at pulling carts. He imagined the look on Annabelle's face if he drove up to the door of the inn in such a vehicle.

The image struck him as funny and he began to chuckle and then laugh, and then he couldn't stop. Lizzie, concerned, tried to discover what was wrong, her worried face close to his. Finally he sagged against a brick wall, weak at the knees, wiping the tears from his eyes.

"I'm sorry," he said, sobering. "I have gone a little mad, I think."

And then he noticed that they had walked to where there was a canal running right through the city. An idea came to him and, grasping Lizzie's hand, he climbed up onto a hump-backed bridge that spanned the canal and they leaned over the edge, watching as narrow barges made their busy way along the greasy stretch of water, drawn along by tow ropes attached to horses and steered by the bargees at the helm.

"Do you think we could hire a barge?" Terry said, grinning at her. "I have heard the canals run into the north. We could travel a good distance without needing to ride in a coach or on horseback."

Surely Annabelle would not be able to complain about that?

They began to walk along the canal until they found one of the barges being loaded with bags and boxes and dressed timber, and made some inquiries. The deal was quickly done and by the time they headed back toward the inn Terry felt his old self again. Indeed his step was quite jaunty, and Lizzie, squeezing his arm and smiling up at him, appeared merry, too.

Maybe, just maybe, he told himself, everything was going to turn out right after all.

Chapter 31

L ord Ridley's narrow boat was a long low craft, designed to move easily through the narrow waterways, with their aqueducts and locks and bridges. It was painted in bright blues and yellows and reds, and as Eugenie picked her way down the stairs into the inside of the vessel, she found it quite pleasant and roomy. The captain, known as Johnno, was a short wide man with tattoos of mermaids on his forearms, who informed them he had once sailed the oceans but after one shipwreck too many had decided the inland waterways were far safer.

"Rufus will get you to Wexham," he said, nodding to where a large feathery footed shire horse stood on the towpath, tethered to the boat by the length of the tow rope. Rufus would pull them along the canal while his master steered.

"As long as we make good time," Sinclair said brusquely.

The captain gave him a look and a nod. "Never you mind. Lord Ridley has given me me orders, Your Grace."

Why didn't that fill him with confidence? Sinclair asked himself, as he went below. Uneasily he glanced about at his surroundings. The interior of the narrow boat was very luxurious, almost dangerously so in the circumstances. They were on a mission to rescue his sister, after all, not taking a holiday.

"I knew this was a mistake," he said. "At least I know where I am with horses."

"You hated that coach, remember?"

"We could have had my uncle's coach."

"We'll find them," Eugenie soothed, feeling the need to say something positive when he looked so dour.

But Sinclair was no longer listening to her. He was staring at a small pencil sketch hanging on the wall. He took a step closer, as if he couldn't quite believe what he was seeing, and then with a curse he swung around and caught Eugenie's arms, hustling her back toward the stairs.

"What is it?" she cried nervously, trying to see behind him. "Sinclair, whatever is the matter?"

"We can't stay here," he muttered.

"Sinclair, what are you talking about? We have no choice. Stop it!"

He did stop, and met her eyes, and she saw that there was something in his that was close to fear. It struck her as so unlike the Sinclair she knew that she pulled away, stepping around him, and making her way purposefully toward the framed sketch.

"Please, Eugenie. Don't." He made another grab for her, but she avoided him, and then she was standing before the sketch.

It was a drawing of a naked woman, standing by an open window, her hair unbound and curling about her hips. Eugenie didn't consider herself a prude, and there was nothing obscene about what she saw now, but it was very sensual. There was the sense of something, or someone, beyond the window who had caught the subject's attention and the fact that she was standing naked led Eugenie to believe whoever was outside was the woman's lover.

Sinclair had followed her, and was standing behind her. He was very still, almost as if he was holding his breath. She understood then that it wasn't fear she had seen in his eyes, but vulnerability. She saw it now in his stance, in his expression, as his dark eyes searched hers as if waiting for an axe to fall.

"Whatever is the matter?" she said. "Sinclair?"

And then she remembered the conversation she'd had with Robert Coachman and she turned again to the framed sketch and searched for the artist's signature at the bottom. Just as she'd thought: *S St. John*. This was one of Sinclair's works from his brief career as an artist.

"You did this?"

He nodded his head, but his eyes remained on hers, searching, as if he was desperately uncertain of her reaction. As if her opinion mattered. Of course he would feel like that after his mother's attitude to his art, but he should have known Eugenie would never destroy his confidence in such a way.

"Sinclair, it's beautiful," she said gently. "Really beautiful."

His shoulders relaxed, his mouth twitched into a relieved smile.

"Although of course I disapprove of you having naked women in your company. Who was she?"

His eyes gleamed with humor. "A model I hired. I didn't know any young women willing to undress for me then."

Eugenie tilted her head, examining the sketch again. "Why did you stop?" she said blithely, as if she didn't know.

He didn't answer, saying instead, "I've wondered whether you might be willing to pose for me. With your clothes on, of course."

She smiled a wicked little smile. "Where's the fun in that?"

He reached for her, tugging her close. She tilted back her head, watching the heat gathering in his eyes, waiting for what she knew would come.

To her surprise he didn't carry her to the bed, but lifted her onto the table in the central part of the boat, edging her thighs apart and standing between them. Slowly, intently, he began to unfasten her bodice. Her breath caught in her throat as first his fingers and then his mouth began an intense exploration of her breasts. She cupped the back of his head, pressing him close, lost in sensation.

By the time he reached beneath her skirts, she was damp and aching, wanting him urgently. It was her fingers which opened his breeches and caressed the hard length of his cock, drawing him to the entrance to her body, wrapping her thighs about his hips as he drove forward.

Voices sounded outside and then their captain,

his voice drifting down from the deck. "We're about to head off. Do you need anything, Your Grace?"

Their eyes met. Eugenie bit her lip. "No, thank you," Sinclair called in reply. "I have everything I need right here."

The boat rocked, began to move.

With his eyes closed and beads of sweat on his brow, Sinclair groaned softly as he thrust again, taking his time. Their buildup to ecstasy was gradual, relentless, and she wondered if she would ever reach her peak, and then when she did it was so tumultuous she felt as if her heart might stop altogether.

Afterward they clung together, weak and shaken. Dreamily she said, "Why did your uncle hang that sketch?"

He lifted her in his arms and she clasped her hands about his neck, resting her head against his shoulder.

"He admired it," Sinclair admitted. "He was the only one who didn't think I should take up more gentlemanly pursuits, like horse racing. He even encouraged me to keep drawing and painting. He did a little sketching himself but he always claimed he didn't have my talent."

"And yet you stopped?"

"Yes. At least . . . lately I've been playing about with my paints again," he said wryly. "Much to my mother's disgust."

"Well, as far as I'm concerned you can paint from dawn to dusk."

The words came out before she considered

them, and then she flushed and hid her face from him. "That is, if I had anything to say about it. Which obviously I don't."

He set her down on the lavish bed and she watched him as he began searching through some of the drawers in the table. "My uncle said he'd left some here somewhere . . ." Soon he found what he was looking for, a sketch pad and pencils, and held them up.

"You said you wouldn't mind," he reminded her, rather diffident.

Eugenie, who wasn't at all sure about this, managed to put on an air of ease. "How should I . . . eh . . ."

"Just like that. Perhaps lean back a little, and hold the blanket to your breasts. Like that." He smiled at her. "Oh yes, very nice."

After a moment, with the silence broken only by the scratching of his pencil on the paper, she said, "You won't hang this one in someone's boat, will you, Sinclair? I don't think my family would appreciate it."

He grinned. "This one is strictly private," he answered her. "This one is for me."

"Good."

They smiled at each other and Eugenie knew with a sense of sheer relief that Sinclair, *her* Sinclair, was back.

She'd fallen asleep.

He wasn't surprised. She must be exhausted after all their adventures, despite their brief respite at Framlingbury. He leaned back in his chair, stretching out stiff muscles, raising his arms over his head, opening and closing his fingers. He'd enjoyed drawing her, and then watching her sleep. Her riotous hair fell over her cheek, tangled strands tumbling down over the side of the bed toward the floor. Her arm, soft and pale and rounded, was caught in a shaft of light from a narrow strip of window in the deck above, and she breathed softly, peacefully, like an innocent child.

He felt happy. A sense of deep contentment he couldn't remember ever feeling before. The movement of the narrow boat, the occupation of his eyes and his fingers, the making of a work of his talent and imagination. All in the company of a woman he was besotted with. If only life could always be like this.

But of course it couldn't. How could it be? The world was still outside and soon it would interfere with them, tearing them apart.

There was another possibility.

Sinclair rubbed his hand across his jaw, feeling the beginnings of a beard. He could take Eugenie's hand in his and they could face the world together. People might sneer and mock, but such things couldn't hurt them.

Not unless they allowed them to.

Chapter 32

For two days they made their way along the waterways, feeling as if they were in a secluded world all of their own. Captain Johnno went about his work with Rufus for company, saying little and paying them no attention. Lord Ridley had chosen him well, Eugenie thought. She wondered, too, whether Sinclair's uncle might have had something else in mind when he insisted they take the canals north. Something other than catching up with Annabelle and Terry, that is.

Could His Lordship be playing matchmaker for his favorite nephew? Was he giving them the present of this idyllic time together before the real world intruded once more?

Sinclair sketched her in various stages of undress, all of them flattering in Eugenie's eyes. But the one she liked best was a sketch he did of her face, half turned away, a little smile tugging at her lips and her lashes lowered, as though she was thinking pleasant and slightly wicked thoughts.

She probably was, and all of them about Sinclair.

And then they made love, for hours, lying in each others arms, falling asleep and then waking up to make love again. She had never been so happy and she believed Sinclair felt the same. Perhaps that was why neither of them mentioned what might happen when this interlude was over. They did not speak of the future, or even the possibility of a future.

To speak of it was to make it all too real and then they would have to make decisions. Every other time they had begun to discuss their future they had fallen out. So Eugenie preferred to drift, with the narrow boat, and enjoy each moment as it came.

But of course their journey had an ending, and now it was fast approaching. When Johnno informed them they were approaching the last lock on this stretch of canal, the last lock before Wexham, where they would take to the road once more, Eugenie was shocked. The last lock had a certain significance. She could no longer pretend they would go on forever, drifting like flotsam, careless of what was ahead.

Sinclair seemed to feel it, too, although he didn't say so. But he was quieter, more introverted, caught up in his own thoughts.

Of course she didn't ask what those thoughts were, and if he wondered the same about her, then Sinclair didn't ask, either.

The lock consisted of wooden gates and levers, and by the working of these the lockkeeper allowed the narrow boat to pass into a closed off section of the canal. The gate behind the boat was then closed while the level of water was altered by sluice gates. When the level was the same as the canal in front of the boat, the other gate was opened to allow the boat to continue on its journey.

Sinclair and Eugenie had already passed through numerous lock gates on their journey, and rather than staying on board they climbed up onto the towpath while the sluice gate was open and the water rushed in, raising the level of the river. This was an isolated stretch of canal, with meadows and fields surrounding the lockkeeper's cottage, and they strolled through wildflowers and long grass, the sun warm on their heads.

Eugenie expected Sinclair to speak about his uncle's horses waiting at Wexham and the journey north and what they must do, but he said nothing of it. There were willows growing in the marshy land south of the lock gates, and instead they found a place to sit in the shade, watching the water birds going about their daily tasks.

Sinclair was wearing shoes without stockings—he'd taken to wandering around barefoot lately—his trouser bottoms rolled up, as were his sleeves. He'd taken to the narrow boat as if he'd lived on one all his life, and the change in him was remarkable. Eugenie, glancing at him surreptitiously, wondered how long it would be before he reverted to the arrogant duke, once he got back to Somerton.

She dreaded that.

But still she said nothing.

When he reached for her hand, turning it over in his, lifting her palm to his lips, she smiled at him. She knew there was love in her eyes and that he could probably read it plainly, if he wanted to, but she didn't care.

He sighed and rose to his feet, bringing her with him. The sun was lowering in the sky, the day waning. Another day gone, another day closer to whatever lay before them. Suddenly cold, Eugenie shivered.

Sinclair didn't ask why. He simply slipped his arm about her waist and held her close.

On their way back to the narrow boat the lock-keeper's wife spotted them and called out to them. Would they have tea in her cottage?

Her name was Mrs. Burdock and she sat them down at the tiny table in her little kitchen and proceeded to set out her best teacups, blue with pink flowers. As Mrs. Burdock chatted away, her northern accent difficult for Eugenie to understand, she glanced at Sinclair and caught his smile. And for a moment she felt as if they were an ordinary couple.

"Such a pretty time of year," Mrs. Burdock went on. "You wouldn't believe how cold it gets in the winter. Frost an inch thick on the canal some mornings."

Eugenie's gaze rested on a tall dresser opposite her, with its proud display of patterned china, her best wares probably. Mrs. Burdock had been baking and now she produced a plate heavy with large flat cakes with jam in the middle. Eugenie accepted one with pleasure, and the warm crusty texture crumbled into her mouth, the jam sweet and hot on her tongue.

Sinclair complimented Mrs. Burdock on them and she promptly handed him another.

"Captain Johnno says that you're an artist, sir."

"I . . ." Sinclair pushed a lock of his hair off his forehead. Under the table his feet in their shoes and no stockings were truly Bohemian. He gave Eugenie a smiling glance and said, "Yes, I am."

She thought it was probably the first time he'd ever called himself an artist out loud and was proud of him.

"And your wife? Are you an artist, too, ma'am?"

Eugenie shook her head. Her hair was tied back loosely with a ribbon and her curls danced about her. Sinclair had made her a daisy chain on their stroll through the meadow and set it on her head like a yellow crown.

She could feel Sinclair's eyes still on her, caressing her, and the warmth flooded her body as she thought about what they would do, later, when they returned to the boat. Although now her anticipated pleasure was streaked through with the unhappy knowledge that this may be their last time together. Maybe another day, or another hour, but soon it would end.

"Well," Mrs. Burdock was looking from one to the other of them with an indulgent smile, "you're young and together. I don't think it matters as long as you're together, eh? Especially when anyone can see you're so much in love. I can remember when me and my Jack first married, we couldn't keep our hands off each other." She gave an earthy chuckle. "My father was against our wedding from the first, made all sorts of excuses why we'd never be happy. But we went ahead anyway and here we are, forty-two years later, still in love. Just shows it doesn't go to pay too much attention to other people when your own heart is telling you what's best."

"Yes," Eugenie whispered. She reached over and touched the woman's reddened, work-worn hand. "Thank you."

Mrs. Burdock's merry face creased in a frown. "My dear, what is it?"

Eugenie shook her head, her throat closing, suddenly very near to tears.

"Now you take heart," the woman insisted. "No matter what others do and say, you still have your love for each other, and if you hold firm that will pull you through the bad times. Believe me, 'cause I know."

Abruptly a call came from outside, and then voices arguing.

Mrs. Burdock lifted her head. "Now who could that be?" she murmured, puzzled. "We're not used to this many customers in a day."

But Eugenie had recognized the voices and she knew who it was.

Sinclair recognized them, too. He rose to his feet. He'd hardly worn shoes since they boarded the narrow boat and now when he put them on they felt tight and pinching, as if his freedom were somehow being curtailed by their restriction. If he'd had time, he might have drawn parallels between his shoes and society, and his need to be free of them both, but there was no time for philosophizing.

"Why did you let me persuade you into doing this?" Annabelle's voice was a wail, on the verge of tears. He knew that tone well.

"I must have been out of my mind," another voice groaned, and he recognized Terry Belmont.

Eugenie jumped up out of her chair and was hurrying to the door of the cottage. He reached it just behind her.

Outside by the lock gates a strange scene confronted them.

Annabelle was standing on the towpath while Terry was walking away, to where the upper lock gate had opened up to let Lord Ridley's narrow boat through. A slight fair-haired woman stood between the two of them, as if caught in the middle of their argument—Miss Gamboni. There was a barge tied to the bank by the narrow boat, facing away from Wexham. Terry and Annabelle's? The lockkeeper, Mr. Burdock, and Captain Johnno stood close together, attention fixed on the arguing couple, enjoying this unexpected entertainment.

"You must hire a fast coach, one that doesn't rock about."

"And how will I do that? All my money is gone."

"When I return to London and marry Lucius, I will repay you every penny."

"Do you expect this Lucius to want to marry you? Now? What about your reputation?"

"Terry . . ." Miss Gamboni warned, but it did no good.

Annabelle choked. "You are hateful to remind me! What will I do? Oh what will I do?"

Terry sighed. "I'm sorry," he said, as if it was now a common refrain. He turned back to her and tried to take her in his arms, as if to comfort her, but Annabelle pulled away. She was close to the towpath and when her foot slipped she teetered on the edge of the canal. Terry made a grab for her but it was too late, she was already falling. The next moment she hit the water with a splash.

Eugenie cried out and Mrs. Burdock clasped her arm tightly, as if afraid she might jump into the canal, too. Sinclair ran toward the towpath where Terry stood, his face chalk white, almost colliding with Miss Gamboni, who was also running. He pushed them both out of the way in his impatience to save his sister.

He could see Annabelle's dark hair beneath the brown water, her clothing rising up in clouds as the air bubbled out of it. He had only a few brief moments before she was dragged down into the depths, vanishing forever in the muddy canal.

He jumped in as close to her as he dared.

The water was very cold. His body was shocked into inaction. He could not even catch his breath. And then he gasped and flailed out, hunting for his sister in the murky water. He dived, feeling with his arms for any sign of her, but there was nothing. When his head rose above the surface again, he heaved in a deep breath and then another.

Terry was above him.

"There!" he shouted, pointing a little to Sinclair's right.

Sinclair caught sight of a fold of cloth, drifting down. He struck out, grasping at it with his outstretched hand, and felt the material brush his fingers. His grip tightened, and then he was reeling the folds of cloth in toward him. She was heavy, weighed down with skirts and petticoats. Then he felt her body, limp, and pulled her close.

Her head tumbled forward, dark hair trailing in ribbons, and he lifted it out of the water, onto his shoulder. Her face was white, eyes closed. Was she breathing? But he couldn't worry about that now. He had to get them both out of this freezing water. Sinclair struggled toward the steep bank of the canal.

"Here you go, sir." The lockkeeper was there with a pole, and Sinclair caught hold of the end of it, using it to help him onto the wooden ladder that hung down from the path. Then there were hands, pulling him upward, lifting Annabelle's limb body from him. It seemed only a moment later he was sprawled on the towpath, shivering with cold and shock.

A group had gathered, hiding the prone body of Annabelle from his view. He couldn't see what was happening and he was too exhausted to get up. Seconds passed, then minutes. He began to believe the worst. Then there was a shout, and Eugenie came hurrying over to him, her face alight with good news.

"She is breathing. Sinclair. She is alive."

Chapter 33

R elief washed over Sinclair. His sister was alive. All was well. He pulled himself awkwardly to his feet, leaning on Eugenie as she slipped an arm about his waist, her clothing soon soaking in the water from him. The group shifted to allow him in, just as Annabelle vomited up some of the brown water, and began to indulge in a fit of sobbing hiccups.

Mrs. Burdock slipped an arm about her shoulders and helped her to sit up, murmuring sympathy. Miss Gamboni had come forward but, seeing Sinclair, backed away again. Annabelle's dark eyes scanned the faces looming over her and widened when she realized that her brother really was there.

"You saved my life," she croaked. "Sinclair, you were right all along. I should have listened to you. Anything is better than this. How could I have thought I wanted to live the life of a simple girl?"

He knelt and took her hands in his. "Hush, Annabelle. Now is not the time. We will talk about these matters later."

"My life is ruined," she wailed.

When it was obvious she wasn't going to calm herself, they carried her into the cottage and up the stairs to the Burdocks' bedroom. There she was left to the tender care of Mrs. Burdock and Eugenie. Sinclair, who'd followed them in, sat at the same table he shared with Eugenie only moments ago.

Captain Johnno placed a blanket about his shivering shoulders and he thanked him, holding it close, feeling the warmth of the stove gradually seeping into his bones. Or was it his heart? Why did he feel so worried? He should be happy and relieved. Annabelle was safe, all was well, they could go home now. It was over.

But perhaps that was the trouble. It wasn't over. He didn't want it to be over.

He noticed Terry hovering in the doorway, peering up the stairs, clearly worried about what was happening up there. Sinclair eyed him a moment, wondering if he had the strength to punch him in the nose. After a brief struggle with his wobbly legs he decided he didn't.

"Sit down for God's sake," he growled instead.

Terry eyed him nervously. "Only if you promise not to call me out."

Sinclair snorted. "I don't have my second here at the moment. Sit down, Terry. I have no intention of calling you out."

The boy—and suddenly he seemed little more—edged toward the table and sat down. There was a strained look about his eyes. Sinclair realized he felt, if not sorry for him, then at least a little less inclined to blame him for the whole situation. Annabelle could be very strong-willed when she wanted something and Terry had little experience of strong-willed dukes' sisters.

"Do you think she will recover?" Terry said, glancing toward the door to the stairs again. "I would have jumped in, sir, but I never learned to swim."

Sinclair rubbed a hand over his face, feeling the grate of his unshaven cheeks. When had he last shaved? He couldn't remember. It hadn't seemed to matter . . . until now. "She's in good hands. Your sister will take care of her and Mrs. Burdock seems to me a capable woman."

Terry nodded, and when he looked at Sinclair again it was with speculative eyes. "May I ask, sir, what my sister is doing here?"

Sinclair wondered how much to tell him, or how much Eugenie would want to tell him. In the end he said, "She wanted to find you. She was worried I might do you an injury if she wasn't here to stop me." His mouth curved into an involuntary smile, and he saw Terry's gaze sharpen. Quickly he made his expression stony again.

"Is my sister's virtue intact?" Sinclair asked bluntly, thinking he may as well know the worst so that he could deal with it.

Terry's eyes opened wide. They were green, like Eugenie's. "Yes, sir! It was never . . . we were never . . . We are friends only! And Lizzie was with us all the while. Miss Gamboni, that is. She was chaperoning your sister. None of it was her fault. We sort of—sort of kidnapped her, you see."

He looked so indignant, so eager to impress upon Sinclair his innocence, that this time Sinclair had difficulty subduing his smile. Then he thought of something else.

"Then what on earth did you think you were doing eloping for the border?"

"We weren't eloping," Terry groaned. "I was escorting her to Scotland, where her friend lives. She could not marry a man she didn't love and live a life she despised, and she begged me to help her escape. She wanted . . . she said she wanted to be an ordinary woman living an ordinary life." His voice trailed off at the end, as if he'd realized that Annabelle's declarations were no longer to be trusted, and perhaps they never had. He knew now he should have listened to Lizzie when she warned him, but he'd been too caught up in the romance of rescuing Annabelle, of being her hero.

"I see."

And reading the misery in Terry's face Sinclair did indeed "see" the truth.

"Will there be a terrible scandal, sir? I don't care what happens to me but please don't blame Lizzie for any of this. It wasn't her fault."

Sinclair rubbed a hand across his eyes, feeling the weight of his responsibilities, of being the Duke of Somerton.

"We had turned back," Terry went on to explain. "We didn't even reach the border. Annabelle wanted to go home. She decided she didn't want to be an ordinary girl after all. She wanted to marry this Lucius fellow and live in London and go to parties and balls and . . ." He sighed, as

if all his beliefs had been shattered. Sinclair had a
fair inkling that the boy had imagined himself in
love with Annabelle, and planned to be her heroic
savior. Now he probably felt like a complete idiot.

"You understand I will have to send you away
from Somerton," Sinclair said, watching Terry's
face to see how he'd take the news.

He took it bravely, straightening his shoulders,
although there was an expression of misery in his
eyes. "I know that, sir."

"So where is it to be, then?"

Terry shrugged a shoulder. "I thought about en-
listing as a common foot soldier, just to get away
from . . ." He swallowed. "I always hoped for a
commission but my father . . . It was not possible."

Sinclair could read between the lines. He considered the matter. "Very well, I will buy you a
decent commission. But you will repay me by
being a model soldier. If I hear of any schemes to
make money and defraud anyone, any gambling,
any drunkenness . . . you know the sort of thing
I'm talking about. If I hear of anything like that
then I will pay a call to your commanding officer
and see you thrown out. Do you understand me,
Terry?"

The boy blinked in amazement. "I . . . I don't
know what to say, sir."

"Thank you and good-bye, in that order," Sinclair said. He looked at the door that led to the
stairs. "I wonder what's taking her so long," he
murmured, and realized he was thinking of
Eugenie.

"You will look after Lizzie, won't you, sir? You

will take her home with you and write her a good reference?"

"Yes, all right." He eyed Terry with sour interest. "Are you planning to marry *her* now?"

"She wouldn't have me," he said glumly.

"Give it a year or two and she might forget what a fool you've been over my sister," he felt impelled to say. The boy looked so forlorn, and the fact that he could feel so when he'd just been given the commission he'd always wanted said something for his genuine feelings for Miss Gamboni.

"Might as well be a lifetime," Terry sighed.

Upstairs, Eugenie had helped Annabelle to undress and rubbed her warm and dry with towels provided by Mrs. Burdock. They tucked the girl into a bed with a hot water bottle, and eventually her shudders began to give way to yawns and sighs.

"What is my brother doing here?" she asked, eyes beginning to close. "I did not expect to see him here."

"He was trying to catch you before you reached the border," Eugenie explained. "We have been following you since the night you left Somerton."

"We?" She gave Eugenie a scornful look. "What, were you traveling with him?"

"Terry is my brother," she said with quiet dignity.

"Oh yes, so he is." Annabelle yawned again. "It wasn't his fault," she said. "He only did what I wanted him to do. I thought I knew what I wanted but I didn't understand what it would be like. Being a commoner."

A commoner, thought Eugenie, as if she were royalty! She supposed with the Somerton wealth and power and family background, she was the next thing to it. Eugenie felt her spirits sink as once more Annabelle's attitude brought back to her just how large was the gap between a duke and a Belmont. As wide as an ocean.

Or it might as well be.

"Do you think Lord Salturn will take me back?" Annabelle was nearly asleep, struggling to keep her eyes from closing.

"I'm sure your brother will persuade him to do so."

She managed a smile. "Sinclair can be very persuasive."

"He can."

"Why is it I never realized how much I—I wanted to be Lucius's wife until it was too late?"

"Perhaps it isn't too late."

Annabelle's breathing finally deepened and slowed.

Mrs. Burdock glanced at Eugenie. "She's asleep," she said, with obvious relief. "When I saw her fall into the canal I thought she was a goner for sure. I can't tell you how many dead 'uns my Jack hauls out of that canal, some fallen in by accident, others by purpose. Breaks your heart, it does."

Eugenie managed a wry smile at the mention of broken hearts. She knew it wasn't Annabelle's fault the magic spell that had held Eugenie and Sinclair in its thrall had unraveled.

If Sinclair hadn't been here when his sister fell, then she would have drowned and then where would they all be? No, it was just the way things turned out. She'd known all along that the end must come to their idyll at some point, and now it was here.

Mrs. Burdock was kind enough to agree to sit with Annabelle, and Eugenie made her way downstairs.

Terry was seated alone at the table, but he jumped up as soon as he saw his sister. .

"Annabelle . . . ?"

"Lady Annabelle is asleep," Eugenie said briskly. Then, taking pity on him, she said, "She's perfectly well, Terry. Just a little shaken."

He looked exhausted and relieved, and for a moment he seemed so much like the little boy she remembered from their childhood that she put her arms around him and held him close.

"You are a fool," she said huskily. "How could you have done such a thing? She would never have married you, Terry."

Terry squeezed her tight before letting her go. "I know. She isn't so bad as you think, Genie. Besides, I met Lizzie, and that made it all worthwhile."

"Hmm. Lizzie, is it? You realize Father and Mother were quite mad with grief when they read your letter. Mother thought you'd go to gaol for certain."

"I'm sorry," he muttered, and then gave Eugenie a sly look. "I'll bet Father wasn't mad with grief. He probably thought he'd have a wealthy daughter-in-law to borrow money from."

"Terry," she said sharply.

"Somerton has offered to buy me a commission in the army," he told her proudly. "He just wants to get me away from home, of course, but I think it's decent of him to offer, don't you? I always wanted to go into the army, Genie."

It was generous, but then Sinclair was a generous man. She told her brother she was glad for him, scolded him again for worrying them all so, and then gave him another hug.

"Here now, girl, I'm going to be a soldier now. Soldiers need to be brave. They can't be cuddled like babies."

She chuckled. "Well, soldier, here's a question for you. How are we to get home? Have you any money left?"

He looked comically blank. "I thought . . ."

"That the duke and his sister would take us? No, Terry, we can hardly ride in their coach now can we? We are trying to avoid a scandal, not make another one. You and I must find our own way home."

"But," he began, eyeing her knowingly.

Eugenie gave him a stern look. "But?"

"Well, it seemed to me that the duke and you might be . . . well, that he was more fond of you than you let on."

"Don't be silly, Terry," she said, her voice giving away the lie. "He is a duke, after all, and dukes don't allow themselves to become fond of women like me. Now you come with me while I talk to our captain and see what ideas he has. Maybe he can take us as far as Manchester."

Captain Johnno was brushing down Rufus, the big horse standing patiently, enjoying the attention. They both glanced up as Eugenie and Terry approached along the towpath.

"The young lady has taken no permanent hurt then?"

Eugenie assured him Lady Annabelle was resting but should be perfectly all right when she woke.

Slowly, a little embarrassed, she explained her and her brother's predicament. Johnno thought a moment and then suggested they make their way to a town some five miles to the east of the lock, where they could get the mail coach south. "There's a reasonable coaching inn you can wait at," he said. "It's clean and the landlord is an honest man."

"We have no money," Terry informed him bluntly.

Johnno thought a moment more, until Rufus stirred and nudged his shoulder. "His Lordship left me some blunt, in case," he admitted. "He was worried that the duke might fly up into the boughs about something or you'd have a barney, or so he said, and you'd be left high and dry, miss. You may as well have the blunt, if it'll get you home safe. His Lordship would want me to do that."

"Tell Lord Ridley we'll pay him back as soon as we can," Terry said seriously.

Eugenie felt like sagging with relief. They would be able to get home safely, thanks to the kindness of Lord Ridley. The next emotion that swept through her was sadness, like a dark cloud, the color of mourning, because this really was the end of all her hopes and dreams.

The end of love.

Chapter 34

⁓ ◦◦ ⁓

Sinclair had changed out of his wet clothes and returned to the Burdocks' cottage. The sun was setting, the long evening beginning, as he climbed the stairs and found his sister still asleep. He reached for her hand where it lay curled on the bedclothes and her eyelashes flickered, lifted sleepily, and she smiled.

He shook his head at her in mock anger. "What a mess, Annabelle. You should be ashamed of yourself."

Her mouth turned down, but he could see she wasn't as repentant as she was pretending. "I thought I wanted to be ordinary but when it came to it . . ."

"You didn't."

"No. That awful coach Terry hired. I was so sick. I've never been so sick. That's why we decided to use the canal."

Remembering the coach he himself had hired Sinclair understood her objections completely. "Just as well you took to the canals or I wouldn't have found you."

"No." She sighed. "I've decided I do want to marry Lucius. Do you think he'll still have me?"

"As I remember it Lucius is so besotted with you he would marry you if you grew another head."

She giggled. "He is, isn't he? I've been such a fool. But at least I know what I want now, at least I will never die wondering if I've made the right decision."

"You've chosen rather a desperate way of discovering it."

"I know. I'm sorry. But Lizzie was with us, you know. I think Terry prefers her to me," she added with painful honesty. "Not that I mind, of course. They deserve to be happy, too."

"Of course."

Sinclair watched her, but he wasn't seeing Annabelle. He was seeing Eugenie, with her freckles and her wild curls and her wicked little smile. He didn't want to die without having the happiness of her in his life every day and every night. It would be such a waste. What was the point of living a life without love in it?

"Sinclair?" She was looking at him oddly, and he realized she'd been calling his name while he'd been miles away. "What is Terry's sister doing here with you?"

He thought about his answer.

"I was a little surprised to see her. She's hardly in your class, Sinclair, is she? Mother will be cross when she finds out. What a scandal!" She gave a false laugh, but her eyes were watchful, doubtful, waiting.

"Do you know, Annabelle," he said, "I have an

urge to discover what it is like to be at the center of a scandal?"

"Whatever do you mean?" Her eyes were big.

"Well . . . I have been so good all these years. I think it is time I was bad."

Annabelle sat up. "Sinclair, you had better tell me what you mean!"

"I have decided to elope with Miss Belmont, Annabelle. I think that is the best way of diverting the scandal from you. In fact we can turn it all around and say that it was Eugenie and I who were heading for the border while you tried to stop us. No, that would not do. Best just to pretend you had nothing to do with it, while I take all the blame. Do you know, I am quite looking forward to it?"

She seemed to be finding it difficult to speak.

"You see, Annabelle," he said, leaning closer, "I am in love with Eugenie Belmont, and I don't think I could live my life without her. I don't think I would want to live my life without her."

"Sinclair, you can't mean it! Mother will be furious . . ."

"I know." He grinned. "But I won't be there to hear her scalds."

"No, but I will," Annabelle said glumly.

"Yes, but when you tell her about me then she will forget all about you, Annabelle. And she will have your wedding to busy herself with. No, I think she will put me aside and never mention me again. And do you know? I think being on the outer with Mother will suit me quite well."

His sister put her face in her hands.

Sinclair hesitated. Her shoulders were shaking.

She was crying. He hadn't meant to make his sister cry, but he couldn't help it now. He wasn't about to change his mind because of Annabelle's tears.

She lifted her face and to his surprise he saw that she was laughing, not crying.

"Oh Sinclair!" she gasped. "This is wonderful, truly wonderful! I will be Mother's favorite at last."

Sinclair felt as if a great weight had been lifted from his shoulders. He'd walked into the lock-keeper's cottage as one man and walked out another. Why had it taken him this long to recognize that responsibility and position did not mean he had to be miserable all his life? He could be happy. He could do all the things he did, that it was his duty to do, but with Eugenie at his side.

And that was exactly what he intended.

It was only when he reached the narrow boat and went below that he saw it was empty and, worse, Eugenie's flowery carpetbag was gone. Which meant that Eugenie was gone.

She had left him.

Eugenie glanced back over her shoulder yet again and sighed. Terry was ambling along in the twilight as if he had all the time in the world while she wanted to get to the town and arrange for their seats on the mail coach before it was completely dark. Once that was done she could close her eyes and try to forget any of this had ever happened, try to put it behind her.

A moth fluttered against her cheek and she brushed it away.

How long did it take for one to recover from a broken heart? A month, a year, a lifetime?

"Terry, do come on."

He put his hands on his hips. "I don't know why you're in such a hurry, Genie," he grumbled. "I didn't even get to say good-bye to Lizzie."

"I would have thought you'd be grateful for that," she said tartly.

"Do you know, when we were in the coach, Annabelle was ill?"

"Coaches have that effect on some people."

"But you don't understand. She was ill on me. And then Lizzie sewed on my button and stuck me with her needle and I didn't even care. Do you think that's love?"

Eugenie blinked at him, uncertain whether she wanted the image of Lady Annabelle being ill on her brother in her head. "How would I know, Terry?"

"Because you love the duke," he said bluntly. "Don't you?"

She opened her mouth to deny it but the words caught in her throat. Tears sprang to her eyes and she turned blindly away, stumbling on the road. "Nonsense," she said huskily.

"I'm not an idiot, Genie. I know you do," Terry retorted. "And he loves you, too. I could see it. Why are you running away from him? You're not even giving him a chance."

"I'm running away because if I do, as you say, love him, then there's no future in it. How can there be?"

"Well, you'd better tell him that." Terry spoke

just as she heard the pounding of hooves approaching from behind her. She spun around, wide-eyed, and there was Rufus looming up behind her, and seated on his broad back was the duke.

"My—my goodness me," she managed.

Terry smiled and turned without a word to begin the walk back to the lock, lifting his hand in a wave as Rufus went by. Sinclair drew the big horse to a halt and slid down to the ground, his feet bare and, now, dusty. He was panting, his eyes were wild, his hair windblown, and . . . he was the most handsome, the most wonderful man she had ever seen.

"Where do you think you're going?" he demanded, and spoiled the image with that arrogant duke note in his voice.

"Home," she snapped.

"What, by foot? A singular plan. Was that one of yours or Terry's?"

"There's a mail coach from the next village," she retorted coldly. "I intend to take a seat on it."

"I have a better idea."

He took her hands in his and, although she tried to shake them off, held on tightly. "Eugenie . . ." he began, then shook his head. "No, not like this." And he dropped to his knees on the dusty track, still holding her hands and gazing up at her. "Eugenie, will you elope with me to the border?"

"Elope?" she croaked.

He searched her eyes but found only mistrust and confusion. Impatiently he shook her hands. "I'm asking you to marry me, Eugenie. We can elope to the border if you like, or we can go home and get married at Somerton. I'll even ask your family, *all* of your brothers. I suppose it'll be impossible to ignore them when we're related."

She seemed stunned to silence.

"Eugenie, I know I've taken some time to come to this decision. I know I've fought against it. But that was because I didn't understand. I do now. I want to marry you and live my life with you."

"Sinclair," she murmured, "how can we? It's impossible. The—the scandal! And your family . . . no, I can't allow you to do it."

Sinclair had a sick feeling in his stomach. It had not occurred to him that she might say no, that she might not want to marry him for the very reasons he'd used before. He didn't know if he could bear to hear her reject him.

"My family will be polite, I will make certain of it. They may not approve, they may not love you as I do, but why should we care for that? As for the scandal . . . there are new scandals every day. Something bigger and better will soon come along and occupy the minds of the gossips. Perhaps when they see how happy we are they will be shamed into letting us be."

"They will never forget, Sinclair, and you know it."

"So what? I will be the Bohemian duke who paints naked portraits of his wife, and you will be the girl whose great-grandmother was the mistress of a king. We will be asked everywhere; no society function will be a hit without us."

For the first time Eugenie giggled. The shock

of his proposal had swamped any joy she felt, but now the happiness was rising up to drown all doubts and negative considerations. And then she remembered the letter she'd written to her friends and the nonsense of the Husband Hunters Club.

"Sinclair, I should apologize again. I never meant to tell my friends I was going to marry you. They are all so much more eligible than me and I felt as if I should have something exciting to tell them, a possible husband who would be better than all of their choices. And you were the best, the most wonderful, man I could think of."

"You can talk about this later. Right now I would like an answer. Will you marry me?"

He looked overwrought, as if he thought she was going to refuse him. What a turnup that would be, Eugenie Belmont refusing the Duke of Somerton! Turning down a proposal from the most eligible man in England!

She smiled.

He finally stood up. "Say something, for God's sake!" he roared.

Eugenie put her arms about his neck and kissed him.

"Yes, Your Grace," she whispered. "I will marry you."

He gave a shout of joy, and then he lifted her and swung her around on the dusty road. Rufus raised his big head and gave them a quizzical look, and then, satisfied all was well, went back to cropping the grass.

*   *   *

Lizzie was sitting on a bollard by the towpath, gazing into space. She didn't hear him approach and he hesitated, wondering whether he should just creep away and leave her alone. She deserved better than him. And what if she rejected him in her kind, gentle way? No, he couldn't bear that. But neither could he bear not to know.

Gathering all his courage, Terry walked toward her.

She must have heard him then because she looked over her shoulder. Something flashed through her eyes but it was getting too dark for him to read, and then she had dropped her gaze and turned away again.

"I thought you had gone," she said.

He tried to read the emotion in her voice but failed.

"My sister was eager to leave as soon as possible, but the duke had other ideas."

She looked at him then. "Oh." Her soft mouth curled into a smile.

"He's promised me a commission in a good regiment in the army."

Her smile faded but she forced it back, pretending at a joy she didn't feel. Watching her closely he thought he understood her now; it was time to take a chance.

"I'm glad everything has turned out as you wanted it," she was saying, still with her fake-happy smile.

"Somerton has promised not to punish you," he added. "He knows none of this was your fault, that you were only trying to help."

"I expect I will go home anyway," she said. "I won't feel comfortable staying."

"There is another option."

She stiffened as if preparing herself for bad news. Terry decided it was time Lizzie learned that the world held more than disappointment. "Oh?"

"You could come with me."

"With you?" Her eyes were wide now, and he could see hope in them, mingled with doubt.

"You could be an army wife, Lizzie. I don't know whether you'd want to travel about and live in barracks and set up camp in far and foreign lands. But for me it would be so much better if you were there."

Her smile was broader now. Her eyes shone.

"Yes," she said. "Yes, yes, yes!"

He caught her as she flung herself at him, happiness overflowing. And Terry knew as he held her that this time he had made the right choice.

Epilogue

The ball was one of the grandest of the season, but then the Duke and Duchess of Somerton had the means to see that it outshone all the others. Greenery and flowers were banked against the walls and satin hangings and ribbons fluttered in the breeze from the open windows. Hundreds of society guests chattered and danced like peacocks beneath the glittering chandeliers.

Sinclair was speaking with his uncle Lord Ridley, when he heard her voice behind him. He came to with a jolt, only then realizing that he'd been waiting for her like a thirsty man longs for water.

His wife. His duchess.

She was making her way toward him, her fashionable gown molding the swell of her bosom and her waist, before flaring out in a waterfall of ribbon and lace and silk ruching. A necklace of green emeralds rested about her neck and her wild curls were contained, for the moment. She was smiling and elegant, perfectly at ease in the company in which she found herself and if she was aware of his eye upon her she didn't show it.

Sinclair knew she'd always had this quiet dignity. It was just that he'd been too blind to see it. Like a precious jewel, Eugenie shone in whatever setting she was placed.

He'd been surprised how soon she was accepted by most of the members of society. There were a very few who still refused to acknowledge her, but that was their loss. The others found her charming and refreshing, and the story about her great-grandmother was a great hit.

"You have royal blood?" they cried, eyes wide. "How marvelous! Does Her Majesty the Queen call upon you, Your Grace?"

"I could not possibly say whether she calls or not. It is rather a scandal, you know."

Sinclair, who'd always thought of her royal blood as a minus, was amused by Eugenie playing up to her heritage, and rather nervous. "You know how your tongue runs away with you," he murmured. "I don't want you falling into another scrape, Eugenie."

"I've learned my lesson," she assured him.

He hoped so. Eugenie's friends from Miss Debenham's Finishing School had come to the wedding, and he'd been sorely tempted to tell them the truth. Eugenie had sworn him to silence and, he had to admit, she'd behaved herself—more or less—ever since.

Still he couldn't help but admire her ability to play the duchess. Was this the same girl he had met in the lane long ago? The girl who rode bareback, showing her legs, her curls tumbling about her?

That was why he loved her.

Because in a moment he could brush aside the elegant duchess and bring out that hoyden again. She was always there when they spent time on their narrow boat on the canals. Sinclair, painting in the sunlight, shoes off and trousers rolled up, while Eugenie paddled in the water or sat dreaming.

"Lucky old you." His uncle was watching him, smiling with satisfaction. "You made the right choice, eh?"

"She's been the making of me. Everybody says so."

Eugenie had reached them and now she took his arm. The curve of her growing belly beneath her gown was only visible to him, and he felt a swell of pride. Their child. An heir to the dukedom, or perhaps a girl with wild curls? Whatever it was they would love it.

Sinclair was happy, and gazing into Eugenie's emerald eyes he saw his happiness reflected. Even his mother had come around, now she knew there was a child on the way. Eugenie said the dowager duchess was lonely, without Annabelle to fuss over. His sister was happily married and reigning queenlike in London society.

Even having the Belmonts for in-laws was not quite as bad as he'd feared. The house he'd bought them was far enough away that he did not have to see them too often, although he was happy to have Jack stay at Somerton whenever he wished. Jack had always been his favorite Belmont.

Apart from Eugenie.

At night, when he closed the bedchamber door, he had her all to himself. Then they were simply Eugenie and Sinclair, wife and husband, together. No one to judge them with cynical eyes, no one to care about who they were or had been. They were perfectly matched.

"Sinclair," she whispered, her breath warm against his skin, "I can read your mind."

He smiled and lifting her hand, kissed her fingers, heavy with rings. "Can you now? What am I thinking then, Duchess?"

"You are wishing you were a wicked baron and could ride off with me into the night."

She'd made him laugh. "You know me very well."

Her green eyes glowed. "What if I dared you to abduct me?"

His eyebrows rose. "Here? Now?"

She thought he wouldn't do it. She didn't believe him capable of it. Sinclair grinned and reached for her. They were about to create another scandal and he was looking forward to every moment of it.

978-0-06-200304-1

978-0-06-202719-1

978-0-06-206932-0

978-0-06-194638-7

978-0-06-199968-0

978-0-06-201232-6

*At Avon Books, we know your passion
for romance—once you finish one of our
novels, you find yourself wanting more.*

May we tempt you with . . .

- **Excerpts** from our upcoming releases.

- Entertaining **extras**, including authors'
  personal photo albums and book lists.

- Behind-the-scenes **scoop** on your favorite
  characters and series.

- **Sweepstakes** for the chance to win free books,
  romantic getaways, and other fun prizes.

- Writing **tips** from our authors and editors.

- **Blog** with our authors and find out why they
  love to write romance.

- **Exclusive content** that's not contained
  within the pages of our novels.

Join us at
www.avonbooks.com

AVON

An Imprint of HarperCollins*Publishers*
www.avonromance.com

Available wherever books are sold or please call 1-800-331-3761 to order.

FTH 0708